A Belfast

Angeline King

ISBN13: 978-1530952373
ISBN10: 1530952379

Second Edition

Editor: Donna Moore

FOR

Christopher and Eliza

May you always live in a country of peace.

A NOTE ABOUT DIALECT

'A Belfast Tale' is written in Standard English, but I wanted to pay homage to the heritage that I was given. I have sprinkled a wheen o Ulster-Scots words throughout the prose and within the dialogue. I hope you enjoy their resonance on the page as much as their relationship with the soil from which this story was extracted.

PART ONE

A Belfast Tale
By Angeline King
CreateSpace, £10

"You say a married couple is having troubles, not a nation." This line, striking in its simplicity, says a lot about how the Irish deal with really big issues. It's 1990, and eye-popping synthetic 1980s fashions linger while advances in technology are beginning to affect the traditionally manual workplace. In this self-published book Angeline King tells a tale of misplaced passion and the common problems of Annie and Jean, Protestant mothers who meet at a gathering of Project Children, the organisation that sends young northern Protestants and Catholics to the United States each summer holidays, for a break from local politics and a chance to play together. The friends' marriages are troubled by actual and imagined injuries; their children are living with both the jaded fear of ongoing violence and the growing movement towards cross-community co-operation; and families still live in the streets and houses their parents grew up in. Eventually, even grand passion loses significance to love in the face of harsh reality.

CLAIRE LOOBY

THE PRISON BUS
1990

Heels clattered, seats shuffled and voices clanged through the Great Hall. Annie located a seat two rows from the back and settled under a spray of ecclesiastical orange light splitting from latticed iron on vaulted windows. The order of service was a glossy itinerary, shimmering in shamrocks, stars and stripes. An American woman with long, brown hair stood in the pulpit and tested the microphone. Annie sat upright on a hard wooden chair and scanned the oak panelled walls, walls that were imbued with the academic endeavours of ghosts of the past and the silent fears of the women present. Two hundred mothers, divided by politics and religion, were united in plans to deliver their children to America for a peaceful summer.

A refreshing scent of flowery perfume bustled past Annie's legs and nestled beside her. Annie turned to the left and met a face charged with electric blue eyes, a figure slick with a curt coif of carefully crafted black hair and a smile gleaming with bountiful red lips. 'Jean Adams' was printed on a name badge in black letters and Jean was hovering above her seat and stabbing the badge onto her jacket. Her voice flurried, 'Hello there, love.' Annie smiled and reached up to help her neighbour remove a baggy leather jacket with wide padded shoulders that contained a compact and sprightly woman dressed to the nines in a black suit with patent heels. Jean flicked through the programme, fiddled in her bag and floundered in the air between sitting and standing. She turned to Annie as her hand patted the top of the immaculate creation on her head. 'Here, love, you wouldn't check my hair, would you? It's blowing a gale out there.'

'It's sitting perfect,' Annie laughed, beguiled by the heady mix of motherly charm and prevailing fashions.

The voice came again in a gust. 'It's him!' Jean said, clinging onto Annie's arm. 'It's Honky Tonk! He's my son's host dad from last year!'

'Honky Tonk' laughed Annie. She wondered at the words and the storm of their articulation and looked towards the front to locate the object of Jean's trouble.

'Your big fella in the red jumper!' Jean signaled, tossing her eyes to the right. 'Our wee neighbour saw him in a picture and called him the Honky Tonk man.'

Annie's misgivings about attending the induction workshop dissipated as the words 'Honky Tonk' re-awakened her spirits and her childhood. There in the small living room of her past, was an LP sleeve with a man in a cowboy hat, and as she drifted contentedly through her early years, a record player sang, 'I love to give the girls a whirl to the music of an old juke box.'

The invitation to the Project Children event at Queen's University had alerted Annie to the reality that she was sending her son far away from home, and her imagination had cast up a terrible fear of a child lost in a wilderness before Jean had arrived with her red lipstick and country song. Annie relaxed and regained some of the zeal she'd had when the school principal had approached her about sending James to Washington D.C., and just as Annie's mind settled on a house with a swimming pool filled with happy children dipping and diving in a world far removed from Belfast, the colour red appeared in the periphery of her right eye.

'Jean. It's you!' came a soothing voice.

'Shaun, lovely to meet you at last,' said Jean, holding out hands to Shaun across Annie's body.

Annie, caught in a crossfire of red wool and spiked hair, remained stationary to avoid severing the beauty of the exchange, but as the tall, broad American pulled away from Jean, she caught his brown eyes and pictured them set in the shadow of a cowboy hat.

Jean clasped Annie's arm without pausing for breath. 'This is my friend,' she motioned.

Annie smiled and watched Jean assess the white sticker on her black polo neck jumper. 'This is my friend, Annie Steen,' continued Jean with an air of authority. 'And Annie, this is Shaun.'

'Good to meet you,' said Shaun as he reached down and enveloped Annie in an unexpected embrace. 'Do you have a kid on Project Children?'

'Yes, my son, James.' said Annie. 'He's nine and—'

'Shaun is my young fella's host dad,' interrupted Jean with a confident blast of voice that demonstrated pride tempered with stage fright. 'This will be Robert's second summer with Shaun,' she added.

The shriek of a microphone cut short Jean's discourse and Shaun stepped back, 'Looks like we're going to begin,' he said. 'I hope you ladies have a great day. I'll see you at the end.'

Shaun walked away and Annie felt a pinch on her arm, 'Holy God,' she heard from the woman who was using her other hand to fan a flaming face. 'He's coming to dinner tonight and I'm a married woman. Here,' she said, turning to face Annie, 'Is thirty-five too young for hot flushes? It's probably hot flushes, isn't it?'

Annie smiled, 'You're too young for hot flushes. Was that the first time you'd met him?'

'Yes, but I've seen photos of him and his wee fella. Robert says he lives in this big fancy house in Washington D.C. and you'll never believe this.'

'What?' enquired Annie, mesmerised by this pint-sized wonder of a woman.

'Robert said there was a laundry room and three toilets in the house.'

'Three toilets! Why would anyone need three toilets?'

'I know! That's what I thought. Anyway, God only knows what he'll think of the Shankill.'

'I'm sure he'll love it.'

It had been a long time since Annie had visited the Shankill. She had worked in an office in the mill at the height of the Troubles, and had developed an immediate affinity for the laughter of the people there despite the undercurrent of sadness.

'And guess what else?' said Jean as the first induction speech began. Annie leaned in and Jean whispered in husky tones, 'He's a widower.' The last word could just as easily have been murderer or terrorist, such was the gravity on Jean's face.

'He lost his wife two years ago!' she exclaimed in whispers.

Annie's eyes moved to the front and back to Jean, nodding.

'Terrible thing,' said Jean.

Annie attempted to lead Jean to a place of silence with her eyes.

'And Annie.'

Annie smiled and repeated the journey of her eyes back towards her neighbour.

'I think you should stop talking,' came Jean's chastising voice. 'The speeches are starting.'

Annie tried to hush Jean, but the ripples of laughter caused each person in her circumference to turn and stare.

Jean threw Annie a flash of mock censure and nudged her elbow, 'Seriously love, you need to focus.'

Annie listened to each speaker as they discussed the aims of the Project Children program, and wondered what it would be like to be back in school with Jean. The teenager who had grown reluctantly into a young woman almost twenty years ago was re-surfacing as an American woman told the audience how twenty-five thousand children had completed the journey to the US since the summer program began in 1975.

Jean pulled a face, and Annie was swiftly learning that Jean had a repertoire of faces to exemplify her emotions, each expression formed in a conspiracy between the direction of her head and the length of her neck.

Annie returned to the American lady on the stage, whose

voice was so strong that it should have deterred Jean from mischief.

'Here,' Jean's voice flexed. 'Why is it that Americans all have such lovely hair?'

'Jean!' Annie was scolding a women she had known for less than twenty minutes, and the thoughts of it and the woman's perfect hair were distracting Annie from listening to a story about an Irish gentleman in New York who, fifteen years previously, had started to bring Protestant and Catholic children to America to escape the violence on the streets of Belfast.

Jean's head was cocked to one side, her lips pouted into self-enforced silence, and Annie's mind returned to the Honky Tonk man. She was curious about what had compelled him to take Jean's son into his home last summer, and her mind drifted back to an image of the American dream with children splashing in swimming pools as mothers watched on from their spectacular kitchens. Her fantasies of American laundry rooms and multiple bathrooms came to an end and she noted that half the people in the room had their hands raised. Annie looked around and then back to Jean with beseeching eyes.

'Tut tut. You haven't been taking heed, have you?'

Annie shook her head.

'Well, since we're good friends, I'll tell you what she said.' There was a pause. 'She said, hands up if you're in Shaun's group.'

Annie raised her hand.

'You're a disgrace of a married woman,' said Jean as she eyed Annie's wedding band.

'Why? What group am I in?'

'You're with Stella, the lady with the nice hair. Look at your induction page.'

Annie scanned the sheet of paper with a watermark of an American flag and said, 'Oh.'

'But the good news is that you're with me for the next two hours.'

'Oh dear,' said Annie with feigned disapproval.

'Hmm, and I was going to invite you for a cuppa, but now

I'll have to think about it.'

'Is there a chance of coming around to your house tonight?' smiled Annie.

'Oh that would be lovely,' enthused Jean.

'I'm working tonight,' Annie laughed. 'I just fancied a whirl to the music of an old jukebox.'

Confusion beckoned another tilt of Jean's head.

'You know... the Honky Tonk man,' Annie explained.

'Oh flip, ay,' said Jean. 'I haven't heard those words in a long time.'

The most toneless song that Annie had ever heard subsequently emerged from Jean's lips en route to their workshop. Annie's face was hot with laughter as she walked through a room of bemused women with the most disruptive girl in the class. The laughter continued throughout the induction with Annie's country accent falling under Jean's scrutiny at every opportunity. Jean's voice descended from its mountainous range of rocky vowels into rippling glens of soft consonants until Annie was certain that Jean had acquired her voice. 'Annie, you're no wise in the heed,' she'd say. 'Annie, what d'ye think o thon?' she'd whisper, until they both exited the gates of Queen's University with linked arms, united in a coalition of words.

The wind was sweeping up the rain and bristling it in spots across Jean's pop socks. Annie walked with a sense of newness. Jean was hanging off one arm, and she elbowed Annie to alert her that Shaun was walking alongside them.

'Och hello there,' said Jean, as though it was the first time she'd seen him that day. Only minutes before, they had said an extended goodbye. Jean then took the opportunity to run through a second verification of Shaun's tastes in spuds, scallions, cabbage and beef, whereby Shaun repeated his promise that the proposed menu for dinner would not offend him in any way.

'Ladies, I have to go this way,' said Shaun nodding to the right at the corner of University Square.

'Annie, love, are you not getting the train too?' asked Jean.

'I am indeed.'

'There you go! Annie will walk to the train station with you.'

Annie looked down to avert her eyes from Jean's amused grin.

'I'm going the other way to get the bus,' Jean added.

'No problem,' agreed Annie, with a feeling that Jean had been giving her directions all her life.

'And, Annie, remember what I said about taking a scoot up the Shankill for a wee cuppa. It's the first house on Snugville Street, right opposite the benefits office.'

'That'll do,' smiled Annie.

Annie was saddened to be parting company with the woman whose presence was as strong as the hairspray holding its matter in vertical fortitude against Belfast's rain, but was resolved to end the farewell before pneumonia set in. She looked at Shaun as Jean waved goodbye. 'We should start walking,' Annie laughed. 'I'm foundered!'

Shaun stopped and turned to Annie several paces into their walk. 'Should I be concerned about scallions?'

'Scallions? Why would you be concerned about scallions?'

Shaun's neck was tinged with red and he spoke slowly. 'What are scallions?'

Annie laughed and skirted the puddles on the cracked pavement, 'A scallion is a type of snail,' she explained. 'It's a local delicacy. Tell Jean you don't want any snails in your champ.'

'Champ?' asked Shaun.

'Potatoes mixed with milk, butter and scallions,' said Annie, retaining her straight face despite the look of bewilderment in her companion's dark eyes. Annie cleared her throat audibly and turned into Botanic Avenue with a confident stride. She checked the expression on Shaun's face.

'Okay, you got me,' he smiled. 'Help the poor American guy with the gullible face out. What's a scallion…Really?'

'A long, skinny green onion.'

'And champ?'

'I didn't lie to you about champ.'

'I don't think Jean has left me in safe hands. Are you guys old friends?'

'No, we met today for the first time,' said Annie.

'You're kidding.'

'Sure, isn't a stranger just a friend you haven't met.'

'True,' said Shaun. 'Are you a Yeats fan?'

'Yeats?' Annie imitated in confusion, relieved that the rain had started to filter out the conversation.

'You know, the poet?'

'Yes, the poet.' Annie paused as she searched for a response, clamouring over some words in her mind. She opted for a smile and a silent reply before the conversation took her to a place where her lack of poetic insight would be revealed.

Annie walked on and recollected the other Americans she had met. Lilting voices had breezed in and out of the factory, whistling compliments and attesting good manners around the small kitchen where she prepared lunch for the directors and their visitors each day, but she had yet to move beyond pleasantries in her transatlantic conversations.

'Where are you going?' she asked as they entered Botanic station.

'Carrickfergus.'

'We're on the same train then. We go this way.' Annie motioned Shaun towards the correct platform.

'Why Carrickfergus?' she asked, hiking her long coat up to stride the high step of the old train.

'I wasn't sure if I should stay in Belfast.' Shaun lowered his voice and surveyed the empty carriage before continuing, 'I wasn't sure if it would be safe. It's my first time in Northern Ireland.'

'I see. You didn't want to stay in the most bombed hotel in Europe, then?'

'Maybe not. It's in Belfast?'

Annie nodded as she closed the rickety train door.

Shaun settled opposite Annie on a red, high-backed, velvety seat. 'Where do you live?' he said, adjusting his long legs into the aisle.

'In Whiteabbey. It's a couple of stops from Carrickfergus. They call our estate Bethlehem.'

'Bethlehem?'

'The houses in the Fernagh Estate are white with flat roofs. Some people call it Jerusalem too. You'll see it from the train.' Annie nodded towards the window where a pale face with straggling dark hair peered back. It remained stationary as Belfast moved behind her own reflection. She turned swiftly to Shaun, disconcerted by the haunting image she had seen in the window pane.

'I live in Bethesda,' said Shaun. 'We share biblical place names.'

'Oh ay? Like the pool of Bethesda?'

'It's a suburb on the edge of Washington D.C. Is Whiteabbey worth a visit? I'm here for the rest of the week.'

'I'm not sure about that,' laughed Annie, imagining an American visitor walking into her home to find the shameful disorder of her life. 'I'm originally from Glenarm on the Antrim Coast. You should go there. You'd like it.'

'I'll be going on a bus tour of the Antrim Coast. I'll look out for Glenarm.'

Annie stood up minutes into their journey, 'Here we go,' she said, Bethlehem in all its biblical glory. What do you think?'

Shaun followed Annie to the door and looked out the window.

'It looks great,' he said and glanced at Annie with a knowing smile after surveying the white cubed homes that could be seen through the serrated iron fence.

'Goodbye,' Annie said, pulling down the window and turning the door handle from the outside. 'Enjoy the summer with Robert and if you see James, tell him to make sure he calls his mother.'

'I'll do that,' smiled Shaun. 'It was good to meet you. I'll let you know if I survive the scallions!'

***

The journey on foot to Robert's house from the train station in Belfast was longer than Shaun had expected. He passed Snugville Street before doubling back, furtively checking his map in the quiet evening repose of the Shankill Road, conscious that he was walking alone on one of Belfast's most notorious streets.

Snugville Street appeared to be as warm and still as its name, the forebodings of violence and despair somehow neutralised by the designation. Shaun looked down the street at the row of red-bricked terraced homes, each of them no more than twelve feet wide, and wondered how men of a certain stature lived comfortably in such restricted space.

Jean's face flashed across the first window on the street, and there followed a disoriented blur of words, arms and one silk peach cushion that was being thrashed into shape through a cavalcade of words, 'Hi Shaun, welcome to Belfast. Come on in. Harry, would you come on! Shaun's here! Robert, Shelley, Hannah, come and see who's here!'

Shaun's coat was taken from him in a foray of nervous energy and one by one, children appeared in the narrow stairway. Shaun recognised them from pictures Robert had shown him in Washington D.C. the previous summer. First came Shelley, a girl in a red velvet dress with blonde curls tied in white ribbons.

'And what's your name?' asked Shaun.

Shelley looked at her sister.

'Her name is Shelley,' replied Hannah.

'How old are you?'

Hannah, who had dark curls, blue eyes, and the fiery expression of her mother, voiced her sister's response. 'She's two and a half and I'm four and a half.'

'And do you guys like candy?'

'Yes!' came a flutter of voices as Shelley unfurled herself from the bannister.

'Well, I have some candy all the way from the United States of America. I can give it to your mom for after dinner.'

Shelley walked past Shaun and huddled into her mother's legs as Shaun handed the coveted bag to Jean.

Robert arrived at the top of the stairs, shrinking behind his sister. Shaun looked up and smiled, 'Hey, Robert. How are you?'

Robert glanced at his mom, self-conscious and unsure and

Jean placed her hands on her hips. 'Robert, son, are you not going to come down and see Shaun? Come on. Get down the stairs. And what did I tell you about wearing that football top? I left your shirt out on your bed.'

A mumble, hardly decipherable, and similar to the stilted collection of syllables Shaun frequently heard from his own son, Toby, followed. 'I want to wear my Northern Ireland shirt. I want to show it to Shaun.'

Shaun read the dynamics between Jean and Robert and filled the muted gap. 'Is this the shirt you were talking about? Well, that's pretty neat. I need to get Toby one of those.'

'We have one for him, don't we Robert?' heralded Jean.

Robert finally approached with his hands in his pockets.

'Hey buddy! I've missed you,' said Shaun.

Robert looked up and revealed a shy smile, 'Come and see my dad,' he said quietly. 'He's in the kitchen.'

Surveying the living space, Shaun soaked up a woman's touch. The windows were treated with pink satin curtains, dark wooden furniture gleamed against an array of china dolls and the unfortunate cushion was in its place with the others, all tilted at angles on the sofa and chairs.

'Sit down, Shaun,' said Jean. 'The tea's nearly ready. Harry, where are you, Harry? Shaun's here.' The voice was ever expanding against the diminutive figure of its owner.

'Keep it down woman!' steamed a response from the back of the house. 'You could hear you at Killarney!'

It was Harry, a formidable man, built like the stern of a ship and towering above Jean as he reached out the coarse hand of a welder. 'How are ye, Shaun? Welcome to the Shankill.'

'Good to meet you,' Shaun replied, trying hard not to stare. The physical dynamics of this couple, a titanic ship with its tugboat, intrigued and enthralled him. Robert had often boasted about how his father worked at Harland and Wolff, and Shaun realised the might of a shipyard man.

Harry led the way into the kitchen where steam was swirling a foot high from three small plates heaped with champ, beef and cabbage. In between sat three side plates with a scattering of fish fingers and fries for the children. Shaun smiled as he recalled the battle he'd had enticing young Robert to eat normal food in his home. A solution of fish sticks and fries every night for three weeks ensured that the boy didn't starve. Shaun watched Harry dig a fork into the pile of food and followed his lead, relieved that he hadn't been a second late for the six o'clock dinner appointment. The steam filled his lungs and the mashed potato subdued his hunger. His lips burned and his tongue burned, but his fork accelerated at a pace as he consumed the heartening remedy to the damp he had carried around in his bones since his plane had touched down at Aldergrove airport three days previously.

'The food is great, Jean. Thank you. You're quite the chef.'

Jean's face turned scarlet with Shaun's words, and as Shaun smiled in her direction, a white mountain, volcanic with steam, landed on Shaun's plate. Shaun raised his eyes to Harry who was refilling his own supply of spuds with a large pot in one hand and a ladle in the other. He had known Harry for less than ten minutes, but recognised at once that he was witness to an unlikely match of apparatus and man. Jean stood up and took the pot from Harry's hand. 'Shift over,' she said. 'I'll do it.'

'Jean's a great cook, isn't she?' Harry smiled with pride gleaming through his long, white teeth. 'When I married her I was only eight stone in weight. Look what she's done to me.'

'Would you listen to him?' said Jean, her wrist turning the spoon with expertise.

Shaun inhaled the steam, ploughed his fork into the pile and welcomed the taste of home cooking once again.

He addressed Hannah as the last spoonful warmed his stomach, understanding her position as spokesperson of the children present. 'I met a woman today who told me that scallions were snails. How do you like that?'

'Yugh,' sang a chorus of children's voices. 'That's disgusting,' added Hannah. 'Do you eat snails?'

'Well, no, but this lady was a bit of a comedian and she thought it would be funny to tell me that champ was made of snails and spuds!'

'Timmy Robertson has snails in his back garden,' said Hannah.

'Everyone has snails in their back garden, dummy,' retorted Robert. 'Timmy Robertson's my friend. I'm going on the prison bus with him tomorrow.'

'No, you are not indeed,' drilled the voice of Jean.

'Come on mum, it's only a prison bus. You get free lemonade and crisps.'

'Not a chance, son! Don't even mention it again.'

Robert sulked with one hand on his cheek as he moved around a fish stick on his plate. Shaun retained a look of neutral observance whilst Jean and Harry glared at one another and back to Robert. Harry finally looked up to Shaun to explain, 'The wee lad wants to go on the prison bus with his mates. A few of them have dads in prison. He thinks it's a great adventure.'

'Our daddy doesn't go to prison,' Hannah said, in a tone that voiced disappointment. 'But mammy says daddy'll end up in prison if he doesn't start coming home at night.'

Shaun looked from Hannah to Jean and tried hard to avert Harry's eyes. A smile emerged from the edges of Jean's quivering lips. Harry retained a dignified air with blue eyes resting on a distant place before finally turning to Shaun and releasing the first sounds of amusement. Within seconds, Shelley had followed her daddy's lead, and soon, Harry's bellowing laughter filled the room.

'Hannah, love, there are some things you're not meant to say to people,' laughed Jean.

'Leave the wee girl alone, Jean,' said Harry. 'Sure she only learns it from her mammy.'

Jean was standing with her hands on her hips, 'I'm sure Shaun doesn't want to hear any of this nonsense. I bet there are no prison buses in America.'

'No,' Shaun hesitated. 'It's not something I've ever paid attention to. But the lemonade and chips part, you know, I get it, and Robert is in luck because I'd love to take you guys to the cinema on Sunday afternoon. We'll have popcorn and soda and we won't have to worry about that bus. How does that sound?'

Shaun was unprepared for the volume of affirmation, as noise escalated from the children's mouths.

'That's lovely,' said Jean with a smile. 'You're a kind man.'

Jean sat back down after clearing the plates. Although she appeared more relaxed cradling a piping cup of tea, two large blue teardrop eyes assessed Harry each time he opened a new tin of lager. There was a distilled beauty in Jean's face that softened the hard ridge of her dark hair, and Shaun detected an old soul in the eyes of a woman whose young heart prevailed upon the trends she followed.

Jean and Harry narrated stories of the Shankill of their childhoods, stories of how things used to be before violence and despair took hold of their community, and when it was time to put the kids to bed, Harry gave Jean a beseeching look that led to her hands firming in around her hips again. 'If you take Shaun to the pub on a Thursday night, be home at a decent hour! You've to work in the morning.'

Shaun watched again as Jean washed the dishes and busied herself with the children's bedtime routines. Domesticity was not in Harry's realm and Shaun thought about what a contrast Harry's life was to his own. Apart from the plod of spuds on Shaun's plate, Harry's strong hands were solely occupied with the pouring of lager, while Jean fulfilled every other chore, the same chores that Shaun had once shared with his wife.

Shaun looked at Harry and was transported to his childhood home in Silver Spring, a modest bungalow replete with faces and voices. There in the small brown and yellow kitchen of his youth was his father, furtively reaching his head around the door after an opportunist trip to the bar, and close behind the muffled rattle of a closing door came the bellowing sound of his mother's chiding. Shaun could see his parents in the two people at the table who were a generation younger and he could see his mother's sadness in Jean's eyes when it was time to say goodbye.

Harry's brother, Sammy, was in front of the house in his car, the engine running throughout the farewell. Jean's goodbyes were as long as his mother's and Shaun regretted leaving her alone when she had been so happy to have the men there at the table.

At the car door, Harry caught a glimpse of a small woman

with curlers in her hair peeking through her drapes next door. He smiled and the drapes folded swiftly. Shaun then took in the length of the red-bricked houses on the dimly lit street, and saw the same twitch of drapes in every home as far as the eye could see.

Sammy dropped them off next to a barricade. The city hall was in the distance, a grey, domed monument sitting in darkness like a sombre father at the head of a table of subservient children. One light shone above the entrance, a watchful eye on a city steeped in quiet.

Shaun followed Harry to a narrow alleyway with white-washed walls, cobbled stones and the unmistakable trace of urine.

'Joy's entry,' said Harry. 'Where a United Irishman was led en route to his hanging.'

The bar was old and the smell of burning peat was a retreat from the dark alleyway. Harry explained that the United Irishman, a mixed group of Catholic and Protestant dissenters, had met in the bar two hundred years ago. Today it was hard to imagine anyone awakening a sense of rebellion in the sleepy men with their tweed jackets and bowed caps.

'Is this where you drink?' enquired Shaun when Harry returned to the table with two pints.

'No, I brought you here because of the history thing,' said Harry. 'Did you know that it was the Presbyterians from Ulster who got the people of the colonies all fired up about their freedom. Next thing you know, you lot were dumping tea into the ocean!'

'Is that how it all began?' laughed Shaun as Harry handed him a glass, 'It's as well those ships weren't packed with ale if the Irish were involved. So, can I clarify, you're a Presbyterian?'

'Non-practising Anglican. The wee neighbour takes the kids to church.'

'And you're a Unionist?' Shaun was aware that most Protestants fell into the British camp, but knew better than to generalise.

'I'm a non-practising Socialist, and non-practising man of

temperance,' said Harry holding his lager aloft.

'You have a lot of free time,' Shaun stated as two glasses with pale ale and froth merged in the air.

'I'm in the Argyle Temperance Flute Band, a world champion band filled with several other non-practicing men of temperance.'

'So, how does a non-practicing Protestant, Socialist and man of temperance vote at the ballot box?'

'With lead in his pencil and lead his heart. There isn't a party in the country trying to lure me in.'

'But you want to stay in the UK?'

'You know, if I thought the fine lady that is Eire genuinely wanted me for herself, I might give the whole idea of Nationalism some consideration. The truth is that the people of Dublin couldn't give a cup of Barry's tea about the North.'

'But that can't be true.'

'Look mate, the British couldn't give a mug of Tetley's brew about us either. We're unwanted. We're what you might call the fourteenth colony, only our forefathers signed the declaration of American independence and then forgot to send ships back to collect us.'

Shaun laughed. 'You know, I belong to the Irish Society in Maryland. I have to mention the tea situation to a man I know who dreams of a United Ireland.'

'There's no harm in dreaming of a United Ireland. Here's what I think, Shaun.'

Shaun awaited Harry's voice as the liquid drained from his glass.

'The lines on the map of Ireland aren't all that different from the lines on the map of a marriage. Ireland needed her independence from Britain for her own sanity, so she took it. And she believed she'd come back some day for her children in the north, but half the children in the north were loyal to their father. And so the children of the greatest divorce to ever shake Irish soil have been paying the price ever since. The Catholics in the north know that they belong to the land of their mother and the Protestants in the north know that they belong to the land of their father.'

'Harry Adams, you're a poet,' said Shaun, as he looked into Harry's distilled blue eyes.

Several more yarns and pints passed by and Shaun swiftly learned that 'I'll tell ya another one, mate' was a green light to a whole new version of Ireland. 'I had this mate once,' was the second preface to Harry's world.

Harry laughed raucously at one of his own stories before Shaun checked, 'Should I be concerned that you shouted my name all over this bar? I was told by your son to change my name to John in the Shankill.'

'You're fine here. I'd be more worried for my own safety. I sometimes get mistaken for my younger brother.'

'I assumed you guys were twins.'

'Non-Identical twins. He's ten minutes younger and nowhere near as handsome. Anyway, I'll tell you a good one about twins.' Harry leaned in and lowered his voice. 'So, I'm sitting in a football club about ten years ago with a neighbour called Johnny Sharpe. He was older than me and he'd gone away to join the British army when he was younger.'

'Okay.'

'Johnny was telling me stories about his time in the service. He said that in the early seventies, right in the middle of a summer of riots in Belfast, he took leave to come home. While his fellow soldiers were on one side of a barricade defending themselves against bricks and bottles and petrol bombs, Johnny Sharpe found himself on the other side pelting bricks and stones at the army.'

'So, slow down and let me get this straight,' said Shaun, his mind decelerating in pace with his speech. 'This guy is from the Shankill, a Protestant area within the United Kingdom, where the folks don't give a Tetley's tea bag about Northern Ireland, and he comes home and attacks his own people, his own army, his own comrades?'

'That's right.'

'But I thought you guys were on the same side.'

'Hey, don't include me in this! I've never attacked a soldier in my life.'

'But the people of the Shankill attacked the British army?'

'A few of them did. Mate, the folk along the peace line don't get much sleep at night. They trust no one and take no one's side.'

'Is it the same everywhere?'

'Not everywhere. The Falls is of a similar disposition.'

'The Falls?'

'Other side of the peace line, only Catholic and Republican.'

'I see,' said Shaun, 'Back to Johnny.'

'Well, I look up and there's a fella on TV and his name is Shauny Sharpe.'

Harry's arms were conducting his story.

'So, I looks back to Johnny and then up to Shauny and I think I'm seeing double. Shauny Sharpe was a Republican who had been freed for murder due to some mistake the police had made.'

Harry downed the remaining half of his pint before proceeding with his account.

'I point to Shauny and say to Johnny, "You'd think you were related to him." Well, Johnny was a bit vain you know, a real lady's man, so he's raging. He says, "What do ye mean? Thon ugly pachle? Sure he's as broad as he's long."'

'As broad as he's long,' Shaun sighed in a Belfast accent before finishing his own pint.

'Not bad, mate,' smiled Harry. 'Johnny and Shauny were both a bit on the short and stocky side and it turns out that they were indeed cousins. Johnny, by that time, had left the army and graduated to Loyalist terrorism, while Shauny was an entrenched Republican terrorist.'

'Johnny the Protestant and Loyalist and Shauny the Catholic and Republican,' confirmed Shaun, his mind misty with alcohol.

'Exactly. The mothers were two Catholic sisters who married two Protestant brothers. One convinced her man to turn Catholic and together they had eleven children, including Shauny Sharpe. The other sister turned Protestant on account of her husband's job and had eight children with her man, including Johnny Sharpe.'

'Nineteen cousins!'

'That's not the interesting bit. Johnny Sharpe and Shauny Sharpe both lived in relative poverty right next door to each other, and they saw each other every day of their lives. They were practically brothers, but at the start of the Troubles, Johnny's family had to get out of the estate they were in and they moved to the Shankill. The two families haven't spoken to each other since.'

'Not even the brothers and sisters.'

'No, there would be too much suspicion. They would be accused of being informers.'

'That's the saddest tale I ever heard,' said Shaun, certain that Harry's story contained at least an element of exaggeration. 'Man, you Irish know how to tell a sad tale.'

'You could call it a Belfast tale and it's as true as I'm a non-practising man of temperance. What's worse is that the devil sent Johnny, Shauny and several of their brothers out to kill.'

'I thought you said you were non-practising Anglican,' said Shaun.

'I don't need a church to know the devil, and do you want to know something, Shaun? The work of the devil has no end.'

Shaun was facing the bar as he nodded and a line of bottles caught his eye. 'See that bottle of whisky over there,' Shaun said, pointing to the wall. 'That's where the devil lies for me.'

'Oh ay,' said Harry, 'He's dancing in the swirling syrup whisky for you and he's stirring the creamy froth of Guinness for me.'

'You're a poet,' said Shaun as he staggered to the bar. He returned to his seat moments later with a thump as his long legs wrestled with the trestle of the table. 'Bar's closing,' he said, 'Two double whiskies and two pints of Guinness coming up. Your Guinness is apparently settling.'

'Cheers,' said Harry, holding up his glass and smiling. 'We shall repent tomorrow!'

'Yes, we shall be great men on Friday.' said Shaun. 'And at least no one's going for a ride on that prison bus,' he added, the flame of whisky kindling his body.

'I don't know,' said Harry, standing up and looking into the distance. 'I might have reserved a place on that prison bus by

Saturday.' Harry collected his Guinness from the bar and held his glass aloft, 'From this day forth, let us not dance with the devil or ride on the prison bus!'

'Agreed, and cheers,' laughed Shaun.

'Cheers, mate,' said Harry against the clang of a glass. 'And thank you.'

'What for?'

'For taking care of my son,' said Harry. 'To Robert! And to Toby!

'To Robert and Toby!' retorted Shaun. 'May they be great men!'

'May they be great men!' smiled Harry, his eyes blurred with tears.

'With great fathers,' added Shaun.

'With great fathers,' repeated Harry, draining his Guinness. 'With great fathers, who know when to stop dancing with the devil!'

THE CASTLE

Annie had applied her makeup in the reflection of the train window and tied her hair back into a neat bun, but two small red rashes remained like stained maps under each eye.

The windows to the soul, her dad had often said, and he was right. Her face was now defined by colour, but the cartography of her marriage was etched in her eyes.

She worked back through each minute of her return from work and tried to understand the mistakes she had made. She always did so after an argument. This time, there was little to unravel. She had momentarily lost her mind, and there was nothing redeemable about how she had behaved.

Returning home from another day of cleaning dishes and preparing meals, Annie's retreat from work closed in on her. The boys' pyjamas were still sprawled across the living room floor, plates lay encrusted with tomato sauce and grease, and the sink in the kitchen was spilling over with bean-stained pots and pans. A collision of coats, clothes, books, and mucky shoes all combined to send her head into a whirl of voracious fury.

'What the hell have you done all day?' she'd said piercingly to Roy when he had appeared in the doorway.

Roy had stood startled, unable to react in the no man's land of Annie's mind.

'Don't ever speak to me like that!' he'd said.

'Why not? You do nothing. I'm fed up. I can't do this anymore.'

'You can't do what anymore?' Roy had retained control as his shoulders moved back and arms spread out to the sides. 'Run around like a martyr looking after your cripple of a husband? It must be awful for you, but I will tell you something, you are not the girl I married. You yap from the minute you wake up that the place is a mess. Well, guess what? It's not bloody important!'

Annie had remained static while his voice soared. 'A yap? Is that right?' she ventured weakly. 'I work myself to the bone and that's what you think of me.'

'As I said, you're a martyr. You do everything. Did you congratulate me for putting the washing on? Did you say thank you to me for walking the kids to school? Did you notice that the boys had a proper cooked breakfast this morning instead of that crap you give them from a box? You only see what you want to see. Well I can tell you that that I won't be treated like a charity case anymore.'

Roy's body had swept across the living room, his prosthetic leg trailing half a second behind the other. He had snatched the plates up from the floor and banged the kitchen door with his fist. A clatter of crockery had come from the sink in tandem with incoherent words. The words had moved closer as he had returned to the living room. 'I tell you what, Annie, you can tidy up yourself because there's not a chance I'll do it properly. I'm away to the club.'

Annie had run after him, tugging at his arm. 'You can't go! Wait! I'm at the castle tonight. Who's going to look after the boys? You promised James you'd take him to football.'

'You fix it. You tell James that his dad has gone out because he can't bear to be in the same house as his mother. Sort out your own mess.'

'It's not my mess. Roy, be reasonable. I need to get to work. James' trip money is due. I need to go.' Annie was clutching at his shoulder by the living room door. 'Stop. Please. It's cash-in-hand. Mr Moffit will sack me if I let him down tonight. Don't make me cancel.'

Roy's face was close to Annie's. Too close.

'I couldn't give a shit about Mr Moffit and your precious job. You need to take a long, hard look at yourself in the mirror and see the person you've become. You're self-important and nasty.'

'You hateful…' she began, but Roy's blue eyes were cold and she stopped.

She tried to speak again, but he was tall and strong and stationary and words eclipsed her as her mind raced. She pushed him. He stood still. She tried again. His eyes were stone. She pounded her fists on his chest in an affray of energy and released everything that had been contained since the warmth of their marriage had disappeared.

Roy remained still.

Annie's rolled fists had landed on his chest one more time, but silence had reflected off her last pathetic thump as her fists came undone.

She stood back. There was a darkness in his eyes. She turned the palms of her hands towards her face and stared in disbelief.

And she realised she had done something wrong.

She looked up. Roy remained motionless.

'Say something,' she said.

'I don't have anything to say.'

Roy's voice was small and distant.

Annie searched again in his vacant eyes and the lack of response reduced her further into herself. Repelled and stunned by her own behaviour, she hugged herself and looked into her husband's eyes. 'You said I was self-important and nasty.' Her words were feeble. She wiped her hands on her thighs and began to shake. 'It's who I've become. It's not who I am.'

Roy's head moved. He stepped back. What was that look? A glimpse of sadness? A pang of regret? No, there was nothing. There was nothing because Roy had finally flipped the switch. This was Annie's crime.

Annie watched Roy make his way down the path and fell to

her knees. A sound broke free from her chest. A cry. She rocked and felt a deep and unknown pain cut through her.

And on the train to Carrickfergus, she stared at her own reflection, unsure who exactly was looking back.

A violent woman, a lost woman, a contemptible woman filled with self-loathing. He was right. She was not the girl he'd married, and more than ever Annie needed to know the girl that Roy had married.

Did she regret it? What was the reflection telling her? Do you regret pounding your fists off your husband's chest? Annie didn't know. She felt repelled by her own image and yet the woman whose cheeks were burning and who felt life return to her body didn't feel remorse for what she had done. Instead, she was glad because she knew it was the last battle.

The pale woman she had seen only days before was glowing in the train window in colour where hatred had triumphed. The look in Roy's eyes was hatred. It had to be over.

And she couldn't regret anything knowing that it might be over.

***

Shaun looked around the room at the other guests, most of them seated in couples. He pictured Sarah's face among the people there and tried to recall how she used to be, her freckled face always alive with vitality. And then she was pale and weak, and it was hard to imagine which version of Sarah was sitting beside him, the woman who had once confidently walked across a bar to speak to him, or the woman who had so desperately cried out to God to take her in the night and to bring her to her destiny.

Carrickfergus Castle was the location of a St. Patrick's Day party organised by the American Embassy. Stella from Project Children had been invited too, but family commitments had led her back to the U.S. early. Shaun was alone.

The music began, and a strong pale arm, defined by taut veins and ridges of fine muscle, lifted his plate. The arm was on the other side of the table, clearly recognisable by its strength and deftness. He followed the line up to the hem of the white, satin shirt and felt two eyes inspect him before he met their reflection. It was Annie.

She looked relieved, as though she had been trying to capture his attention. A broad smile fanned her lean face. It was a darker face than the one he had seen in the rain, her cheeks tinted red and eyes speckled black. He smiled. 'Annie.'

A man with grey and black curled hair appeared behind her like a dragonfly. She saw him and sped away, turning back to shrug in Shaun's direction like a scolded child. Shaun watched Annie flit through the room. She wore a black skirt, skimming her knees, her legs also concealed in black. Large plates lined up her arms as she weaved in and out of the guests, raising her arms, twisting and turning purposefully. She looked back as the waitresses left the room and her lips smiled.

Shaun waited for a chance to leave and it came when the bow of a fiddle collided with strings in a buoyant melody. Feet tapped and hands clapped in time to the fiddler's refrain, and Shaun walked towards the stairwell. He descended the stone steps and passed a door with a sign, 'Staff only.' Should he tap the door? No, it was too foolish to go there and ask to see a waitress. He fastened his coat and walked outside.

This was a milder version of Ireland than the one he'd learned to battle with rain hoods and umbrellas. It was cool, but clear and the sky was a sheet of hazy black. Twenty minutes passed by and there was no sign of Annie. Shaun felt too awake to go back to his hotel, but too weary to be in the midst of a party, and just as he contemplated confiding his spiritual disquiet to the sky, a voice pulled him back to reality.

'Are you aware that you're standing under the statue of a hero?'

Shaun turned to find Annie, her face half covered in the layers of her purple scarf, looking up at a floodlit statue of a gentleman with long flowing hair.

'No, I didn't know. Enlighten me,' he smiled.

'The king you see before you is a hero because he saved my ancestor's horse! Do you know who he is?'

'No, I don't.'

'That's King William III, King Billy between you and me.'

'Ah, I see,' replied Shaun.

'Can I check that you know who King Billy is before I continue with this life-changing information?'

'Yes, I know a little bit about King William of Orange and King James II, but please tell me more.'

'King James' army ransacked the ancestral home of John Roxboro in Cullybackey in the year 1690. His men killed Granda John and his wife and made off with a beautiful bay coloured horse. John Roxboro was my Great Great Granda's Great Great Great Granda.'

Shaun looked up to the left and made a swift calculation. 'Are you sure there are enough greats there.'

'Roughly.'

'Well, that's a tragic tale indeed.'

'The good news is that John's baby boy survived, hidden as it was in the covers of the bed, and today a descendent of that very baby stands before you.'

'And what role did Billy have to play in the horse's fortunes?' Shaun asked, enlivened by Annie's words.

'King Billy was a Dutchman who came to these shores in 1690 to chase the Catholic King Jimmy away. He popped into Carrickfergus to this castle on the way to battle. Once he was fed and watered in the banquet hall where you just had a feast, he rode off to the Boyne river and battled a thief on a special horse, a special horse stolen from my ancestor's farm in Cullybackey.'

'And what became of the thief?'

'I'm not entirely sure,' answered the lilting voice with its peculiar musical accent, 'but I think he fled to France.'

'And the horse?'

'That's precisely why King Billy is a hero. He returned the horse to the farm in Cullybackey and it lived a long and happy life.'

'You know, you remind me of a man called Harry Adams.'

'I don't think I know him.'

'Harry, Jean's husband.'

'Oh, I've never met Harry. I only met Jean the other day for the first time. Does he look like me?'

'Not quite, but he tells a good yarn.'

Annie laughed. 'What are you doing out here? There's plenty of free drink in the castle.'

'I think I had enough drink with Harry Adams to last a lifetime. I'm going for a walk if you'd like to accompany me. I'd love to hear more of your history lessons.'

'Oh, I'm not sure. I've got a train to catch. I need to get back to my...' Annie paused and looked around. She spoke hesitantly, 'I can spare another hour before the last train home.'

Shaun chose not to ask any questions. He knew that Annie had at least one child and it was probable that she had a husband too. He shrugged off any thoughts that might make her change her mind and focused on the path ahead. They continued past the castle towards the promenade in silence.

He needed to hear Annie's voice again. 'So, tell me, do you get to work in this fabulous Norman castle every day?'

'Just two nights a week. I work at a telecoms factory in Whiteabbey during the day. I make tea and serve lunch to the directors and visitors. What about you? What do you do?'

'You really want to know?' Shaun inquired, holding back a smile.

'I think so,' Annie replied nervously.

'I'm a professor.'

'A professor,' Annie stated, her eyes pinned to Shaun's.

'A professor,' smiled Shaun. 'At a university.'

'A professor at a university,' Annie repeated, her top lip folded between her teeth.

'A professor of history at a university.'

'History,' Annie said, her brows dipped to the centre of her face.

'History,' said Shaun, hiding the grin that was trembling in his cheeks. 'Specifically, Irish History.'

'No,' a wince came from Annie.

'Yes,' Shaun smiled.

'My thesis was on the history of the Scots-Irish in America, so I spent a summer in my twenties in Dublin immersed in public records on those who boarded ships to America in the decades after a great battle.'

'A great battle on a river called Boyne, by chance?'

'The very one.'

'So you know a little bit about King Billy and King Jimmy.' Annie said, her face now hiding in the fabric of the winding purple, scarf.

'A little.'

'I'm affronted.'

'Don't be...affronted? I knew absolutely nothing about the famous Roxboro clan of...where did you say?'

'Cullybackey. Actually, it's an old yarn that's been handed down over generations, so you may need to check its accuracy.'

'I'm sure it's true. And the kid was wrapped in a blanket, huh?'

'So it goes.'

'It sounds like a good story to me, although we do have that issue of trust regarding the scallions.'

Annie smiled. 'How did the dinner go?'

'It was fun.'

'Jean's a laugh. You know, she got me into a wile lot of trouble at that induction. I wish it was me going to America. Me and Jean together in Washington, D.C. We'd have a brave time of it!'

'A brave time of it, indeed!' echoed Shaun, surmising there was more entertainment than courage in the bravery to which Annie referred. 'Jean would certainly make an impression.'

***

The last train had already departed, but Annie made no effort to find her way home, grounded as she was to the timelessness of the present moment. The memory of what she had done to Roy was buried in some mechanical part of her being that allowed reality to sound its dull tone far from her mind. She walked and freed herself from the boundaries of her moral compass. She led Shaun along the promenade and the highway and onto on a narrower road with houses on either side. On the edges of a black country road, a car approached with headlights blaring at full beam, and she knew that it was time to turn back.

The wide walls of the castle were in front of them again, illuminated against the darkness, and casting their ancient, stony splendour into rippling flags of yellow on the black sea.

Annie recalled her own castle set in a forest of a glen. She remembered strolling with boys along the edge of a dark forest path, where the only pointers were the sound of the gushing river and the rocky, sludgy earth below her feet. She had stopped and she had kissed them under black skies skinkled with stars. It was innocent back then, and Annie yearned for that innocence as a temptation to reach out and take Shaun's hand awakened her sense of the past.

After the bomb, Annie had fulfilled the promise she had made to care for Roy in sickness and in health, and when Roy's wounds had healed, daily existence had dragged them through chugging motions of quiet resentment, forgiveness, animosity, contentment, bitterness, stalemate, greedy hatred and cold indifference. Annie had finally been reduced to her knees and the walk with Shaun had pulled her back to standing.

She turned to Shaun. There was a sadness about him, a sort of melancholy warmth, as though his eyes were fixed on a distant place.

'What was she like?' Annie asked.

Shaun raised an eyebrow before acknowledging his understanding of the question.

'Sarah?'

'Your wife. Jean said you were a widower.'

'Yes, her name was Sarah. She was….let me see.' Shaun paused. 'Lively, crazy, strong. She was beautiful.'

'She sounds special, the crazy and the beautiful. Do you mind if we sit down?' Annie gestured towards a bench. 'I've been on my feet all day.'

'Sure.'

'Did Sarah help with Project Children too?'

'No, after Sarah died, a friend told me that bringing a kid from Ireland over on the Project Children program would help Toby heal. She was right. Toby had a blast with Robert, but that one Irish kid helped us both heal in the end.' Shaun seemed distracted. He looked out to sea and breathed deeply before posing a question that Annie knew would unsettle the night. 'And you?'

'Me,' she responded, looking Shaun in the eye, 'I'm married to Roy.'

Shaun's face remained composed. Could that be enough information to close the discussion? She waited.

'What does Roy do?'

Annie smiled inwardly at the juxtaposition of questions. 'Roy runs the house and looks after the two boys while I'm here or at the factory.'

There was a betrayal of curiosity in Shaun's composed face and Annie continued with the reality she could no longer hide. 'Roy lost his leg in a bomb eleven years ago.' She became aware of time and her surroundings and of the day she had had. 'A unilateral transfemoral amputation. That's the technical term. He was a fitter in Standards, and before that, he worked as an engineer on bridges in Holland.'

Shaun was motionless. He then spoke thoughtfully. 'You carry a great deal.'

Annie's face reddened. She wanted this part of the conversation to end. 'Roy looks after our boys. He runs the house. He's busy. I didn't want you to think I was complaining.'

'It's okay. I didn't think you were.'

'He was in a lot of pain in the beginning. He could only work part-time and by the time we would pay for...'

Annie stopped. She needed to change the subject. The reality of her day was striking a match against the dark grace of the night.

Shaun spoke first. 'You know, it's late. Your train will have gone.'

'It's okay. I'll get a taxi. Can we keep walking? Maybe you need to go, though?'

'No.' Shaun said swiftly. 'I do have to get up early, but I'm wide awake. Let's walk.'

The conversation returned to an easy stream as they each

shared the story of their lives. Shaun seemed intrigued by Annie's transition from college to working in a kitchen, and she tried her best to explain how working in an office had stemmed her freedom. When Andrew was born, Annie had been glad to have an opportunity to leave the workplace, and she had been content to live on less to escape the burden of sitting still. High energy had always consumed her body and her mind, and fate had granted her an uninvited acknowledgement of her ability. Annie's legs had moved swiftly when her eldest son had walked towards the fire, and Annie's arms had swept him up promptly when he was inching towards the deep bath she had prepared for Roy. Roy had remained stationary, with only a voice to caution.

It was a Loyalist bomb that had severed Roy's leg, but it was Annie's refusal to leave Northern Ireland at her husband's request that had splintered the tracks of their marriage.

As Annie walked with Shaun, they didn't discuss Roy or Sarah. Annie narrated stories of her childhood in the coastal village of Glenarm, her mind rekindling the past, her body ignited by the present. Shaun, in turn, spoke of his family, his mother's ceaseless reproach towards his father's drinking, and the visits from his loud and feisty Irish-American aunts and uncles from New York.

They strolled in silence through the empty town and as they arrived at the highway by the shore again, Annie removed her hand from her pocket and placed it in Shaun's. Shaun continued to look straight ahead as he led the way across the road, and Annie could feel a struggle in the hand that remained loose and unsure. They approached the castle and stopped by the yachts and the fishing boats anchored to the oily port. A scene that Annie had passed so many times before appeared out of focus and charged with a mass of life that was beyond any fantasy she had ever conjured in her mind. In all the years she had been with Roy, Annie had never once imagined herself touching another man.

Hypnotised by the yellow flames dancing on the water, the chord of the sea beating against the shore and the nervous tension in Shaun's hand, Annie found herself on the cusp of a crime and stoked with daring.

She turned to Shaun and assessed the dark contours of his face, the long line of his nose and his eyes that were glistening black. She lightly touched his cheek and a surge of love and a destructive desire compelled her to reach out and kiss the stranger by her side.

***

Shaun had willed Annie's lips to meet his, yet he knew he had to stop. Sea-gulls circled somewhere in the dark sky and their cautionary cries alerted him to the danger in the woman's eyes. Shaun forced his bewildered face to look away. He needed to look away because his mind was transfixed on the image of a man who had lost his leg in a bomb. He removed Annie's hand from his cheek and held it tightly. He turned to the boats that were moored in shimmering blue and black and spoke carefully. 'With everything in me, I want to kiss the beautiful woman standing beside me, but I know that she would regret it.'

The words were not his own and he realised that his mind had drawn strength from an intangible spirit. He looked up to the empty sky and wondered what force had taken Annie's hand and removed it from his burning face.

Shaun did want to kiss Annie, but he knew that he was acting for two souls lost in the dark. He faced Annie, clasping each of her hands in his. Her dark eyes were pleading and her face was complex with colour.

'Annie, you're married.'

'I know.'

Annie's head had lowered slightly, but Shaun could still see her defeated eyes as her lips turned downwards.

'Why?' he asked.

Annie was looking up but not responding.

'You've never done this before, have you?'

'No,' she said, her lips trembling.

'And something has happened to make you think that you want this.'

She shook her head. 'I didn't want to do the right thing.'

He heard a deep sadness in Annie's words. He held her tight and looked up at the sky. Why? He was unsure if he was speaking to God or to the ghost of Sarah, and he knew that there would be no answers. The woman in his arms was gripping his body, and yet his courage flowed naturally. Shaun knew that kissing Annie and leading her back to his hotel would take him on a journey that was not his own, and his will clashed with his calling like water lapping against the harbour wall. Shaun stared through the yellow light of an old castle and held onto Annie. She remained silent in his arms.

'I'm going to take you to the train station,' Shaun said, but first, we're going to go to the hotel lobby to get a warm drink.' The look on Annie's face told him that he should not let go of her hand.

Shaun had talked to Annie all night, and as he watched the first morning train move away towards the hills around Belfast, a shroud of regret covered his eyes and dispersed the smoky pink glow of dawn on the platform. Annie was gone.

He leaned against the red-bricked wall where they had waited for the train. They had been sheltered under a canopy of wood and decorative wrought iron support beams that had gradually revealed their intricate beauty through the emerging daylight. He thought over the hours that had passed by and he thought of Annie's hand holding his and the heat of her body as he held her to escape the devastating crush of her eyes.

He walked back through the town, the rows of tiny houses huddled together like a blanket around him in the cold March morning. A sheet of grey had replaced the sea and the castle appeared stoic and strong, a castle that had stood, unshakeable for eight hundred years, beating the elements, sea, fire and war. He entered his hotel room and lay on the bed fully clothed. What if he had brought her here?

They had talked for more than seven hours, and yet the conversation was incomplete. Shaun flicked through the Project Children guide beside his bed. There she was, Annie Steen. He couldn't call her number. She was married.

Was that the real reason he had held back when she'd reached up to him? No, some force had been placed in front of him like an unsolicited virtue.

He considered if he should go to sleep before the bus collected him for the Giant's Causeway and the Antrim coast, a part of Ireland that Shaun had always dreamed of seeing. He hadn't been brave enough to visit a war zone in the summer of 1976 when he had studied in Dublin. It took a boy from a war zone to come to his home before Shaun realised that war was a back-drop to the story of Belfast and not a character he was bound to meet.

Shaun's world had been consumed by Ireland since he was a child, but now, he understood that the beauty of the island was a woman called Annie Steen. She had said her name meant stone, and yet, she was floating like a feather in daydreams that pervaded his morning.

Standards, wasn't that the name of the factory? Shaun took a pen and notebook from the side table and began to write.

THE FIRST LETTER

Songs of the seventies rippled from the radio as the fluorescent tube on the ceiling met the morning light from the yard and transformed the kitchen floor into a river of shimmering vinyl. Jean held onto her mop and dispersed Harry's muddy footprints to the beat of *The Hustle* before stepping back to the tune of *The Bus Stop*, dancing and singing and shimmying along the black and white floor, all the while pushing thoughts of Harry's whereabouts away.

Jean remembered the Sunday morning in 1976 when she had befriended Downtown Radio. She was twenty-two and Harry had just asked her to marry him. 'Hello Happiness. Goodbye Loneliness,' were words that had made Jean smile from her duster to her mop. And as the words drifted from the Drifters and into Jean's subconscious, she recalled the look of joy on her brother's face. He was fourteen and covered in pimples and Jean's dancing and singing had made him smile.

Jean hadn't thought of her brother for some time. She had never needed to keep his memory alive, because he was there every day in the shape of her son.

She returned to her mop bucket, inhaled the scent of lemon Flash and wondered why her husband was creeping around the kitchen in the middle of the night. Harry had long ago sworn that he would never enter the underworld of the Shankill and it was his promise in exchange for the family of his dreams.

Four was the number of children that Harry and Jean had planned. The plan hadn't been discussed since the birth of Shelley, but Jean knew that they were both content with a contingency of three. Hannah had been born four years after Robert, and Jean had dared give herself one year to recover before setting her sights on number three. Shelley had been a blessing, but as each person eked out space in the narrow walls of their home, Jean realised that one more child would throw her system into disarray.

Jean's system was a tidy home to master an untidy mind, and she always felt empowered at the helm of her vessel when surveying the majestic calm of her gleaming kitchen floor.

Her eyes travelled to the door between the kitchen and living room, where a crop of disorderly hair offended her sense of order. She tip-toed to the sink, ran her hand under the tap and walked backwards swivelling the mop to restore the floor's twinkle. She then turned, grabbed Robert and trussed the wet strands of his hair.

'There,' she said, as Robert ducked away from her hand, 'That's better. You look like that wee fella from the pictures. The one from Top Gun.'

'Tom Cruise?'

'That's the very one. Here, do you not think there's something funny about that fella? I mean nice face and all, but there's—'

'Mum! I'm trying to go out to football!'

'Alright! Keep your hair on.' Jean stood back and admired her boy with the long piercing blue eyes. 'Tell me this before you go, did you enjoy Shaun's visit the other night?'

'Yes,' said Robert.

'Are you looking forward to the cinema?'

'Yes.'

'And are you looking forward to America?'

'Yes.'

'And do you know any other words apart from "Yes".'

'Yes,' he repeated, this time with a smile.

'And will you miss your wee mammy?' said Jean.

Robert looked up and pressed his lips together. He turned his head to one side as Jean turned her head to the other. Robert was the same height as Jean and, as he looked her in the eye, Jean considered his expression to be the greatest demonstration of his love. She reached out and ruffled his hair. 'You know, son,' she whispered, 'Mammies always love their sons best, but don't be saying to your sisters.' She winked, but she had spoken too soon, and Hannah was in the doorway with her hands on her hips, 'Mammy, you said you loved me most,' her four year-old daughter complained.

'Oh I do. Mammies always love their daughters the most and their sons best, isn't that right Robert?'

Robert bounced a ball off the slippery floor and walked to the back yard.

'For God's sake, Robert. You're worse than your father. Would you watch where you go with that bloody ball. My lovely floor's a mess.'

Hannah, who had her arms folded, looked up to her mother with condemnation, 'Mammy, you can't say that!'

'What? Bloody? Sorry, love. Do not ever repeat that word, understand?'

'Bloody will still get you into heaven, but you did a blasphem…' Hannah stopped and tried again. 'You did a big blasphemenation. That's what you did!'

'A blasphemenation, indeed? And who taught you such a word?'

'The Sunday school teacher did. I said "Oh my god," to her and she said I wouldn't get into heaven.'

'Is that so?' said Jean. 'Well, I'll be having words with that Sunday school teacher of yours.'

'She said bloody and the word that sounds like duck were okay in God's eyes, but you shouldn't say them either.'

'Is that—'

'I told her my mammy says those words all the time.'

'I do not.'

'You do so.'

'I beg your pardon!'

'You say the F word to daddy all the time, so you do.'

'Well—'

'And Robert and Timothy say it too, so they do.'

'Is that right?'

'Yes, it is, so it is.'

Jean smiled, 'You know, you'll be a linguist one day, young lady? You and your blasphemenation '

Hannah smiled and cocked her head to the side with pride as words tumbled down the stairs from Shelley.

'Finished!'

Jean rolled her eyes and called up the stairs, 'Harry, Shelley's finished.'

'Finished!' repeated Shelley.

A bang followed from the wall next door. Jean popped her head out the front door and, as expected, found Mrs McAdam in her curlers with her head out the window.

'I think it's wee Shelley, love,' said Mrs McAdam. 'I think she's finished.'

'Ay, I know. Thanks for that Mrs McAdam,' Jean said. 'The whole bloody street knows that Shelley's finished. You can put your brush shaft away!'

Jean closed the door and ran upstairs. The bathroom was alive with the chemical scent of Vosene shampoo, and there in the pink bath in a mist of steam lay Harry with the offending solution slathered over his hair. His large, hairy chest was disguised with the giant newspaper that was sailing inches above the water. A red facecloth, meanwhile, was anchored to his virtue with a blue tub of bubble bath. Jean looked at the small smiling face on the Matey and laughed, 'I see the wee man's smiling, she said, almost forgetting about Shelley, who was perched on the edge of the toilet, her pale face drawn with frustration.

'In the name of God, Harry,' said Jean as she lifted Shelley, 'Her wee legs are all red. Was there no chance of you getting up to help?'

'I'd only flatten your shagpile carpet with my wet feet, and then you'd moan. Anyway, you're better at that kind of thing.'

Jean was busy attending to Shelley whilst the debate ensued, 'Well, you wouldn't be so slow at getting up with Mrs McAdam scrutinising your parts.'

Harry pulled the paper down in a swift movement. 'Is she here?' he asked.

'No,' she's not, Jean smiled, recalling how Harry had been caught short when Mrs McAdam's bathroom had been under construction. He had been so engrossed in the History of the Monarchy, that he hadn't noticed Mrs McAdam on the throne. Having had no facecloth to hand, Queen Victoria had suffered a heavy drowning, and the book had been returned to the Shankill Road Library with sellotape supporting the entire nineteenth century.

'Where were you last night anyway?' asked Jean as she soaked Shelley's hands in the sink.

Harry peered over the newspaper and replied so swiftly that Jean could have sworn it was rehearsed, 'I went to the club with some of the lads from the work. It was wee Frankie's retirement.'

'Wee Frankie?' said Jean, ushering Shelley out the door.

'Ay, we Frankie the Fitter from Forestside,' said Harry with a wink.

'I'll wee Frankie you. I've never heard of wee Frankie in my life. You need to get home at night to wee Suzie the sexbomb from Snugville Street.'

Harry lowered the paper and smiled with a sparkle in his eyes that Jean hadn't seen in some time.

'Wee Suzie Quatro, eh? I haven't called you that in a while, have I?'

'No, love, you haven't. Now, when I think of it, you haven't.'

'Tell me this, Jean, does Shaun have a girlfriend?'

'I don't think so,' Jean blushed, nervous that Harry had been aware of her musings with Annie. 'What makes you ask?'

'Nothing. Just wondered if maybe he was doing the Project Children program because he'd met someone here. It seems a bit strange that he's so kind to Robert.'

'Well, there's a sad slur on humanity if I've ever heard one. People can be kind for no reason and Shaun is mourning his wife. He probably needed a distraction.'

'Probably,' Harry agreed, his eyes drifting over the

newspaper.

Jean looked back at Harry before leaving the bathroom. 'Harry, love, will you come home next Friday night at a decent hour?'

'Yes, love,' said Harry, returning to the *Belfast Telegraph*.

Jean had given her husband a whole new vice. She had created a liar out of a husband who had yet to lie. He would not be home at a decent hour. Harry was involved with paramilitaries and Jean was sure of it. It was the only reasonable explanation for muddy footprints on a Saturday morning at dawn.

***

The question caught Roy off guard and its vibration around the room brought to Roy's attention the reality that his son was no longer the child he'd been only days before. Andrew was on the cusp of his teenage years, and six months from his twelfth birthday, the boy who had always been playing outside or sitting upright with his toys in the middle of the room, had taken to slumping solemnly on the brown velvet armchair.

'Why aren't you talking to mum?' Andrew repeated.

'That's no your concern.' Roy replied. Andrew was silent and looked towards the TV screen. 'Sorry son,' Roy said. 'I didn't mean to—'

'Why did mum not come home last Friday night?' Andrew interrupted with an accelerated spring of confidence, 'Are you going to split up?'

Roy didn't know the answer. He hadn't spoken to his wife for six days. They had slept in the same bed because there was nowhere else to go, but Annie had been distant and neither of them had made any attempt to engage in conversation. Roy had gone through the motions of a normal weekend, knowing that when marriages were sinking, routines remained hooked up like bridges, supporting all the people who crossed their lives.

Roy had been angry, and his anger had only eased when he realised that his wife hadn't come home. Throughout the many arguments they'd had in the thirteen years of their marriage, there had never been a night when they hadn't slept under the same roof, but Friday night wasn't a normal night.

Andrew's question swayed in the air like a ticking clock. Roy turned to his son. 'We had an argument but it doesn't mean we're going to split up. Have you any more questions?'

The voice of his youngest son circled through the house, bringing the conversation to a welcome close. James seemed to be rapping in time with the music video on the TV. Roy missed the first sentence, but 'You're listening to the boy from the big bad city' was clear. As was, 'This is jam hot.'

Roy looked at his nine year-old son and enquired in words his own mother had frequently used when he was listening to the psychedelic sounds of Pink Floyd 'What was thon?'

James, who was clad in a white shell suit and white trainers, snatched the remote control from Andrew's hands and spread his wings in the middle of the living room in movements resembling a drowning minister bobbing up and down in the water. 'This is jam hot,' he sang as his body mimicked the routine of the other white shell suit in the room, the one that was drowning on the TV screen. James repeated the chorus, and Roy concentrated on the words as his son's body shoogled on the mat. 'Tank fly boss walk jam nitty gritty. You're listening to the boy from the big bad city. This is jam hot. This is jam hot.'

Roy smiled. Whatever trouble Andrew had witnessed between his parents, the war had eclipsed James, the son who could learn rhymes in his sleep and who had excelled at earning sweets in the Baptist church, the Presbyterian Church and the Tabernacle due to an ability to absorb and repeat verses. It was never entirely clear how much meaning he derived, his talents faltering at the school gates, where a barrier went up between the words in his mind and the paper on which they were written.

'What was that?'

'It's Beats International. Shush and listen.'

Roy listened. He could decipher a buzzing hum against a microphone that was increasingly infectious, and he could see a young female singer with an angelic voice and a bun in her hair, crying 'Just be good to me.' Roy looked closer and realised that the woman in the oversized white shirt, plastic leggings and trainers could have passed for Annie. As the thought crossed his mind, Annie appeared at the door in her white shirt with her hair tied up in a bun like the girl bouncing around the TV, and six days of stalemate dissipated in a hip hop song. Roy laughed and broke the ice. 'Annie, you and James could get work as a tribute band to Beats International.'

Annie didn't speak but her curious eyes assessed the TV screen and smiled.

Andrew was next, 'Right enough, mum, all you need is a pair of those shiny trousers.'

'I'm sure I'd look wile nice in one of your daddy's shirts and shiny leggings,' said Annie.

'You're back early,' Roy observed. He hadn't expected to see Annie before ten o'clock.

'I resigned.'

'You did what?' Roy asked, sitting upright on the sofa.

'I resigned. You should be happy now.'

It was true that Roy had been asking Annie to leave the castle for months. His disability allowance was a pittance, but a combination of it, the family allowance and the factory salary was enough to pay the bills, and Roy's uncle had always been more than generous with the boys. Why had Annie finally decided to leave?

'I'd had enough of Mr Moffit. He's a right auld blirt sometimes.'

Roy laughed at Annie's choice of words.

'I've been telling you that for ages,' he said.

'Yes, well, I won't be workin' at the castle anymore. So, shift over and let me sit down. Top of the Pops. Perfect. I haven't seen it in years.'

'Actually, it's over. Your nitty gritty song was number one.'

Roy smiled at Annie. He wanted to place his arm around his wife's shoulder and keep her there beside him, but the cold war of the last six days remained in the room like inertia.

Annie was still distant. Her eyes were often cold by day, her voice strong as it expressed Roy's imperfections, but deep in the night, she was silent, her body stirring, fumbling, clutching at passions stoked in the heat of the darkness. As morning broke through the curtains, Roy would reach across the bed to find that the gleed would have long departed. Annie would go to work, the boys would go to school and Roy would be alone with a long list of chores and a vision of Nina, her silky, yellow hair rippling across his daydreams, her blue eyes furrowing into his mind until he would awake with a bang.

Roy had met Nina at the gatherings of their childhood. The reunions of his father's friends, expatriates of the Netherlands, would commence in faint whispers, a large circle of people seated in measured serenity. It was a contrast to the rowdy festivities of his maternal side. There was little room for silence in the cramped walls of a Glenarm cottage where a clout in the ear was delivered to heedless children and the sound of laughter and foofing rumbled under tables. There was little room to fall in love with the muted lips and intrepid eyes of a girl.

Roy would see her once or twice a year and she would follow him with her haloed, blue eyes. As a teenage boy, it was Nina who filled his dreams when hormones washed over his body. He'd blushed at the Sinterklaas celebration when he was twelve. The gifts delivered by the friend of his father dressed in the green velvet of Sint Nicolaas meant little contrasted with the beauty of Nina. Then, when he was fifteen, she had pulled him behind a doorway of a friend's home. She had unbuttoned her blouse and allowed Roy's abashed eyes to rest on her swollen breasts. There was a look of knowing that day in her powerful eyes.

Roy would be a father with an expectant wife before he would hear the sound of Nina's voice, and then he would learn the danger of following a silent woman.

He looked back to Annie. How different she was from the Frisian girl who ran screaming from his dreams.

Each time Roy imagined a new chapter of his life without Annie, the pages would start to curl, and he would think of the mute girl and he would know that Annie's voice was safe.

***

Mr Haas's secretary was timorously clinging to the doorway of the small kitchen. She reached an arm out to Annie, who was busy refilling the coffee machine. 'This letter is for you. It got mixed up with Mr Haas's mail,' she said. Annie had delivered his mail that morning with his breakfast and hadn't seen it. On closer inspection, it said clearly on the envelope, 'Mrs Steen, Catering Services, Office of Mr Haas.'

The stamp was an American one, the writing similar to that on letters she had received from the Project Children team in the US, and Annie knew instinctively it was from Shaun.

She poured the rest of the water into the percolator, closed the lid and made her way to an empty conference room. Opening the window to disperse the stale air of smoke, she pulled up a seat and carefully removed two small note pages from the envelope. The paper was headed with a logo for the Coast Road Hotel, Carrickfergus, and it was packed with the same elaborate script that Annie had come to know as American.

March 18, 1990

Dear Annie

As you can see from the paper, I am snatching a short moment before my coastal tour. I didn't want to leave without thanking you. Carrickfergus Castle spoke to me like no other place I'd ever been, and the legend of King Billy and King Jimmy will forever bring a smile to my face.

I will meet your son, James, in July and I will be sure to arrange some time for him to play with Toby and Robert. I also wondered if you might be interested in helping out with Project Children in Belfast. This may be presumptuous, but it would be wonderful to have you on board, and Stella could certainly benefit from your advice. I know how busy your work schedule is, but I could pass on your details to her if you could spare an hour or two per week to help.

My flight leaves in the morning and I wish I hadn't left some things so undone. It would be good to stay in touch.

Yours sincerely,
Shaun Kelly

Annie touched her neck and read the words again. She folded the letter, placed it in her pocket and returned to the kitchen. Catching her reflection in the metal door of the dishwasher, she saw that her neck was red and blotchy.

The cold war had ended the night she had resigned from the castle, yet a chill was ingrained in the walls of her home because neither she nor Roy would ever discuss what had happened. Annie was tired of fighting and ashamed of facing up to the crazed soul who had flung her mind onto her husband's chest. There was a calmness in her marriage, a release of months of tension, and a feeling of sanity.

Annie ran her fingers across the paper in her pocket. She had tried to kiss another man and the paper grazing her stomach mocked the calmness. She touched it and walked to the drawer beside the sink. She lifted the jotter and skipped through the scribbles of orders until she found a clean, white, page.

Uncertainty prevailed upon Annie's hand, and as she tracked back through the road she had travelled, sanity and insanity conspired to form words on a blank page, words that were actions in the life of a woman who was accustomed to moving fast, yet going nowhere at all.

***

Shaun took some quiet time to drink coffee and read his mail before his first tutorial. He had returned home late the previous night after yet another extended Irish Society meeting, and caffeine was required to brave the morning and remove the voice of Eamon Fitzgerald from his mind.

Eamon Fitzgerald had single-handedly transformed the

Irish Society from a fund-raising charity to a blatantly political organisation. And his voice and his politics were gradually quashing Shaun's will to follow in the tradition of his grandfather.

Shaun's grandfather had been an illiterate labourer who had boarded a ship to New York in the early twentieth century with nothing but his good looks and a tonne of muscle, a legend that he had passed down to his own son, who also lay claim to the same attributes. He was the first in a line of three generations of men with an anglicised variation of the name Seán, and he had been a founder member of the Irish Society, which had eventually become a source of assistance to Irish tradesmen in search of work.

Shaun was the only member of his family who had retained the connection to the Irish Society and who had any real interest in the country of his forefathers, but there had been a shift in his perceptions. The poetry, the Guinness and the wild rugged coast were still there, but his mind was alive with murals of a divided land, the voice of a boy who lamented his passage to a prison bus and the pleading eyes of a woman. Annie's eyes had borrowed his mind and removed any former notions of his homeland.

He turned to his desk and picked up some mail. After three weeks, he'd stopped checking for a response from Annie, aware that that the madness surrounding his search for her every morning served as an extension of his mourning. Yet, there it was: a small envelope with Queen Elizabeth's head. His body jolted and he ripped open the envelope.

The neat lines of careful handwriting were Annie's. He sat down, moved his coffee to the side, and began to read.

13th April 1990

Dear Shaun

Thank you for your letter. It was a lovely surprise. Thank you also for offering to meet up with James. My mother, who wouldn't be one for believing in streets paved with gold, said I need my head looked at sending a nine year-old boy to America on his own. She fears that America is beset with gun-crime, drugs and excessive materialism. If you could ensure he retains his distance from at least the first two things, my mother would be most grateful.

As for the Project Children program, I'd love to help out once a week. I recently resigned from the castle, so my Thursdays and Friday nights are free. You'll need to explain to Stella that I work in a kitchen and that my administrative skills, which were once good (I came first in my Business Administration course at the Polytechnic, if you don't mind me saying), are now fairly inadequate. I don't even know how to use a computer. The boys want one for Christmas though, so there is hope.

It's interesting that Carrickfergus Castle spoke to you. It's not famed for its voice. Also, it may have been a little bit more decorated than usual the night that you saw it.

By the way, I forgot to tell you about Jean's name for you. She'll kill me if I tell you this, so don't breathe a word. Jean told me that she and her wee neighbour refer to you as the Honky Tonk man. I'm certain this will make you smile!

Yours sincerely,

Annie Steen

Shaun laughed aloud at the last line. He was tempted to write back straight away, but he stopped and reflected.

There were many married women in Shaun's life. There was Stella from Project Children, who'd held him close when Sarah had died. Then there were his university colleagues, Patricia and Francine, friendships that were all bolstered by a safe mutual flirtation.

The problem with Annie was that there was no flirtation. And there was nothing safe. There was a long conversation and danger masked in the recesses of two beseeching eyes.

Shaun was afflicted by a wholly irrational feeling that ran into conflict with a desire to remove some of the pain from those unrelenting eyes. He knew that he would write again. He would write and be wary of an unsafe flirtation and the tempered threat of getting close to Annie Steen.

THE TROUBLES

Annie passed by the Whitehouse, an old fort less than a mile from her home. She ran her hands across its ancient walls, dusting the nostalgia nestled in the mortar of each flaky stone. Ahead there was the sound of sticks cracking and the memory of two little boys in wellington boots running towards the shore. There were no little boys now, just a tangled sense of restless disquiet, and the realisation that Andrew and James had long lost interest in kicking in the sand.

She lay her jacket on a patch of grass by the water's edge and looked out to sea to Belfast Lough, where a belt of motorway arced around a small forgotten patch of water, leaving a sludgy lake of mudflats that nature had reclaimed. Hundreds of mallards bobbed up and down, the beautiful male emerald heads rising supreme from the water, shadowing the female in her camouflage of speckled brown.

In her hands, Annie held another letter. She had already ripped it from its envelope in the factory and greedily consumed its contents. Now she had to destroy it. Life in her home had returned to the way it had been before she started spending evenings in the castle, and she and Roy were once again living out an unspoken coalition of consensus. Life was flat, but it was easy and Annie knew that the letter she held could unsettle that refreshing sense of calm. She read the letter one more time.

May 6, 1990

Dear Annie

May is a wonderful time of year in Washington D.C. The winter can be pretty harsh, so we welcome the spring like a new beginning. Here at the Catholic University of America, the flowers are blooming in spectacular colour and the breeze is providing a welcome breath from the high temperatures.

It won't be long until the Irish kids get here, and there is a flurry of activity in preparation. I have been busy with work since Spring Break, but I managed to make it to a Project Children fundraising event last week in an Irish bar in Virginia. A record number of host parents have signed up this year. I was the first single man to take part, and I believe I may have set a trend. Once word spreads, everyone wants an Irish kid to come and stay for the summer. I was speaking to some of the host parents from last year at the fundraiser and, although most of them have entered into this program with altruistic intentions, I couldn't help but pick up on a few things that people were saying, especially after a few drinks.

One guy, whose children have grown up and left home, told me that he couldn't handle another holiday alone with his wife, so he had brought a Protestant boy and a Catholic boy to America to distract her! He said that Project Children had worked well for them and they'd had the best holiday at their lake house ever. The Irish parents are probably unaware that their kids are keeping the peace in homes across Virginia and Maryland!

As for you, Annie, you do not lack the skills that Stella requires. Regardless of your profession or standing in the world, you'll be handed a pile of envelopes and be told to start folding and sticking. You are an intelligent lady and I'm glad that we're going to be working together. I look forward to hearing from you again.

Yours sincerely

Shaun

The letter didn't contain any information that Annie couldn't keep at home, but her hands automatically tore it into tiny pieces and scattered it in the muddy water. She watched as the pieces pulled back towards the shore, resting together in a rock pool above the sludge.

The letter had said so little, but it was filled with words that had served a purpose, words that kept a perilous conversation flowing.

Annie could invent a kiss and conceive a whole other reality in the safe hold of her mind. And while her imagination had already trespassed over Shaun's body, she needed a small piece of his reality. She needed him to tell her how he had felt at the castle when a married woman had reached out to take his hesitant hand.

It could have been a fantasy, a flight of an overzealous imagination and a reaction to the frenzied hatred she had fired at Roy.

Yet, the conversation with Shaun had streamed like easy contentment, and Annie was possessed by the knowledge of how effortlessly her hand had wrapped itself in the hand of a widowed man.

***

Roy retraced the words on the *News Letter* with a burning sense of disorientation. 'IRA attack in Holland', read the headline. 'Two Australians shot in a spray of bullets.'

'Annie, take a look at this,' said Roy.

Annie turned away from the steaming pots in the warm kitchen and sat down beside Roy at the table. She read slowly.

'Oh god,' she finally said, 'How could they mistake two Australian tourists for British soldiers?'

'They had British registration plates,' Roy explained.

'I don't understand.'

'I told you before that it's a mad war.'

'The terrorists all seem to know what they're doing, if you ask me,' said Annie.

Most of the terrorists had no idea what they were doing, and that was what Roy needed to believe. He needed to believe that the men and the women shooting bullets and planting bombs had long ago lost their minds.

The physical pain after the bomb at the McNeill bar had sent Roy reeling to a dark place, but as he recovered, he had resolved that he would not be broken by the Loyalist organisation behind his bomb. It was the footsteps of Nina and the clicking of her heels on the cobblestones that still haunted him every day.

The birth of James came at the right time, and Roy understood that his legacy was to ensure that his children would never suffer the mania that had oppressed the country of their birth for so long.

'Ierland is ziek.'

Roy said the words and Annie looked up. 'Ireland is sick,' she translated. 'Yes, I remember you said your father used to say that. Those words certainly mean something today.'

'He said that if a nation was starved, the madness would last for generations.'

'I remember your father as this mysterious man walking through Glenarm. I always thought it was nice that he was different, that he was Dutch. I suppose I liked that about you too,' smiled Annie. 'I don't know about that famine theory though. It was such a long time ago and these terrorists, all of them, the Republicans and the Loyalists, are destroying communities for no reason.'

'You know, when I was a boy I was proud that my dad had been in the Merchant Navy and that he'd seen the world, but now when I think of him, I think of the young man who survived a famine. He was a true hero.'

Annie stood up and placed her hand on Roy's shoulder. 'James told me you're his hero too.'

Roy smiled. James had always boasted to his friends about his father's leg, as though it was a rite of passage for James to be in command of every wayward escapade among the boys on the estate, but James' grandfather was a real hero.

Jan Steen had survived the Hongerwinter of the

Netherlands in 1944, only six years before he had docked in Ireland and fallen in love with Molly Magill. His father had told him that hunger tears at a man's mind like a wild beast, and that nothing he would ever experience in life could compare to its maddening cries. The honger had eventually killed Jan's infant nephew, the only son of his brother, Dirk, and in Dirk's eyes the lack of food supplies and the hunger would forever be linked to the Duits. Once the Germans were equated with starvation, there was no way of reversing the association in the minds of the generation who had felt hunger inch from their bodies to the frontier of their minds.

Roy had often wondered if there was merit in his father's theory that Ireland still carried the burden of a Great Famine. Starvation, scurvy and diarrhea may have killed the bodies of one million people one hundred and forty years ago, but Jan had said that it was hunger that had stolen the minds of the survivors, and whilst historians might attest one hundred explanations for a famine, when a man is reduced to hunger, generations will feed off the resentment of ancestors who had to scrape the earth like wild animals for nourishment.

'Look at that,' said Annie, breaking the flow of Roy's thoughts, 'One of the victim's father lived through the Second World War and the Greek Civil war. He survived all that and moved to Australia.'

'And his son was caught in a mad war in a country of peace,' said Roy.

He thought of the impact of the shooting across the world. There would be tears in London among the friends and colleagues, shock in the town of Roermond in Holland, so ashamedly pillaged of its innocence, mourning in Greece and grief in Australia.

'Roy, you know I do understand why you want to move there,' said Annie, moving back towards the cooker.

Roy kept his eyes on the newspaper and didn't look towards his wife. It was the one subject he had promised not to raise again. They had tried living in Holland, and she had missed home. After the bomb, Roy knew that Holland represented the best chance for them both to have a good quality of life and he had pleaded with Annie to move there. Roy's uncle, Dirk, needed someone to help him run his engineering business in Leiden, and Roy could have had a meaningful job that fitted around his disability. Dirk had said that they could live with him and that one day the house would be left to them in his will, but Annie was intransigent.

'I know it wouldn't work,' Annie said carefully.

She was granting Roy the opportunity to talk about something he had long desired, but he knew he had to be careful not to shatter the peace they had practiced for two months.

'You might meet more folk this time, parents at school and the like,' Roy suggested.

'But the boys have so many commitments. It would be too much to uproot them.'

Roy knew Annie's rationale by heart. 'Annie, let's face it. You won't entertain the idea of leaving your mammy.'

'Yes. I still have my parents and I want to be here for them. You'd feel differently if yours were still alive.'

Roy didn't respond. He had loved his parents, but Annie's words were untrue. It was Jan and Molly who had always encouraged Roy to leave Ireland. Having a son so late in life gave them a more practical view of his future. They had endowed him with the skills to survive alone. Molly had died when Roy was living in Holland with Annie, but he had never connected her passing with the fact that he wasn't at home.

Annie had. She believed that his mother's death would have been less sad, somehow, if they had both been in Glenarm to see it happen. And so, Annie's freedom had always been bound up in a perpetual fear of her parents' death. All Roy could do was explain to his own children that his love for them would never change if they left these shores, and that their childhood years were compensation enough for him if they ever decided to do all the things that Roy knew he would have done if an illegal army hadn't tried to steal his mind.

***

Shaun perched restlessly at the bar as a fog of smoke and stale ale wrapped around the clients of Flanagan's in the easy communion of Friday night drinks.

The latest letter from Annie had unsettled him. She had spoken with truth marked out with anger, darkness and guilt, and she had written in a prose so enrapturing that he began to feel he had lost his sense of reality. Who was Annie? What did she mean to him and why did he suddenly care about her destiny in the world? He wanted to hold her hand and walk with her down a snowy canal. Yet, how could he wish himself to be part of someone's past and simultaneously regret the future he had never had with Sarah? His mind was flooded with the intangible kinship of love past and present. He held out his hand and watched his fingers flexing to reach for something that wasn't there.

Shaun finished his beer and made his way upstairs to the meeting. Eamon Fitzgerald took the chair and went through the minutes. Fundraising for political prisoners, British government collusion with Loyalists. Words. So many words from Eamon Fitzgerald. The stories of political prisoners paled against the imagery painted in Shaun's mind. As jails continued to swell in the north of Ireland with terrorists, the Irish Society had started to raise funds for the families of Republicans. The children of those locked away in prison needed food and clothing, yet bound up in the image of neglected children was the sound of a mother's cries, the mother of the boy in Annie's letter. As Sarah's face became entangled in the vision, Shaun shook his head and looked up to the man with the mousy curled hair and clear blue eyes.

Eamon reported a donation from a wealthy Congressman. Shaun spoke finally, 'Why don't we use the money for the kids. What about making a donation to Project Children?'

'Project Children,' said Eamon. 'I don't agree with it. What purpose does it serve to give these children a taste of rich America, when they only return home to the reality of their plight? Money needs to go into the heart of these communities in Belfast and Derry. Shaun, that young fella from the Shankill...did you visit his home in Belfast?'

'Yes, I did.'

'And what was it like? Was there a swimming pool? Was there a large, sunny backyard?'

'No,' Shaun said, incredulous that his one idea was being knocked down so swiftly.

'And how do you think he feels knowing how the other half live?'

'It's not like that, Eamon. You're mistaken if you think that these children return home in despair that they lack wealth. Robert's household was one of the most loving I'd ever seen. The only thing I gave Robert was a holiday and a chance to see what it looks like to live in a peaceful country. The kid thinks it's normal to spend a Saturday afternoon on a prison bus.'

'We'll move on if you don't mind. There are more important matters.'

Shaun was tired. He'd had enough of politics and his mind was flagging against the prescriptive negativity of the meeting. The Irish Society had once been about jobs, about helping Irish tradesmen in Maryland. It had gone underground when McCarthy's men were sniffing out any hint of red, and it remained steadfastly green, its origins disguised in St. Patrick's Day parades and ceilidhs. Had the Irish in Maryland become so socially mobile that they no longer required help? Shaun knew that the Troubles in Northern Ireland had touched many people in his social circle, but the Irish Society was fast becoming a fundraising group, dangerously political and opposed to the founding principles of fair work and fair pay.

The meeting closed and Shaun stayed behind to co-sign the treasurer's cheque for the American office of the political prisoner's charity in Ireland. He opened the letter when he was alone in the empty reception room above the bar and read it once again.

28 May 1990

Dear Shaun

There are some things that happen in this country that make you reflect more than others. Sometimes the deaths and the injuries pass you by in a wave. Perhaps the exhaustion of daily life dilutes the horror of each person's individual story or maybe our minds can only withstand so much. Today I read the story of two Australian tourists who were shot by the IRA and it took me back to a time that I haven't visited for a while.

Before Roy lost his leg, the one story that enveloped my heart and soul, was that of a little baby, killed by the IRA at the harrowingly incomplete age of fifteen months. After a bomb warning in Glengormley, only a few miles from here, his family was about to evacuate the area in a car. The bomb exploded and the debris struck the baby in the safety of his mother's arms as the family tried to get away. The screams I never heard still fracture my dreams.

At that time, Roy and I were newlyweds. We had moved to our new home in Fernagh estate outside Belfast. I was twenty-one, a young bride, and I was in a hurry to start a family after finishing college. I don't know why the story affected me in such a physical way, but I felt the loss in the pit of my stomach.

Roy had dreamed of living in the Netherlands and when we heard the news on New Year's Day in 1977, we started to think about moving, knowing that we wanted to live in a safe place where we could raise our own family.

Roy's uncle, Dirk, his father's brother, had work planned for him in the Netherlands from day one. He owned an engineering company, specialising in tension testing on bridges. Roy loved his job there. He suited being out in the wind and sunshine, climbing to the top of bridges, viewing the world from the sky.

We lived in a modern apartment block in the centre of Leiden. The windows in the Haagplein were huge and the small balcony overlooked the old town with a spectacular view of a windmill that would light up the sky at night. On Fridays, I would buy myself tulips from the stand at the corner of Haagplein. I guess you could say I was a housewife. I cleaned the flat, bought fresh food from the market and cooked meals for Roy coming home.

In the afternoons, I walked the length and breadth of Leiden. The cobbled streets were filled with vintage bicycles and rivers of people flowing over stone bridges, whilst the rows of brick houses were brimming with charm. As I walked along the canals, there was so much to take in, from the reflection of the bikes on the water, to the unadorned windows revealing small rooms crammed with books and plants. I would end my journey on the Rapenbug, where the elegant houses glistened on the water. I would crane my neck to take in the detail and wonder if I'd ever grow tired of it. The Rapenburg was at its most striking in the snow. Imagine an impressionist painting where white rooftops blend into a pale sky and where the weeping willows cast ice tear-drops onto the glass rivers and canals.

The Leidse Hofjes were my personal sanctuaries; secret gardens hidden right in the centre of town. I used to read my books there in the summer. I dreamed of having a little garden like that one day.

I didn't tire of the walks, but I grew weary of my own company. Roy's uncle encouraged me to sign up for a Dutch class. I did and I worked hard to learn the language, but I never felt part of a community, as I do now here in Fernagh. More than that, I missed home. The Troubles raged on and my mother encouraged me to stay in Leiden. What future was there for a twenty-two year-old woman in Northern Ireland? She didn't understand that I missed her. And I missed my two sisters. Their families were growing and I couldn't imagine not being there to see my nieces and nephews. In the end, I broke Roy's heart and asked him to come back home.

Sometimes I feel I am paying the price. You were surprised by how much I work. I do it because we need money and I do it because of the guilt. If we'd had stayed in Leiden, Roy would never have walked into Belfast on the day of the McNeill bar bomb and he would still be climbing up great bridges in his beloved Holland.

When I wrote that first letter to you, I promised myself that I would not write about the Troubles. I hate showing people abroad that part of who we are, but sometimes it's all too impossible to escape.

Yours sincerely

Annie

DISTANCE AND TIME

Annie's eyes flitted back and forth towards the smoke-stained melamine clock in the kitchen as the small hand inched II on the roman numeral dial. The delegates from Sudan had taken a long time to leave the boardroom, and just as Annie was ready to set off for an empty conference room, a Sudanese visitor, who had revealed impressive manners during lunch, called her from the kitchen door.

'Excuse me, Miss. May I?'

Annie brushed down her apron and stood to attention. 'Of course, come in.'

'I am Ibrahim,' he said, revealing a silver smile.

'I'm Annie.' Annie replied, bemused by the exchange.

'Annie. Ah. This name contains so much beauty.'

'Oh,' said Annie, failing to locate a measured response in her pre-occupied mind.

'Your lunch was very special.'

'Thank you.'

If there was one thing that Annie knew for sure, it was that lunch was not special, at least not in the way that Ibrahim's smile dissimulated. Mr Moffit, having forgotten about the booking, had discharged a large pot of stew from one of his local cafes, stew as pale as water that Annie had doused in Bisto gravy granules and pepper to bring back to life.

'In my country we give gifts,' Ibrahim continued.

Annie found herself spreading her arms to receive the proffered parcel. In the join of the exchange, Ibrahim looked longingly into Annie's eyes. Annie quickly placed the small package bearing the strong scent of leather on the bench, and smiled a wide grin of gratitude that was not quite as genuine as the leather.

The man from Sudan then walked backwards, his striking smile visible below a bowed brill-creamed head, an impressive head of hair given that he was around thirty years Annie's senior.

Ibrahim clashed shoulders with Mr Haas upon exiting the kitchen and Annie almost forgot about the time as she realised how unusual he appeared without a desk attached to his ribs. Kok Haas, the Dutch Managing Director, who was never called by his Christian name, and who rarely extended his conversation beyond one syllable words, glanced disapprovingly at the gift on the kitchen bench and said, 'I think Mr Mahmood may be seeking another wife. I doubt Mr Moffit will find a replacement with such poor Dutch if you accept his offer.'

Annie, more disoriented by the fact that Mr Haas had spoken to her than by the concealed compliment on her Dutch learnings and unexpected attempt at humour, smiled and wondered if there had been a magnetic shift in her relationship with the world. Her imagination was pinned to a needle that was pointing east to the birthplace of Mr Haas, south to a dusty desert in Sudan and west towards the sender of the note that was burning a hole in her apron pocket. Her life was no longer fixed on true North.

Mr Haas was gone and Annie followed the flight of his short footsteps to the door. She watched him enter the lift with the man from Sudan. Once she was certain that the lift had departed, she walked across the hall to the empty boardroom, her hand cradling the short note in her pocket, the heat in her neck rising.

June 1, 1990

Dear Annie

Could you call the number below? I know you shouldn't do this at work, but I could call you straight back to avoid any charges. Leave it until you are on a break some day. I'd like to talk to you for a moment.

Yours Sincerely

Shaun

The lengthy bleeps of the international call lingered before a familiar voice sounded, 'Hi, this is Shaun Kelly.'

'Hello, Shaun,' said Annie in nervous, yet energetic tones, the unusual events of the past five minutes still nurturing a warm smile within.

The faint rustling of an intake of breath momentarily cut the wires.

'Annie. It's you. You called,' Shaun replied.

'I did indeed.' Annie laughed, unable to disguise her enthusiasm.

'Could you give me your direct line and I'll call you back?'

Annie read out the factory number and added the boardroom extension. She waited and rubbed the front of her neck again as a carousel of images flicked through her mind: Shaun walking in the rain towards Botanic station, the deadpan look in Roy's eyes as his wife stood back and stared at her own fists and the tall shadow by a bronzed statue at the castle. Annie wondered for the first time if there had been a connection between meeting Shaun and the fight with Roy, not a sequential link where one thing follows the other, but rather a pull of gravity that led Annie, Jean, Shaun and Roy to the same place.

Finally, a voice on the phone, 'Annie.'

'How are you keeping?' Annie asked.

'I'm good, thank you. This is pretty amazing. Thank you for

calling'

Annie relaxed as the aperture of a memory widened in her mind. She swivelled in the chair by the desk at the side of the room and turned away from the digital clock that displayed 09:05 beside an American flag.

Shaun spoke again. 'I couldn't reply in writing. I needed to talk to you. Your letter moved me.'

'Sorry about that,' Annie replied, hoping he could detect her smile.

'Don't be sorry. It just brought me right back to the castle.'

Annie relived a feeling of disappointment and wondered if what Shaun had said was true. Had he wanted to kiss her?

'You know,' Shaun ventured hesitantly 'I thought of a butterfly when I saw you wait tables in the castle. I was in a trance watching you.'

Annie's chest tightened as the compliment crushed the ease of the call. She was not accustomed to this kind of admiration, and the verification of Shaun's feelings reminded her that she had almost committed adultery. In that one moment, she understood the magnitude of what she had been prepared to do.

'I watched you, Annie, and you were beautiful.'

Annie listened, Shaun's words resting on the wires.

'I can't write any of this down, so I'll say it. I did kick myself about not kissing you. I regretted it, but I knew that it was the only choice I could make. I needed to speak to you because I want to confirm in my mind that I understood why.'

There was a long pause as Annie tried to compose the right words.

She spoke carefully. 'The night that you saw me, I had an argument with Roy and I did something wrong. I felt young again when I was walking with you. Do you ever feel like time is slipping away from you and you're not moving?'

'Yes. I do.'

'I felt like I was moving again. You have to believe me when I say that I didn't ask to walk with you because I had those intentions. I don't think I even realised there was an attraction until we'd started walking. Don't take that the wrong way because it didn't escape me that you were handsome when I imagined you as the Honky Tonk man.'

Annie paused to hear a soft cough of laughter. She smiled and continued. 'It must have looked so bad and I'm sorry.'

'You know, I believe that something happened at Queen's university, but we both recognised it at different times.'

'What do you mean?'

'Something happened. I felt it as your train departed that morning and it was too late by then.'

Annie recalled the train departing. The carriage had been empty except for a man who resembled Shaun in his height and breadth. She hadn't looked at him, but she had seen the contours of his face in her own reflection in the window.

'I don't have a definition for it,' Shaun continued, 'and I'm not going to throw some romantic veil over it, but I can tell you that there was an occurrence and what I'm trying to figure out is how I can continue to write to a married woman when it feels both right and wrong.'

'But we didn't do anything. You saved me from making a mistake. Could it be that a friend would have saved me like that? You know what that fella Yeats said about friends.'

There was another breath of laughter. 'Yes, I do recall. You didn't want to talk poetry though.'

'I don't know anything about it.'

'I'll send you a poem then.'

'But I might mistake your poem for a veil of romance.'

'I'll avoid the poetry.'

'Good. I think it's the only possible option, given that I have been promised to a man from Sudan.'

A questioning 'Okay' followed.

'A visitor in the office bestowed me with gifts, held my hands, stared into my eyes and told me that my name held some beauty. Then Mr Haas, who has never before to spoken to me in full sentences, warned me that the man from Sudan may be in search of a wife.'

Shaun laughed. 'Well. It sounds like your magnetism may be drawing the wrong kind of attention.'

Annie blushed and checked the clock. 'Listen, I have a

booking now for coffee. I need to run. I don't know if phoning you again is a good idea. I might get into trouble if I'm caught, but please send me a letter. The letters are okay, aren't they?'

'It's all relative, Annie. The letters are okay in isolation. But if the letters are happening when another man's wife is running away from her marriage, then they aren't okay.'

'I'm not running away,' Annie said faintly and with that same sense of disappointment she had felt when Shaun had reasoned away a kiss at the castle. 'Roy and I are okay. Things will work out fine. Our marriage has never been so peaceful.'

'I will write to you, but you need to tell me the minute you feel it's not right. I think I'll know anyway. I hope we can be friends.'

Annie checked the clock again, 'I have to go. Goodbye.'

'Bye, Annie.'

She sat back on the leather chair and stared out the window. She had lied to Shaun. There were at least another five minutes before she had to go, but she knew that if she stayed on the phone one more second, she would have told another lie.

There was peace in her home, and it was like a truce of hot air rising before a storm.

***

Thank the Lord for Project Children, thought Jean as she surveyed the queue for check-in. There, at the desk was a veritable Empire State of a man. He had light hair that flitted over a bronzed face, a torso that was long and lean and covered in a white T-shirt, and his muscular arms were lifting yet another suitcase. Beside him stood a dark-haired boy of Robert's age, whose browned cheeks emerged in contrast to the line of lightly baked heads. Whilst a tint of red blusher guaranteed that at all times, and in all moods, Jean had the fiery blaze of a hearty loaf, the Irish faces of the children of Project Children were almost all united in their scorn of the July sunshine. There was no doubt that the boy and his father were of sunny American stock.

Averting her eyes from the spectacular example of male architecture, Jean caught movement to her left. It was Annie and she was crossing the blue carpet tiles of the airport lounge with hair like an autumn gale and a smile like summer. Jean felt instantly less alone. Harry had let her down and the statuesque American chaperon had been the only distraction to take her mind off the fact that most of the other children were represented by at least two parents.

'Hello there love,' said Jean, wondering if it would be appropriate at that moment to settle the most offensive hair into place. 'And aren't you looking gorgeous today,' she continued, untangling the hair with a swift movement and diverting Annie's attention with a gush of a words, 'I wish I'd skinny legs like yours. When I wear a skirt, I look like wee Jimmy Cranky.'

'Thanks for fixing my hair,' laughed Annie, 'And lovely to see you again.'

'Are you alright?' asked Jean, conscious that Annie was also flustered in the face.

'Yes, I'm fine,' she said, kicking off a pair of black stilettos. 'We just had some trouble with the car we borrowed from my sister. It's about three miles down the road, but we're here now. I don't normally wear high heels.

'And you must be Annie's son,' said Jean as she searched in her bag for her purse. 'If you look over there, you'll find my Robert at the slot machines. Here's a pound. Go and knock yourself out.'

'Thanks!' said the boy, his blue eyes lighting up under a curtain of wispy white hair. If Jean had learned one thing in life, it was that she could make any child smile in a second with the touch of a weighty pound coin.

'As for you missy, did you walk three miles in those shoes? Come here and I'll cheer you up. Look over there and check out your man.'

'Which man?' smiled Annie

'Thon yin! The tall American.'

'The tall American with the fair hair?'

'Ay, the tall American with the fair hair.'

'The one helping that lady with her suitcase?'

'The very one,' smiled Jean.

'The very one standing beside my son, James.'

'Oh,' said Jean, her face burning with force of a fan oven. 'Sorry love, I thought he must be the American chaperon. He's been up front helping everyone with their bags.'

'Roy has?'

'Yes, here, you're not annoyed at me saying that are you?'

'Don't be daft!' laughed Annie. 'Is your husband here?'

'No, he's at work.'

Annie's eyebrows were hiked up in a question mark.

'He's a foreman at the shipyard,' Jean explained. 'He's doing over-time this week. He doesn't normally work on a Saturday.'

The words had barely left Jean's lips before she recognised their significance. What was Harry doing working on a Saturday morning? She blinked away the thoughts and continued. 'I sent Robert over to the machines to take his mind off the flight. I think he's nervous.'

'James seems alright so far, but then it's all new to him. Here they come.'

Roy and James approached, and Jean's curiosity grew when she realised that Roy was walking with a limp.

Annie was looking at Roy and then back to Jean and smiling. Jean was mortified, but an uncontrollable reflex to talk served as an affliction and a cure, and before she knew it, she was speaking to Roy in the exalted tones that often controlled her voice in moments of panic, 'I was just saying to Annie, that's a terribly handsome man up there helping with the bags.'

Roy checked Annie's face with a bemused grin. 'Nice to meet you,' he said, reaching out his hand to Jean. 'I'm Roy.'

'Jean,' said Jean, taking Roy's hand and repressing an unexpected desire to curtsy. 'I heard all about the car and don't worry one bit. Jean will fix it. Harry's brother is a dab hand with cars and he'll be back in an hour. We'll get you on the road,' Jean searched in her purse for another pound. 'Here, love, she said to James. 'Away over the video machines there with your brother.'

'That was very generous. Say thank you to Jean.' Roy

directed the words to his son.

A mumble of gratitude followed from James.

'I'll get you both a cup of tea,' said Roy.

'Tea in this place? You must be joking,' said Jean. 'Tea bags in plastic cups and long-life milk for the price of a fine bone china cup. No thanks, love. You have the great fortune to be in the company of Jean Adams, who's never a sandwich short of a picnic.' Jean pointed to her bag and opened it to reveal two flasks of tea, four porcelain cups, fresh milk, a variety of sandwiches wrapped in cling film, Tayto cheese and onion crisps and a bag of apples. The looks of relieved astonishment on the faces of Roy and Annie filled Jean with pleasure, and she experienced that same sense of satisfaction that came with giving a glimmering coin to a child.

Having checked in the bags, Jean found herself seated at a table opposite Annie and Roy with a picnic between them. The boys ate their sandwiches while kicking around the sides of the departure lounge.

Jean spotted Stella O'Reilly in the distance and waved energetically. Stella's trousers and jumper were simple and navy, but the freedom of her long hair and the large piece of metal twisted jewellery around her neck stood out like individuality. Jean, who always liked to look her best, usually found that her best matched the latest high street fashions. Stella O'Reilly had something else. Her clothes expressed their own inner confidence.

'Would you like a nice fresh cup of tea?' asked Jean, motioning Stella to sit down.

'Thank you. I'd love to join you, but I need to check the kids are okay. Some of the parents have already left.'

'Och, they'll be fine, love. Sit down. The security in this place is better than any airport in the world.'

'I know, but we'll be boarding soon. I'd better round everyone up. I'm so glad to finally meet you two ladies though, and I'm delighted that you'll be helping out with Project Children. As you can see, it takes a bit of organising.'

Jean was mesmerised by Stella O'Reilly's voice and as her aura departed, Jean leaned in to Roy and Annie, 'I think she might have been a hippy in her day. What would you say?'

'I'd say she still is,' replied Annie. Roy looked up over his paper and smiled in the way that men do when a woman's conversation is about to ensue.

'I can picture her on a lawn with flowers in her hair,' said Jean.

'I wonder why the peace movement didn't catch on here?' asked Annie.

'All that wet grass, love. Sure, wouldn't you get piles if you sat around singing about peace in the Woodvale park? And the price of flowers nowadays! No, I don't think we'd have much hope of flower power at fifty pence a rose.'

'I'd join a movement for peace if there was one.' It was Annie's voice and it was in tune with her dreamy gaze.

Roy's newspaper fissled as he looked up to Jean again, his blue eyes wide with surprise.

'I'm fed up with this bloody war,' Annie continued, 'Why do we call it the Troubles anyway? You say a married couple is having troubles, not a nation.'

Jean detected a blush before Annie continued. 'There are guns and bombs, and as far as I can see it's a war.'

'Ay, 'tis indeed. At least you live in a nice peaceful place,' replied Jean.

'Well that's one way of describing it,' laughed Annie.

'You know,' said Jean. 'I can nearly predict bloodshed like I can predict rain. There's this thing in the air like...I don't know how to describe it.'

'Like weightless time,' said Roy, resting his *Belfast Telegraph* to look Jean in the eye.

This time it was Annie who scrutinised her husband, and Jean felt like the earth wire in a conversation that had never happened between the party of people facing her, each of them conducting their words safely through Jean with little energy passing between them.

'Roy was a bomb victim,' Annie explained.

'Oh,' said Jean. She gave the news a moment's silence, and when nothing further came from Roy's or Annie's lips, she continued. 'I tell you what, Roy. If there's ever peace in this country, I'll have a picnic in a wet field with a flower in my hair just for you, and I won't complain about my arse getting wet either.'

As smiles emerged, Jean sighed with relief knowing that the moment had passed. It was always awkward to react to news that someone had been a victim of a bomb, but Jean was fixated on the troubles of the marriage that Annie had mentioned. It wasn't obvious at first. Jean had felt at ease in the company of Annie and Roy, but she soon realised that her ease was in relation to each individual and not to the union before her.

***

Shaun concentrated on pitching the ball in his backyard, the midday sun blinding his unshielded eyes. If he had learned one thing about Northern Ireland kids, it was that they had no notion about staying in the shade during the hottest part of the day. A mere flicker of a sun ray sent them scurrying into the brightest patch of land in much the same way that children who'd known scarcity were drawn to food.

While James was walloping the ball with all his might, Toby waited under the shade of the oak tree and Robert fielded in the sun with his neck craned towards the sky, his palms opened wide. Shaun looked up to the sun and tried to imagine being so starved of its presence. He narrowed his eyes and willed the hot rays to awaken a memory of winter. In his summer routine of cars and an air-conditioned office, Shaun had lost that innate affinity with the sun.

'You're a fast learner.' Shaun addressed James.

'My dad taught me to play cricket,' James replied, tapping the tip of the grass with his bat.

James was a confident and sporty child and clearly more suited to the outdoors than to the interior of the church where they had all been that morning. Shaun had taken it upon himself to give Robert and James a taste of Catholic America, but bringing three boys to church was an all-round flop. Even Shaun couldn't remember why he had practiced his own faith for so long as his mind drifted during the sermon, the word sin merely awakening an overwhelming confusion over his relationship with God.

'How did you find church this morning? Was it much different to your own?' asked Shaun. He already knew the answer to the first question from the bleak look of boredom in the eyes of the two Protestant boys, but he thought he'd venture for more feedback nonetheless.

'Which one?' asked James nonchalantly as the ball bounded past his bat. He dug the baseball bat into the ground and stood astride it.

'The one you go to.'

'Well on a Sunday, we go to the Presbyterian church. That's our normal church. On a Monday night we go to the Baptist church They do football and free sweets if you learn your verse. On Wednesday nights we go to the Tabernacle. They're a bit zealous in there—'

'Zealous,' interrupted Shaun, intrigued by this boy's theological thinkings.

'Yes, they do all this mad stuff and shout at you to repent and give up your sins for the Lord.' The baseball bat was in the air as James spread his arms into a sermon. 'There's a minister who wears normal clothes and he sort of dances on the stage and calls us all sinners,' he continued. 'My mum told me just to keep going because it's free. She said as long as I learned my verse and got my sweet, I was better off there than on the streets.'

'Wow.'

'Then on Friday night we have BB. It's at the—'

'BB?' Shaun interrupted once again.

'Boys Brigade. You wear a uniform and march and do gymnastics and stuff.'

'Is it like the Cadet Corps?'

'No, we have Army cadets too,' James explained with a face filled with old wisdom, 'but they're a bit more serious and learn about guns and stuff. Dad doesn't want us to join it. He's a bit funny like that. I think it's because he's half Dutch.'

'And so, this BB then?' asked Shaun, knowing that Roy's

convictions were not his concern. He began to question his own rationale for inviting this boy to his home. Was it a genuine act of kindness or a bid to learn more about Annie? Shaun's integrity seemed to be hitched to the ball he had pitched that was now soaring into the sun.

James batted and then stood to attention and saluted as words rattled from his mouth. 'The aim of the BB is the advancement of Christ's Kingdom among Boys, and the promotion of habits of obedience, reverence, discipline, self-respect, and all that tends towards a true Christian manliness.'

Shaun lifted another ball from the bucket and stared at the boy before him. 'Now that's something,' he said with a smile.

'Yes, sir,' replied James. Shaun could have sworn the boy mimicked an American accent.

'Then there's Sunday school in the Presbyterian church. My mum does the housework on a Sunday morning, so she sends us with a neighbour. She says cleanliness is next to Godliness, and that God won't mind.'

Shaun was laughing hard on the inside, but did his best to remain composed. This young guy was a comedian and Shaun felt a mix of embarrassment at the insight into the internal walls of Annie's life, and wonder at the Protestant traditions of Ulster.

Robert, meanwhile, still hadn't progressed to a stage of acclimatisation where talk was forthcoming. His blue eyes fell towards his upturned nose as two dimples closed tightly around his conversation. Having James around prolonged the silence for another day.

'Robert, why don't you take a go at pitching?' Shaun said.

Shaun handed the ball to Robert and watched a shy, skinny boy with boney shoulders and knees transform into a nimble athlete as he widened his legs, planted his left foot firm in the grass, bent his right leg towards his ear and clasped his glove and right hand around the ball. His arms stretched, his eyes centred and the ball flitted like a jet stream towards an unprepared James. In a split second, Shaun could see the panic on the young boy's face as he twisted and received the ball on his left shoulder with a thud.

James remained static, holding onto his shoulder. 'Good shot, his strained voice quivered as he fell to the ground. He puffed out his cheeks to contain the pain that could be heard like a whistle through clenched teeth.

Shaun leapt to James' side where Toby and Robert were both kneeling with their hands held out to their friend.

'Can you lift your arms up?' Shaun asked. James' crinkled brow repressed sounds of discomfort as he tried to raise his right arm above his head. 'No', rattled his voice eventually, and traces of tears trickled from his bright brown eyes, pained eyes that Shaun had seen once before.

Shaun shook the images of Annie from his mind and lifted James to his car. He strapped James into his seat and thought of her face when he realised that his destination was the hospital. What had he done to Annie's son?

Shaun remembered Robert and turned to give him a reassuring pat on the shoulder before opening the driver's seat. 'It's okay, buddy. James will be fine and great pitch!'

Fear was etched in Robert's eyes as he looked in the car window towards James.

Toby followed behind him and placed his arm around Robert's shoulder. 'Don't worry. Dad's right. James will be okay. You get in the back seat.'

Shaun assessed Toby's face to ensure that he wasn't using this as an excuse to claim shotgun, but he could see a kindness in his eyes as he turned to check on Robert.

The rearview mirror on the journey to the hospital revealed a picture of two boys who were far away from home. There was James on the right behind Toby, with tears flowing down his face as he concentrated his pain on the window, and Robert on the left behind Shaun. In that moment, Shaun realised that his deepest sympathy lay with the assailant, the innocent boy who had unwittingly hurt another child. James was clearly in pain, but Robert's invisible wounds were clinging to his face.

***

Annie looked out over the banister as Roy picked up the phone in the hall. His body dipped in motion with his voice as he settled on the phone chair and quietly said, 'Is he okay?' Annie slowly moved to the top of the stairs, her hand trailing across the bannister, her fingers clinging onto the last few seconds before she realised that something was wrong. Something had happened to one of the boys.

Annie will want to speak to you,' Roy said, before carefully resting the handset on the table. He whispered to Annie. 'It's James.' Annie's hand automatically moved to her mouth. 'It's alright,' Roy continued, 'James is safe. He got injured in a baseball game.'

Annie lifted the handset as Roy settled on the stairs, the summer dusky light bending through the glass front doors. The hall clock read twenty minutes past ten.

'Hello,' she said in a broken voice.

'Annie, James is in hospital. The kids were playing baseball and his shoulder took a hit from a fast ball. It's dislocated, but he will be okay.'

'Oh,' said Annie with relief. Then recalling how clingy James was in times of illness, her body crumpled into the leather phone chair and tears edged from her eyes. At no moment in her life had she wanted to be nearer to her son.

'Annie, it's Shaun. I should have said that.'

'Yes, yes, I know,' said Annie, her emotions towards Shaun blunted, as she concentrated on James.

'Is he in hospital?' she asked.

'Yes. We're about to leave the hospital. The Taylors have arrived. They want to take him home. I think they feel a little guilty about leaving James in my care.'

'What's the treatment? How much pain is he in?'

'He's on anti-inflammatories and he has to wear a sling. It'll be six weeks before he's back to normal. He'll need to rest plenty.'

'Rest? Annie repeated. 'James can't sit still.'

'I noticed that. He's a livewire.'

The telling comment about her son seemed wrong and the distance between Annie and Shaun was suddenly too narrow. The thing that had pulled them both together was knowing how far apart they were, and now that Shaun had spent time with her son, the realisation that she had done something wrong was too close. Annie needed to get off the phone, even if it meant not learning every detail of what had happened to James. As she turned to her husband on the stairs, Annie knew where she belonged.

Her mind returned to the call. 'Can we bring James home? Did he say he wants to come home?'

'James hid his tears,' Shaun continued in a matter-of-fact voice, 'but I'm certain he misses home. His exact words were, "I'm not leaving here until I've seen the Orioles."'

'The Orioles?'

'Yes, it's a baseball team and he's supposed to be going there with the Taylor family next weekend. Tom Taylor will call you when he gets back from the hospital. The doctors think James will be okay with painkillers and a long flight with restricted movement might not be the best solution right now.'

'Okay, I'll talk to Tom.' Annie felt more troubled by Shaun's presence on the phone as the call progressed. The voice she was hearing was delivering news in an appropriate way between two people who had behaved inappropriately: the holding of the hands, the letter writing, the call. It all seemed so wrong. Annie had only one thing on her mind and that was James. She wanted James home.

'I should go.' There was a pause and then a slight fracture in Shaun's voice, 'Annie, I'm sorry for not taking better care of your son. I should have given the kids a soft ball.'

There it was, that measured tempo of sincerity she had listened to until dawn.

'We wouldn't blame you for this. It wasn't your fault,' she replied faintly, turning away from Roy and staring through the wall of the hallway. 'Goodbye,' said Annie, replacing the receiver.

She looked up at Roy and breathed a deep sigh. 'Thank God. If anything ever happened to one of the boys…'

'I know,' Roy said. He reached out and held Annie's hand and Annie felt a sickness rise from her body, the bile of guilt for her behaviour and relief for her son.

***

July 21, 1990

Dear Annie

I wanted to tell you how sorry I am for what happened to James. We picked him up today for a walk around the Mall. Robert had been so distant since it happened and I needed to cheer him up. It was my fault for giving a hard ball to a kid with a pitching arm like a cyclone. Robert's a quiet boy, but I know that he is full of soul. He came to me a few days after the accident and asked if he could see James and I knew that it had taken an effort for him to speak to an adult.

James enjoyed the Mall, and I swear your kid has developed an American accent. His knowledge on any subject is boundless, as is his energy. I promise you that I tried to make him take regular rests, but it was easier to keep walking. Every time we sat still, he would start climbing or fooling around with Toby and Robert, and I fear his shoulder is in more jeopardy if he is motionless. These Belfast boys don't like walking in the shade, so in one hundred degrees of heat, we donned our caps and walked in the sun.

The white monuments were luminescent today, and I was reminded of my student days. One night, I drank a little too much whisky in an Irish bar and missed my train home. I walked for a while, sobered up and then watched the sunrise on the Jefferson Memorial. It's a white circular colonnade marooned in a tidal basin. Through the cloud of alcohol, I still recall how the sky and water were in flames as the Jefferson Memorial stood out against the red dawn like a white celestial palace. At least I think that's what happened. I hope it wasn't a whisky-induced dream!

Another stop on our journey today was the Vietnam Veterans' Memorial. I was born in 1953 so I didn't have to go to Vietnam. Many of my friends from the neighbourhood and my older cousins did. I guess we all carry a burden of guilt for something, and I go there to seek penance for the year I was born. I had received a scholarship to go to college and although I'm grateful that my name isn't on the wall of the monument, I still feel that I let my country down by not volunteering.

Going to college was a big deal at the time, and my mother and our priest shared a dream that I would become the first member of the family to join the priesthood. I think she wanted to break the tide of late night drinking from a long line of builders and plasterers. My grandfather resisted. He said, 'Empty and cold is the house without a woman.' He needn't have intervened. My position on women was well established from the moment I set eyes on Laura Mackey at the age of twelve. I confessed to the priest that I had committed a mortal sin by thinking about her all the way through mass. He asked me if the thoughts were sexual in nature and I told him that yes, I had dreamed of holding her hand. I wound up working in a Catholic University, a small token of compensation for a disappointed mother!

I probably won't get the chance to see James before he flies home next Saturday, but I wanted to tell you that you have quite a kid there. He's a real comedian, and I did recognise some of his traits from another walk I took in Ireland. James is his mother's image in so many ways. I hope that his journey home is safe.

Yours sincerely,

Shaun

A MISUNDERSTOOD PLANT

Annie stood at the sink and looked outside. She moved her hands in the soapy water, distracted by the view of the garden. It was the same as all the other gardens on the estate, a square patch of land that was big enough to accommodate a picnic table, two benches, a small shed and a few plants. The fence was the highlight, a wooden fence that Annie re-stained every summer. She could picture Roy building that fence, a younger version of her husband and a more determined man. Roy had had dreams back then. He had promised Annie that they would buy a house with a driveway, and that they would own their own car. Annie didn't need any of those things, but she had been wholly unaware of the contentment she experienced at hearing Roy talk about the future. Then there was a bomb and everything changed apart from the fence that wrapped around them like a safe border between a road filled with traffic and two young boys whose father couldn't run fast.

The house itself was timeless. On 22nd March 1979, everything had stood still. Annie had been working when they had moved to the Fernagh Estate. A few months before Andrew was born, she had been able to buy Ercol-inspired furniture that had lasted. The sofas and chairs had been recovered, but the delicate wooden frames with the fine round pointed legs remained. Many books and papers had been shuffled around the oval coffee table, but it was still there with barely a scratch and it was revived each Sunday morning with a smear of furniture polish and a duster. Even the spider plants sprouting from hanging baskets on the yellow wallpaper flourished against time. When the house was quiet, Annie would transform it back to the space it had been when she was a young woman. She would sit with a cup of tea and stare at the wall of stone cladding around the fireplace and recall that feeling of satisfaction of returning home from the office on a Friday night.

The exterior of Annie's home told a different tale. Nature had found its own way of moving the clock forward. The grass, once a patch of smooth and even blades, was a mass of green clover and weeds. The perennials had survived more than ten years, but the annual trips to buy brightly coloured bedding had ended some years ago. It had never occurred to Annie that the ritual had slipped her mind. The purple dahlia were there, a dozen or so heads of perfection surrounded by weeds. The white anthemis with their rich yellow bellies appeared each year like over-sized daisies inviting Annie to come back to her garden, but she couldn't and time was just an excuse. It was the loneliness of the task. Roy was still strong and could easily have helped, but he chose not to. His weekends were spent watching football with the boys or exploring the lines of books on science and engineering in the library, seeking out his own purpose and forgetting to live. Annie knew that they were both guilty of that. She kept on working, thinking that change would come naturally one day. She was working and Roy was surviving, and no one was putting down roots. No one was creating change and it was a sad garden crying out for change.

'It's the end of July,' said Annie, her hands still swaying in the water. 'Summer will be over soon. Could we do something with the garden?'

A ruffle of the newspaper followed a deep breath. Annie held onto the sink and closed her eyes. Roy was in defence. She felt Roy's eyes on her and turned around.

'I'm reading my paper,' said Roy. 'That's what people do on

Saturdays. They read the paper. They relax.' His voice was gentle and controlled.

'Okay, can we think about doing it some other time then? What about tomorrow?'

'By we, I take it you mean me? Can I do it tomorrow?'

'No, not at all. I thought we could do it together.'

Annie realised then that it was she who was the dreamer. She had a fanciful image in her head of a man and women working in tandem in a garden, possibly a staged image from a *Good Housekeeping* magazine from the summer of 1978.

Roy tossed the newspaper onto the table. 'Right, I'll do it. Where do you want me to start?'

'I'd rather do it by myself if you're going to be like that.' Annie walked towards the back door.

'What do you want, Annie? I say I'll help and you've changed your mind.'

Annie looked up and sighed. 'I haven't changed my mind. I want you to do something with me because you want to do something with me, and I don't want another row.'

Annie was beyond weary of fighting. This was the third time in less than ten days. They had a chance to spend time together while Andrew was in Glenarm and James in America, but instead they had found themselves in close proximity without a child to serve as a shield from their mutual animosity.

Annie ventured on, knowing that she had to explain what she meant, yet ashamed that something so minor had become a knotted weed of overgrown antagonism. 'I wish that you would decide that the garden needs fixed up,' she said. 'Look at it. Are you proud of that?'

'I've told you before,' said Roy. 'I don't care about how things look to other people.'

'But what about how it looks to you? Do you like spending time there? It's full of weeds.'

'A weed is a misunderstood plant. There is no such thing as a weed.'

'Don't be ridiculous.'

'I'm not being ridiculous. You see weeds where I see plants

and you see trouble where I see peace. Now, please, the boys are away. We have a chance to relax, so stop starting arguments.'

'I'm not' Annie complained. 'It didn't start as an argument.' She turned away from the window and looked at Roy. 'A request is not an argument,' she said firmly. 'Can I ask you something?'

'Is this going to turn into a thing?' Roy replied despondently.

'It is a thing, yes. It's an important thing. Do you want to live like this when the boys leave home? Is this how you see our future?'

'We do okay.' Roy's voice had mellowed.

'But I don't know if I can live like this. I'm constantly walking on eggshells. Every time I speak, you automatically go into defence and I'm left feeling like the antagonist. This is the cycle we're in.' Annie reached for Roy's hand. 'Come here,' she said. She pulled him towards the kitchen sink and pointed to the yellow tiles. 'See those tiles, I look at them every single day and I want to tear them down and replace them with something modern, but I'm scared of speaking up because I know that you'll tut and complain and then if we buy the tiles and you start putting them up, I won't want to be within an inch of you while you're working.'

'Don't be daft! You're making me sound unapproachable.'

'But that's it. You are unapproachable. I always know that you'll do the job eventually and I know that you'll do it well, but it's a drama trying to steer this ship.'

'Am I ship?'

'No, you're a bloody great tangled plant that twists everything I say. Look, I know there are more important things in life and that your father survived famine and that you survived a bomb, but sometimes there aren't big things in life to survive and you have to just keep moving on with the small stuff. It's called living.'

'I'll sort out the tiles,' said Roy with a look of confusion.

'No, you won't sort out the tiles. You don't get it, do you? Look at that woman in the reflection of the window and tell me what you see.'

'A beautiful woman?' Roy stammered.

'Well I see a right pain in the arse. And I find it hard to love you when I feel like a pain in the arse every single day.'

'So, you don't love me?'

'I love our family. I love me, you, Andrew and James when we are together.'

'But you don't love the cripple by your side.'

'What do you mean?'

'You don't love this,' Roy looked at his own body. 'What is this about? Do you want out?'

'You threaten divorce every time we have an argument. For goodness sake, Roy, all couples argue over minutia. If you're always planning to walk away, how can we ever have a real future?'

'Well, what do you want me to do?'

'I want to feel love.'

Roy moved back to his seat and lifted his paper, 'Is your sex life inadequate, Annie, is that it? Am I half the man I used to be?' Roy's voice was strained. 'If you want to know the truth about it, I look at you and I think, why does she want to be with me?'

Annie paused. Roy was there in the dark each night and she had become dependent upon his touch to sustain her. The love she wanted was different, but how could she explain that to a man who only knew how to give love with the touch of his body. She spoke quietly and sat at the table, pulling his paper away, 'I didn't say anything about that.'

Roy clasped his hands together. 'I'm trying every day, but it's never enough.'

'I'm tired of fighting,' said Annie, reaching across the table. 'We either need to start working as a partnership or not at all.'

They remained at the table holding hands, and Annie knew that this was the last chance. The house was as it was in 1979, but her marriage, like the garden, had been reclaimed by nature, and it needed to change.

***

Linda moved like air, her long limbs gliding along the gritty path. It was early on a Saturday morning and they were walking under the trees of the Ormeau park, far away from reality and at a shameful distance from the airport where Harry was supposed to be.

Sun droplets dripped through the trees and fell on Linda's face and the scent of nature was so heavy that Harry could taste the earthy sap on his lips. He led Linda towards a black, glossy bench by a bed of white flowers that bloomed like large daisies. He kissed her, tugging at her pulpy lips. He then stood back and held her hands, facing her as the sun continued to trickle over her eye-lashes. 'I want to marry you,' he said. He had never felt anything so sincerely. He needed to be with Linda.

She withdrew from his arms, her lips scarlet red from the kiss, her blue eyes splintered into confusion as her body trembled. Harry pulled her to the bench. 'I mean it, I want to marry you.'

Linda remained silent, a coating of mist hiding her bright eyes. 'You can't say something like that.'

'Why? Why not? I love you and I can't go on without you. Look at you. Look at this!' Harry's eyes moved around the park as he smiled. 'This is it! I didn't even know I was looking for you, but I've found you and we have to be together.'

The mist solidified and tears drained from Linda's eyes. Harry was gazing into them and didn't see the flick of her hand as it scudded towards his face. The slap was hard and firm and the daisies were magnified as the green park faded to a blur.

He held his face and looked at Linda, whose lips were hard and stern. 'Don't ever say that,' her voice quaked. She stood up. 'You don't get to do this. It's hard enough. Don't make promises you can't keep.'

He pulled Linda back to sitting and took her hands. 'I meant what I said. This is everything, but never raise your hand to me again.'

She looked up over sorrowful eyes. 'I'm sorry for slapping your face. You confused me.'

Harry placed his left arm around her and pulled her close. He kissed her fair hair and tasted the tear escaping from her right eye. 'I love you and I know that it's wrong, but it's what's happened and I don't know why. All I know is, I have to be with you.'

'But you're married.'

It was the first time that Linda had acknowledged Harry's marriage. When they had met seven months before, she had been assessing his mortgage application in a bank on the Shankill Road. There had been a bomb scare and Harry had offered to walk her to the city centre in the opposite direction from his home.

On the threshold of a bus by a city hall decked in Christmas lights, Harry had said 'Wait,' and that one word had changed everything. Linda had climbed down the steps and waited, and they had both stood side by side, not knowing why they were there or what they were doing.

'I'm going to keep walking,' Harry had said.

And then he was in front of Linda's house, a terraced house off the Cregagh Road in the east of the city. It was an elegant, red-bricked Edwardian semi in a street far removed from home.

He turned Linda, who was awaiting a response. 'We agreed not to talk about any of that. We agreed not to ask any questions.'

She unravelled her shoulder from Harry's arm. 'We did. Yes. We agreed, but you changed everything the minute you said you wanted to marry me. Did you mean it?'

'With all my heart.'

'What about Jean?'

He looked away. He stared through the park dripping green with reality. 'You know her name.'

'Yes,' replied Linda. 'I know her name. I know you have three children and I know your address on Snugville Street. I spent an hour with you completing a mortgage application.'

'But you never mentioned any of this before.'

'That's because of the agreement we had. You stepped over my door and we kissed and we promised we'd never talk about reality.' She touched Harry's cheek and held it as she turned his face towards her.

He felt her warm hand and the forbidden, tortuous feelings of love, and his eyes welled up against the lucidity in Linda's.

'You're crying,' she said.

He coughed and removed her hand from his cheek. 'It's time to talk. Let's walk.'

She stood up and Harry saw it again, that overwhelming elegance, the thick, blond hair, the perfect proportions of her face and the short, flowery dress that allowed two elongated limbs to crush his sense of reason.

'Come in for a cup of tea before you go home,' she'd said after they'd walked from the bank before Christmas. They had kissed by a steaming kettle that would never be used, and they had made love in Linda's bedroom, two strangers bound together in a peach room with white lace curtains falling like a veil of romance over Harry's sanity.

He had left Linda's house the next morning and returned home to his normal life, but life couldn't be normal. Everything had changed, and eventually he had returned to the bank.

They would meet up in the city centre on a Friday night once a fortnight and they would walk across Queen's bridge, regardless of the weather. They would climb the stairs in Linda's house and make love and, each time, they would cling to each other, moving closer together, yet gliding away from the clarity of their minds.

Harry would sleep peacefully, a deep and sensual sleep. And in the morning, he would wake to see the outline of Linda's body against a backdrop of white lace, and he would say goodbye and walk home across the Lagan river, a natural partition that felt like pain.

'You were shocked when I slapped you,' Linda stated as they walked to the bandstand.

'I'm not a violent man. I wouldn't hit you.'

She smiled. 'I'm sorry and I know you wouldn't hit me.'

They climbed the short steps to the bandstand and Linda held onto the black, iron balustrade and spoke tentatively, 'What about your children?'

Harry understood that the game had changed. He leaned on the railing and sighed, knowing that Linda was merely listening to a song he had begun to sing. 'I wouldn't hit a child.'

'That's unusual.'

'I made a promise once that I would never lay my hands on another human being. There are so many things about me that you don't know. It'll never be the same if we do this. Do you want to do this?'

'Yes. I need to know who you are.'

They settled on the steps of the bandstand. Harry was sure that Linda would never understand. She was a middle class woman. She had lived a sheltered upbringing, her father a minister, her mother a housewife. In 1972, when Linda was only eight years old, when her greatest concern in the world was her ballet grading, Harry had walked into a room above a chip shop with his brother and pledged his soul to a world where the only gradings were degrees of crime. He knew this would be the one thing that would matter.

'On the twenty-third of July 1972,' he began, 'my brother, Sammy and I joined...' He stopped and looked into Linda's troubled eyes. 'I didn't kill anyone,' he said.

'But you joined a Loyalist organisation?'

'Yes, I joined the UDA. It was two days after the IRA exploded twenty bombs in Belfast. I was nineteen and I was angry.'

'I don't know what to say. How long?'

'A year. Are you sure you want to know this?'

Harry was playing with his own future with Linda and he willed her to say *yes* as much as he prayed she would say *no*. A *yes* would tarnish the false world they had inhabited. A *no* would give him more time with the woman he loved.

'Yes,' came Linda's voice, a tangled breath of collected confidence and nerves. 'Why did you do it?'

'To protect my community. There were IRA attacks in the local area. It started out as a vigilante group.'

Linda's face was composed, her eyes concentrating hard on Harry's. He had never discussed the Troubles with Linda, but he had a measure of her naivety after the walk from the bomb scare, and it was part of the delusion they practiced.

'And what did you do?'

'Do you want to know this?'

'Yes. Tell me.'

'We kept a few guns under our mother's floorboards. There was no money and few weapons. Protecting what there was at hand was an important job.'

'It doesn't make sense. I can't imagine you involved in something like that.'

'Nothing makes sense in the times we live in. There's an Irish priest living in the USA who sends thousands of guns to Ireland to murder his own kith and kin. The same man would ask a child for a Hail Mary for stealing a dime. The British government will say they are rooting out all crime, all paramilitaries, but they'll turn a blind eye if a common enemy is about to die. And, you know something, if it ever ends, and people try to sit down and grapple over the details to see what makes sense, they'll only find hypocrisy, lies and madness.'

'Do you think it'll ever end?'

Harry thought for a moment before replying. 'There are two sure things about every story. The first is that each story has a beginning, a middle and an end.'

'Here's hoping we're near the end.' Linda was staring into space and then looked up, her eyes alerted to something. 'I didn't mean us. I meant the Troubles. I hope we're near the end of the violence. What's the second thing?'

'In every story, a man leaves town or a stranger comes to town.'

'A stranger, indeed. I see. And you're my stranger, I take it?'

'Remember we're talking about the Troubles. A stranger has yet to come to town.'

'You're a mystery, Harry Adams. How on earth did I end up walking across the city with a stranger like you? Anyway, I thought people got stuck in those Loyalist groups for life. How did you walk away?

'The leadership has changed hands and the UDA isn't the same vigilante group it was when I was nineteen. I'm not saying it's better, just a different shade of darkness.'

'When did you leave?'

'I was there for a year and I started to hear things and see things that I didn't like. I got scared and I couldn't sleep knowing that the cold metal under my bed was being used to kill people, to kill Catholics.' Harry paused and looked into Linda's eyes. 'There's little light between a man and his conscience,' he said finally, unsure if he was referring to the present or the past. 'I went to Smith and asked to be stood down. He told me I might be needed again one day, but I haven't been bothered since. I got away and then I met Jean a couple of years later. She knew my brother, Sammy, was still active. She made me promise that I would stay out of trouble.'

He watched as colour returned to Linda's cheeks, the colour of curiosity. Harry's face remained still but he smiled inwardly as he recalled the spirit of Jean in her tight leather trousers and leather jacket with her hands on her hips, only one week after they had met. 'Harry Adams, I'll marry you and give you four beautiful children if you stay out of trouble.' Harry closed his eyes to erase Jean's voice from his mind.

Linda was looking and awaiting more details, but Jean's voice was still there and he could see her walk in front of him, laughing and dancing and being Jean.

Harry had left the UDA and he had never looked back, not until now, when flashes of torchlight assailed him in a park where leafy trees stood to attention and Linda's pale hand touched his conscience.

He hadn't killed anyone, but he had manned his own small arsenal of murder weapons and he had turned a blind eye to his brother's crimes, and on a summer morning under a clear sky, he looked into the worried eyes of a young woman whose beauty clashed with the shadows of his past like white lace falling on cold metal.

'Whatever thoughts you're having, you'll have to believe me when I say that I've been there. My conscience has been battered.'

Linda appeared less anxious. 'I've never told you this before,' she said. 'I'm a Christian.'

'That's not unexpected in this town.'

Harry wasn't surprised. He'd always sensed there was something more than guilt playing on Linda's mind.

'My father never once forced religion on me. He said I had to find it for myself. And I did. From a young age, I knew that I loved God. What I'm saying is that I know about a battered conscience. Once a fortnight, I do something that goes against my faith and yet, it is the most beautiful part of my life.'

'If this is the work of the devil,' said Harry, 'Then he has fine hands indeed. I sleep soundly when I'm with you.'

'I don't,' said Linda quietly. 'I stay awake and I watch you and I see a married man and pray for morning so that it will all be okay. I knew there would be something about your past that I wouldn't like. I almost wanted it. I thought that if I knew you were part of something that I hate, then I could find a reason to walk away. We either block out reality or we end this. No more talk of marriage. You have a wife and three children. This isn't real.'

'I know.'

What was real was that Harry's son was coming home from America. He pictured a boy in a Northern Ireland shirt and the two little girls in red velvet dresses in the family portrait that Jean had hung on the wall, and he knew that summer would fade soon and that he had to go home.

***

'Flight's delayed, love' were the first words Annie heard upon walking through the arrivals lounge.

She crossed the grey, sticky carpet to the voice and smiled. 'I'm sitting beside you, in that case.'

'Of course you're sitting beside me,' puffed Jean, whilst patting down a blue corduroy chair. 'Who else would you sit beside?'

'Anyone who makes a picnic like you will do.'

'And I thought you liked me for my intellect.'

'No, I'm just after your sandwiches,' laughed Annie.

'Well that's charming.'

Seeing Jean instantly made the trip to the airport a holiday rather than a chore. 'According to James, we're all meeting up with Project Children to play football next week,' Annie said. 'I'll pay you back with the best egg and onion sandwiches you've ever tasted.'

'Sorry about James' shoulder, by the way,' said Jean suddenly, and with a look of concern. 'Big Honky Tonk phoned me all worried. Robert took it hard and thought it was his fault.'

There it was again. Another reference to a man that Annie couldn't shake from her mind. Her child had a dislocated shoulder and Annie had walked away from the call with Shaun determined not to think about him in that way anymore, but he was still there. Maybe it was the Project Children program. Maybe Annie needed to distance herself from it in order to escape from Shaun and re-connect with Roy. She looked at Jean and registered what she had said about Robert. 'I'll tell Robert myself that it wasn't his fault, she said finally. 'James is always getting hurt. He's been walking into balls for years.'

'Where's Roy today?' asked Jean.

'Roy has started a Saturday course at the tech.'

'What doing?'

'Something to do with computers. Coding or programming. Apparently it's the next big thing. It's all double Dutch to me.'

'You like your Dutch, don't you?'

Annie smiled, 'Actually, Roy's trying to save our marriage.'

'By doing a computer course?'

'Long story.' Annie thought back to the three weeks of war and peace and breathed deeply knowing that it was all over. Annie and Roy had decided to make it work. Roy had applied for the course after Annie had stayed out all night in March, but it had come at the right time. In their last week together before the boys returned from their holidays, they'd spent every evening working on the garden. Roy had even started to remove the kitchen tiles when Annie was at work. The problems they had had were laid to rest in a ceramic pile of dusty tiles as they each made an effort to put down roots in their own home. Annie had begun to investigate buying their house, while Roy had applied for a new disability living allowance that entitled him to support in purchasing a car. Life had started moving through a combination of small things that blocked out the one large transgression that Shaun had stopped Annie from making.

Concern was painted all over Jean's peach cheeks as she concentrated on Annie's face. She then looked at the information screen and back to Annie. 'According to the screen blinking at me, you've got an hour to tell me all about it.'

'Honestly, it's boring married stuff.'

'Well, hopefully Roy will crack the code on that computer course and save us all a bloody headache. If it's not one thing it's another. I tell ya, love, I don't understand that man at all.'

'Who? Harry?'

'Ay, Harry. One minute he's nowhere to be found and the next he's up and down the road to Dublin like a young fella.'

'Dublin?' enquired Annie.

'You know love, down south, over the border.'

Annie beamed and held back a mighty gust of laughter.

Jean retained her straight face and Annie doubled over. 'You're a disgrace,' said Annie, aware that Jean was using all her comic might for her benefit alone.

'Look at you all affronted,' said Jean, nudging Annie hard with her elbow. 'Here, do you think it's an early mid-life crisis?'

'I'd say you're right,' said Annie, who then surveyed the arrivals lounge. 'I wonder what the other Project Children mums are talking about.'

'Oh, I don't know, but by the looks on some of the faces, I'd say they could do with getting out of Belfast.'

Jean winked at Annie and a residue of laughter continued to seep from Jean's lips in a long sigh and when silence was finally restored, Annie turned to Jean again. 'Do you ever hate Harry?' she asked tentatively.

'The man drives me mad. I mean, I've been on a promise of a house for years and all I get is hanky panky. I don't know where he goes at night and I can tell you he has me worried, but I don't think he'd ever do anything to hurt me or the children.'

'That's good,' said Annie, staring at the floor. 'You know, sometimes Roy and I have these blazing rows and I swear I can feel hatred in the room.'

'That's just misplaced passion. You can't hate someone that much unless you love them and they've let you down.'

'That's the problem. Roy hasn't let me down. He does everything right. It's me. I'm the problem. I'm a pain in the ass.'

'Don't be too hard on yourself. I tell ya, love. A man's good for shovelling coal on the fire, but you'll never see him on the hearth with a brush sweeping up the soot. And we all know what happens if you don't sweep up the soot.'

Annie looked at Jean blankly.

'The chimney will go on fire, love. The chimney will go on fire.'

'I never thought about it. I just do it'

'And therein lies the difference between an Ulster woman and an Ulster man.'

Annie laughed.

'We all dream of what it might be like on the outside,' said Jean. 'Marriage is as much a prison as anything else.'

Annie's eyes lit up. 'That's exactly what I've been thinking for years. Day in, day out, I feel like I'm in prison. Then something will happen and I'll realise that freedom is as bad. One night at work recently, I even thought about leaving Roy, but the more I thought about it, the more scared and isolated I felt. I resigned from my job that night and went home and I can tell you I've never felt more relieved to be with my family. It's the security.'

'I suppose you're on the other side. I don't go out to work every day, so I'm the security that Harry comes home to. I envy his freedom sometimes, but I wouldn't want it to be any other way. I get all out of sorts if I have to go away from home. That's why my picnic is so well organised.'

'Well, thank goodness for that. Any chance of a cup of tea?

You near made me choke with your talk of Dublin.'

'Certainly, and I've a wee ham and tomato sandwich with the finest Golden Cow butter Crazy Prices has to offer.

'You're amazing.'

Annie thought about Jean and her picnics and found it hard to imagine that someone her own age was so old in her ways. On the outside, Jean was every inch of a modern woman in her cropped jacket and shoulder pads and pointy red heels, but Annie saw before her the expression of another generation. Jean was more like her own mother and perhaps that's why Annie found her company so endearing. She had managed to crochet a whole world around her of happiness and Annie was sure that it was Jean's sense of humour that kept her marriage alive. Annie resolved there and then to bring laughter to her marriage. She and Roy had been too serious for too long. There was one thing she had to do first. She looked at Jean.

'Jean, tell me this. Is there a post box in here?'

'Yes, there is. It's in departures though.'

'Great. Listen, I'm going to abandon you for ten minutes, and then I'll come back.'

'Oh,' said Jean, with a look of disappointment.

'Don't worry, I think you may have just saved my marriage. Never mind tiles and computer courses.'

'Oh, I see said Jean with a coy smile.

Annie laughed, 'No, not that. The Dutch have no respect for border partitions either. I need to post a letter. See you soon.'

***

28th July 1990

Dear Shaun

Thank you taking such good care of James while he was in America. I know that he enjoyed spending time with you, Toby and Robert. Maybe one day James will take his mum to see the things he saw in Washington, D.C.

I read your story about Vietnam and thought of my father. He served on the Normandy Beaches in 1944. Growing up, I always assumed he'd been a gentle and quiet man all his life, but some years ago, Roy was at the club and met someone who served with him in the Ulster Rifles. He said my father was a real character in his youth. He also said he was a hero. I had no idea, and to this day, he hasn't mentioned what he did. The man said that he landed on a beach called Lion Sur Mer and made it safely ashore. He moved on through the villages and towns of France and reached the Belgium border. The truck he was travelling in was carrying five men who died when a bomb detonated right under it. Only he and the driver made it. Shaun, that wall doesn't need any more names on it and so you should free yourself from any burden of guilt.

This part is going to be hard to write, but I can no longer stay in contact with you. Roy and I have been through our own war for so long that it's time to either make a change or walk away. We have both chosen change. In many ways, I have to thank you because I don't think I realised how unhappy I was until I tried to do something I would have regretted.

When I saw you at the castle, what I experienced felt like love and it had been a long time since I had felt the warmth that comes with that emotion. You acted like a true friend and I am grateful, but to make things right, we need to part ways.

Thank you for the changes you brought to my life. Things are better now.

Yours sincerely

Annie

ONE GOD WITH MANY HANDS
1991

Shaun surveyed the crowds in green on the wide expanse of Constitution Avenue. It was St. Patrick's Day and with it arrived a familiar sensation of grief.

Grief had been part of his life for two and a half years, and it changed shape from day to day, as though the ghosts he'd laid to rest were forming their own landscape in his mind.

The morning had been cold. Shaun had awoken with a chill and had checked that the windows were closed. He had reached for the wedding photograph of Sarah beside his bed, the photograph he had framed despite Sarah's protestations, 'I look so sad, Shaun. I don't want people to think I was sad on my wedding day.'

'Wistful.' That's what Shaun had said. She was looking up and her veil was illuminated against the shadows on her face, her eyes fixed in a future place beyond the day.

Shaun turned to his son as the distant sound of bagpipes reminded him why they were freezing on Constitution Avenue. Toby wore the Northern Ireland cap and soccer shirt that Robert had brought him the previous summer, but there had been a scuffle getting out the door that morning, a debate over an appropriate jacket for the cool temperatures. Toby had insisted that he would wear the green T-shirt and a thin jacket. He was a good kid, but once in a while, anger would run through his body like lava. The outbursts would pass, but Shaun always stood back to watch their progress, a witness in a child's acknowledgement that life was hard.

He reflected upon his own childhood and tried to recall any frustrations attached to being nine. Did everything in Toby's life have a link to losing his mother or were some things simply part of growing up? Shaun's own childhood had been happy. It was only after elementary school that a resentment for his father's drinking had cast a shadow over their relationship.

Shaun and Toby stood below a colossal Stars and Stripes banner, hoisted on cranes on either side of the avenue, and waited. Shaun felt nervous, pre-empting a repeat of the morning's fury, aware that this had been a special day between Toby and his mother. It was Sarah who had had the enthusiasm for the parades, bringing the day to life with her green face-paint and themed parties, and on days like today, when her life seemed so noticeably absent, Toby's emotions were strained.

Finally, the parade began with a flurry of police lights, sirens and bagpipes. A smile spread across Toby's face and Shaun watched the procession through his son's eyes.

His own tolerance for the tradition had waned over the years. Two years on the parade committee had removed the excitement of the festivities, but more than that, Annie's Ireland was now on his mind.

Annie. Why was she here with him on St. Patrick's Day, the anniversary of his wedding day to Sarah? A year had passed since he had taken a walk with Annie by the castle. He looked up to the grey sky and realised that two women controlled him, a serene ghost of the past and the soul of a misplaced future. Sarah and Annie walked side by side.

Shaun's attention returned to his son's drooping shoulders as military bands marched by like rows of antique tin soldiers in their colonial regalia. Shaun and Toby waved at Shaun's cousin, but Toby returned to form when the Metropolitan Police Department moved out of sight.

'Let's go for a walk,' said Shaun, interpreting Toby's despondent shoulders as a green light to move on.

'Where to?'

'I'd like you to see a beautiful ceiling on Pennsylvania Avenue.'

'Okay,' Toby said, with an expression of confusion and relief.

They entered the lobby of the Willard Hotel and were embraced by a warm contradiction of opulence and nature. Gold marble pillars heralded a ceiling adorned with gilt stucco cornices and painted state seals, while a symmetrical series of pot plants created the effect of a garden. They took seats at the back of the lobby and Shaun ordered drinks from a passing waitress. They each sat in silence staring up at the ceiling.

'I wonder if this is what heaven looks like,' Toby pondered aloud.

Shaun smiled. 'I think of heaven as mountain range and my son thinks of heaven as a five star hotel. Where did I go wrong?'

Toby's lips smiled and a further silence followed. 'Dad,' Toby began, nervously.

'Yes, son.'

'Do you think mom is in heaven?'

It had been a long time since Toby had asked that question. Shaun's throat filled. He swallowed hard and answered, 'Maybe your mom is here now, smiling down on us.'

Toby flicked his eyes swiftly towards Shaun. He stared up at him and water began to blur the edges of the blue circles, those sky-blue eyes, lustrous gifts from his mother. Shaun put an arm around Toby's shoulder and looked back to the ceiling. 'Sarah, are you here with us?' he asked silently.

There he was talking to a familiar ghost, just has he had done one year ago in a castle in Ireland.

Dreams of Annie and whispers of Sarah criss-crossed in his mind again like the latticed gilt of the ceiling. Grief was a familiar emotion, but he didn't expect Annie to be caught in its consoling wake.

It had been seven months since she had said goodbye. She had written she had felt love and left him with no opportunity to reply. The walk by the castle had the semblance of love. It was beautiful and charged with something almost mystical, but Shaun knew that love could only be measured by the passage of time.

***

The victorious waves of the six men cleared of the Birmingham bombs of 1974 were still prominent in newspapers three days after the event. Annie scrutinized their faces, trying to surmise her own verdict. They looked like ordinary men. She would have spoken to any one of them if she had bumped into them on the train.

'Do you think they did it?' she asked.

Roy, buried deep in a book on C++ coding, didn't look up. He spoke while simultaneously copying something from the textbook onto the computer screen, 'The British justice system made one huge fuck up...I mean screw up.'

Annie caught his smile. Roy had been making an effort to be less confrontational.

'You can say the word as long as it isn't directed at me,' she said.

She returned to her paper. It was hard to imagine that six men, wrongly convicted, had spent sixteen years in jail. Annie wasn't surprised by the police intimidation, but she felt a mixture of bewilderment and shame, as though she'd found out something awful about her own father.

Annie turned to look at Roy. Why couldn't she share this conversation with him? Why couldn't she bring him into the commotion of her mind? She looked away. After all they'd been through, she was thinking of Shaun. She imagined herself writing to him and she berated herself for thinking of Shaun when she should have been thinking of Roy. She had closed her mind to him until a St. Patrick's Day card from the Taylor family in Washington D.C. had reminded her of the party at the castle.

What would she tell Shaun if she were to write to him? Would she tell him about the money that had saved her marriage? Dirk had given a lump sum to Roy to buy the house in which they lived. They had been renting it for years and were entitled to buy it at a low price under the 'Right to Buy' scheme. Annie was surprised that Roy had agreed this time. He had turned down all the previous offers.

Roy's voice interrupted her thoughts. 'I followed James,' he said.

'When?'

'He disappeared after lunch today. He was at the train track with those wee skitters from the estate. They were throwing stones at the trains.'

'And James was there?'

'Yes, but not for long. I took him and three friends to the police station.'

'You did what? What on earth for?'

'To scare the shit out of them,' Roy replied.

'Why didn't you tell me?'

'Because I knew you'd take James' side and let him off with it.'

'And what did the police say?'

'A police officer had a chat with them. That was enough.'

'It was a bit extreme to take them to the police.'

'No, Annie, it was the right thing to do, and instead of judging me, you might think about, just for once, being on my side. I'll do whatever it takes to protect my sons and make them into decent men.'

'I wish you'd let me know before going to the police.'

Annie saw the look in Roy's eye and understood she needed to change her tone. She lowered her voice and her confidence. 'I don't want him to be tagged as the bad child,' she said faintly.

'I can't get it right, can I?'

Annie waited and refused to respond to the anger leaking from Roy's tone.

'What would you have done? Tell me,' Roy said, his face filling with colour. 'You always know how to do the right thing, so tell me where I went wrong.'

'You didn't do anything wrong.'

Annie took a deep breath and spoke firmly. 'Not until the last two minutes when you showed me that I can't have a conversation with you. You see everything as an assault.'

'That's what it feels like. And it's constant. You once complained that you had to walk on eggshells, well so do I. You know, the sooner this course is finished and I can get back into the workplace, the better. You can take over then and things will be perfect. The house will be perfect, the boys will be perfect. You'll have everything you want.'

There it was. The crooked rhythm of Annie's marriage, chugging along until some misshaped words threw it off track. It was a marriage that was as misplaced as the weeds that once ruled the garden.

She stood up, walked to the drawer on the cabinet and pulled out a notebook and pen. It was a cold, wet day, but Annie needed to walk to the shore and she needed to write. She needed to be reminded of the world outside.

***

Shaun left his car parked on P Street after the Project Children meeting at Stella's house and walked to Wisconsin Avenue, the five mile stretch of road that linked his home in Bethesda to Georgetown. The village glow of Georgetown was a nostalgic contrast to the over-development that was occurring at his end of the route. The lights of small cafes and boutiques with their vibrant coloured architraves and thoughtful window displays gave the impression of a Bohemian hub of artists and scholars, belying the material wealth of Washington D.C.'s most exclusive neighbourhood.

He stopped at the door of the Café Bonaparte, an intimate French café with dark tables and the intimate, red light of candles in glass jars. Couples occupied each table and Shaun became aware of a fresh sense of loneliness as he ordered a solitary glass of red wine at the bar. Despite his family, his social commitments and his career, Shaun was alone.

He opened the letter from Annie with a sense of unease. Curiosity willed him to unfold its contents, but the break in communication had allowed him time to live in the moment. While he had been writing to Annie, he hadn't been tuned in to the fact that he was alone, and the letter contained the risk of losing that realisation again. Shaun took a sip of wine and began to read.

22nd April 1991

Dear Shaun

A year has passed since I first met you and I can see a little more clearly. The break between letters has given me the time to understand that you are a friend. When I wrote that last letter, I was confused and I apologise for having been so open about my feelings.

James' shoulder was back to normal within weeks of his trip to America. I think he was disappointed that he had no war wounds to show off when he went back to school in September. He's a boy who enjoys the limelight. Andrew, meanwhile, went into first year at secondary school in September. He passed his eleven plus, and is attending a Grammar school, which means that James is lamenting the loss of a life-time football partner. Andrew has switched to rugby.

I'm writing this letter to you from a loughshore near the remains of an old fort called the Whitehouse (no relation to the one where President Bush currently resides). Someone recently gave me a little pamphlet on the fort and I thought I'd tell you an interesting story since you enjoy history. I need to warn you that I do not have a King Billy obsession, but he may appear in this story.

When Billy arrived in Ireland he brought some followers with him in the form of dignitaries, counts and kings from around Europe. Apparently, you could have walked the seven miles from Carrickfergus to Whiteabbey simply by hopping across the seven hundred ships that were moored on these shores. An eyewitness account by one of Billy's scribes stated, 'We landed at the Whitehouse, where we saw on our arrival great numbers of poor people. The women are not shy of exposing to men's eyes those parts which are usual for the sex to hide.' (The situation today is perilously close on account of fashions inspired by Madonna.)

As you can see, this is conclusive proof that King Billy was indeed a true hero. Not only did he save my ancestor's horse, but he refused the flirtations of those loughshore ladies and remained faithful to Mary.

Perhaps avoiding temptation makes the true measure of a man.

I hope that you can forgive me for cutting off contact. I miss your letters and it would be a pleasure to hear from you if you can write to me. I will also understand if I have created too much confusion.

Yours sincerely,

Annie

Shaun held onto his wine glass and smiled. He then looked up and searched for an old friend as tears stung his eyes.

God had been there for him when Sarah was dying and God had been there for him as a young man, and he realised that his loneliness was deeper than the plight of a man who had lost his wife.

His role as a history professor at the Catholic University of America was to cultivate and impart an understanding of the Christian faith, and yet, each day in work, Shaun avoided the theology attached to the events of the past and imparted only an understanding of cause and effect. Shaun was not only lonely, but he had lost his faith in God. He was a hypocrite in the wrong job, a man stripped of his own values, a man who hadn't avoided temptation and who couldn't rise to the challenge of being a hero. Shaun was in love with a married woman, and it was a monumental fault in his judgement that he should keep writing to Annie.

He raised his head towards the bartender and scanned the dark labels of the rows of wine and the spirits hooked up to the wall.

There it was, the golden glow of an old friend. Shaun pushed the wine to the side. 'A Glenfiddich,' he said as he folded the letter and placed it into his pocket.

***

May 7, 1991

Dear Annie

I started to write you a letter last week, but I was unsure if it was the right thing to do. It's two in the morning here and I find myself writing to you again.

I have been up watching live coverage of riots in Mount Pleasant, a quiet residential area close to Bethesda. It's truly incredible what is unfolding before my eyes. I'm not sure how much detail you get of American news, but a thirty year-old guy from El Salvador has been shot by the police. A mob is going crazy destroying everything in sight. People seem to have lost their minds. Stores have been looted and police vehicles set alight. The Latino community is literally up in arms about how they are treated. I am thinking of your country and what it must feel like to be so close to such disorder. If I lived in Northern Ireland, I would never be able to take my eyes off the TV. I understand why the children who come to America are so well informed about politics. Politics is everywhere when it is this loud.

Your theory on King Billy is interesting indeed, but it's a cautionary tale. King Billy may have been thinking of his mistress, Elizabeth, in all her finery, when he refused those poor ladies, so shoddily dressed, on the shores of the Whitehouse. A hero is an imperfect man, after all.

Yours sincerely,

Shaun

***

A siren heralded the first electric current and Jean's body began to bob gently in the water. She took a deep breath, pushed away her fear, and spread her arms as the waves escalated and the boys moved out of sight.

'They'll be okay,' said Annie above the squeals of dozens of children whose voices travelled and merged into an acoustic din in the foreground of Jean's mind. The sound was unsettling.

'I'm not worried about James and Robert,' Jean said. 'I'm

not sure that I can do this!'

She shrieked when a raucous swell tossed her body into the air. She felt tears run down her face, tears of fear that were drying into tears of laughter as one large current swept her body up onto a crest of wave. She looked at Annie. Her cheeks were glowing with the joy of a child as she surged over waves in the Shankill Leisure centre on the first day of the summer holidays with a huge, engaging smile.

'I'm gonna kill you,' Jean shouted between breaths as she climbed a lap of leaping wave.

'What for?' shouted Annie, averting a mouthful of water, 'Sure you're having a great time!'

'I'm having a...' Jean concentrated as the next wave swept her up into a ball of flesh and pulled her back to Annie. 'I'm having a heart-attack. I can't bloody breathe,' she yelled, spitting chlorine and clasping Annie's shoulder for support. 'If I'm going down, you're coming with me.'

Annie laughed and took Jean's hand.

'Ah, that's better,' said Jean as she relaxed.

The waves slowed to an even ebb and Jean buoyed back and forth in the safety of Annie's hand.

The wave machine came to a halt and Jean found her feet on the slippery tiles.

'I feel a bit better about life when I'm sitting over there on the side,' she said, freeing Annie's hand and nodding to the seats where other mothers observed their children.

'Och, nonsense! Ye had a brave auld time o it!' laughed Annie

'I did ay, but next time, you get on with all that jumping and diving and let me take care of the sandwiches.'

'You're still young! You should be joining in the fun!'

Jean wondered if she'd ever really been young. She envied Annie's zeal. Annie was fit and active and full of life, but Jean had got used to watching life from the sidelines.

'I tell you what,' said Jean. 'I'll go and get changed and head on up the road to get lunch on. You follow when you're all ready.'

'That'll do. See you soon!'

'Now don't be getting yourself too excited on a high tide!' Jean warned with a smile as she departed.

Jean walked home under the zig-zagging drapes of red, white and blue bunting dipping from post to post across the Shankill Road. The Black Mountain presided in the distance where the sun fizzled the landscape into shimmering light. The Shankill Road was beautiful, yet behind the red-bricked shops and houses, lay an ugly secret and an underground world of violent men whose response was to defend when their community came under attack.

Jean thought of Harry. He was still disappearing through the night, returning home with no alcohol on his breath and shoes caked in muck and grime. She had asked him if he was up to something, if he was part of some Loyalist gang, but he had laughed and kissed her and assured her that he'd stuck to his promise. He had even winked and told Jean that he was waiting for her to produce a fourth child.

She had thought about questioning his brother, Sammy, but something had stopped her. Perhaps acknowledging the reason for Harry's absence would implicate her in his crime.

Jean felt relief as she turned the key to her front door, removed as she was from the crushing fear of being in transit.

She was seventeen when she had first felt the fear, the fear of the loud clap of an almighty hand that had brought her to her knees near the market.

That day, God had had enough of Belfast and all its trouble. The word 'quick' had struck Jean in the legs when a policeman had appeared and alerted everyone to get out of the shop. A shove in the back from a stranger had then sent her falling onto the pavement. Jean's limbs had continued their revolt from her mind until she felt a woman's arms pull her away. Smoke and flames had been rising into the sky when another clap had sounded.

God's fury had been heard as people screamed and scattered. There had been a dense drone like the one that Jean had heard in the swimming pool and screaming voices had merged like white noise. Jean had kept walking with her head down until she had reached Snugville Street. Twenty IRA bombs had exploded within less than two hours, and that evening Jean, her granny, and her little brother had wrapped themselves in images on the TV; stationary and safe from transit.

The taste of hatred Jean had felt on Bloody Friday was hard to swallow. She recalled what she'd said to Annie about hatred, and she questioned if her hatred of the IRA was merely a misplaced passion for masked men who would never love her in return. Could it be that the hurt was borne of knowing that those men were fellow citizens of Belfast, neighbours of the same soil?

And could it be that the hatred was heightened as trust trickled like sand through a cracked hourglass of time?

Jean knew that the hatred was misplaced and that people had learned to watch life with steely glances from the sidelines, each side applauding their own version of a Christian God, a Catholic God and a Protestant God.

One God with many hands.

***

Annie walked beside Robert and James as a welcome burst of sun warmed the faded colours of Belfast's battered façade. A young corporal in uniform with a rifle slung across his body caught Annie's attention. The custodian of a wide helmet resting on narrow shoulders, he couldn't have been more than twenty years of age. He was seated in a doorway beside a group of young children who were eating ice-cream and pushing trikes and scooters across his path.

Annie looked into the eyes of the soldiers as a mother looks into the eyes of a son, and she wondered how the English, Scottish and Welsh mothers felt about this corner of their own divided nation. It was hard to imagine how the mother of a soldier in Manchester or Glasgow would see Belfast through kindred eyes.

'Why does Robert's street have soldiers?' James asked.

'To protect the community,' Annie replied.

'Why don't we?'

'You sound disappointed, son,' Annie smiled. 'It's a bit quieter where we are.'

'I'd like to join the army when I'm older. I'd like to drive one of those Saxons and learn to use an SA 80.'

'I thought you wanted to go be a civil engineer and build bridges with Uncle Dirk.'

James looked thoughtful, 'Could I join the Royal Engineers? Robert's going to join the Royal Engineers, aren't you Robert? They build bridges too.' Robert shot James an affirming nod, and Annie smiled nervously at the unsullied ambitions of two ten year old boys.

They had arrived at Snugville Street and Annie marvelled at what lay inside Jean's home. It was a doll's house of dark, mahogany furniture, peach festoon blinds, velvet chairs and deep, shaggy sheepskin rugs.

'Jean, can I come in?' Annie called.

Jean's voice emerged from the kitchen in a tornado of expletives, 'That man leaves a trail of muck behind him. I'm going to kill him.'

Annie entered the living room with a warm smile as Jean's words continued to rotate.

'He has been out all night. I don't know where he goes or what he does. Ever since he got his hands on a set of wheels, he's been gone.'

'Where did he get the car?'

'He bought it for £1000 with part of our mortgage deposit. Now he has the keys to a whole new way of doing nothing to help me.'

Annie winced and tried hard to separate herself from the similarities between her own life and that of Jean. She looked across the fireplace where a large portrait demonstrated the pride of Jean Adams. There was Robert, a handsome young boy who would surely break hearts one day, and beside him, two little girls in elaborate red, velvet dresses.

'I love that photo,' said Annie. 'The girls' dresses are gorgeous.'

'I made them with my own hands,' said Jean with a swivel of her head and a puckered smile.

'I didn't know you sewed! Your talents know no end!'

'Oh I know! And they said I was as thick as champ in school too! Anyway, what about Operation Adamsteen? Are we going to do it?'

Annie laughed. She and Jean had been on the sidelines of a football match between some Project Children participants when they had come up with the idea of a cross-community trip in Northern Ireland.

They pored over the details on how to get the children on each side of the peace line to meet up in a safe place, and concluded that a trip to the countryside was what was required. Just as they finished discussing it, Shelley and Hannah returned home from the next door neighbour's house, smiling shyly as they entered the room.

'Well, what did you do today?' enquired Jean.

Shelley clung to Jean's legs and looked over her shoulder at Annie in a captivating mix of timidness and exhibition, her blond hair tumbling over her shoulders in curls. Hannah, meanwhile, trailed a multi-coloured towel around the room by the ribbons, dancing and singing, 'Any dream will do.'

'Where did you get your cloak of many colours?' asked Jean.

'I made it for her,' tinkled a musical voice. 'We had some fun this morning, didn't we girls?'

Annie smiled as she took in the sight of a porcelain doll of a woman with a pristine smile. She wore a full length, red dressing gown that floated by the doorway to the living room.

'What are you doing hiding in the hallway?' cried Jean. 'Come on in!' She turned to Annie and smiled. 'Annie, this is our wee neighbour, Mrs McAdam.'

'Nice to meet you,' said Annie.

'Och-a-nee! Is this the wee girl frae the country? Nice tae meet ye, love. I've heard all about you!'

'Not quite the country. I live in Whiteabbey.'

'Are you no the wee girl frae Glenarm?'

'Yes, I am.'

'My mother took me to Glenarm yince to see a freen.'

'Yince,' mimicked Jean. 'Are you frae the country yoursel', Mrs McAdam?'

'I'll have ye know thon's the way all the Belfast folk used to talk Miss know-it-all. Isn't that right, Annie?'

'It is ay, Mrs McAdam. You tell Jean to howl her weesht!'

'I'll have to apologise for the state I'm in,' continued Mrs McAdam, changing her dialect to Belfast as she patted the side of her fluffy head. 'Shelley was practicing with curlers and she had me pulled asunder. I think Santa needs to bring her one of those Girl's Worlds or I'll be in a wig before my seventieth birthday. Anyway, I'd better get in and get changed before the bingo.'

'The bingo's not 'til tonight,' said Jean.

'Oh I know, but a girl needs to look her best. You never know, it might be my lucky night.'

Annie smiled knowing that the old lady wasn't referring to the bingo. 'Well, I hope your lucky number comes up,' she said.

'Oh so do I, love. Number three. You and me. Number four. Knock at the door.'

Annie laughed as Mrs McAdam turned and knocked the front door.

'Number five, man alive,' was next and a loud cackle from Jean and Mrs McAdam sent tears of laughter streaming down Annie's face.

'Number eleven. Legs eleven,' added Jean.

Mrs McAdam projected another mighty titter, twirled and pulled up her dressing gown to reveal a skinny ankle.

'Would you look at them ankles, Annie?' said Mrs McAdam. 'Isn't it hard to believe I've been single for fifty years?'

'It certainly is,' said Annie still awash with tears.

'Right girls, are you gonna go to church in the morning?' asked Mrs McAdam.

'Yes!' came twin voices.

'Good. See you in the morning. Bye, Annie. It was nice meeting you.'

'Bless her,' said Jean as she closed the door and returned to the living room. 'Her husband died in the Belfast Blitz.'

'That's a shame. She seems like a lovely wee woman,' said Annie.

Annie watched as Shelley and Hannah giggled and danced

across the living room.

'You've two dancers there,' said Annie. 'Have they ever tried Irish dancing?'

'Is it not for…' Jean placed her hand to the side of her mouth and bellowed a fruitless whisper, 'Is it not for Catholics?'

'No, it's dancing. And I think they can hear you. It's for everyone. The Festival dancing is cross-community. My friend runs a dancing school in Carrickfergus. If you could meet me at the train some Saturday morning in Whiteabbey, I could take them onto Carrick. It starts back in September.'

'Well, girls. What do you think of that idea? Would you like to learn to dance?'

'Yes please,' another chorus echoed as two little girls jumped up and down underneath a large stripy beach towel.

'Are you sure it wouldn't be too much bother?' asked Jean.

'Not at all. It's all boys and mud in my house on a Saturday morning. It would be a real pleasure!'

***

14th July 1991

Dear Shaun

Apologies for the delayed response to your last letter. It's the July fortnight holidays here, so I've been busy entertaining the boys. We visited Jean at the start of the summer. She's getting a little frustrated with Harry. He's staying out for nights on end and she has no idea what he's up too. Roy said he could take a wild guess.

The other day I took Andrew and James to see a wee country parade in Broughshane. It was beautiful. There were pipe bands, accordion bands, flute bands and brass bands, all dressed up in their flowers and their finery. Sombre men in bowler hats and orange sashes marched under wide banners raised onto wood and brass, and children played with their band sticks and their toy drums along the sides of the kerbs.

There's something about the Twelfth of July that takes a girl right back to her childhood. I don't know if you've ever seen a lambeg drum. It has a wide girth and stubborn sound that rumbles deep into the past. When we were children, we used to go to Broughshane with my uncle and watch the men with long arms and strong backs pound their cane sticks against the stretched goat skins along country lanes. We used to cup our hands over our ears when the lambegs passed by. This year I sat back with the mizzle of 'the Boyne mist' on my face and enjoyed the nostalgic beat under a sky painted in woven tapestries of battles that never ended.

Maybe one day, if you come back to Ireland, I could take you to see a Twelfth of July parade.

I hope you have a lovely summer.

Yours sincerely,

Annie

***

Jessica Dean was long and slender, her body sculpted like crystalline in a pale silver gown. Her smile sidled through the room as her voice pulsed the sultry hum of sixties' rhythm and blues under a square cut of shoulder-length brown hair. Shaun's eyes were fixed on her lips. She was in her late twenties or early thirties and had a fineness of face that demonstrated age and the fullness of lips of a younger woman. Her voice hushed the bar as she sang.

Flanagan's had started to market to a new clientele, and Jessica was there on Friday nights supporting the fresh look of the place. Gone were the tradesmen, the tired wallpaper, the faint smell of damp and the baskets of chicken wings. Rows of wine glasses shimmered under spotlights at the bar and Jessica Dean crooned 'Upside Down' in a mellow voice. Shaun caught her eye as her lips brushed the microphone and he knew that the Irish Society meeting would be bleak in contrast to the beauty on his mind. Making his way reluctantly up the stairs to the room that had yet to undergo a transformation, Shaun stole one more look over his shoulder at the singer and was surprised to find that the singer was looking back.

Eamon Fitzgerald was quiet, withdrawn and keen to

progress the meeting. Shaun smiled as he wondered if Eamon had also fallen under the spell of Jessica Dean. He'd never thought about Eamon in that way, categorised as he was in Shaun's mind as a serious man incapable of demonstrating emotion, a man with a human side reserved for the rights of humans suffering persecution under intolerant regimes.

The meeting revolved around some building contracts for Bethesda. The talk of development and the increasingly high skyline continued for ten minutes before Eamon turned back to the subject of funding for political prisoners, swathing the room in a foreboding cloak. Eamon went over the facts of the Birmingham six trial. 'The British Justice system is rotten to the core. IRA soldiers will never get a fair trial on British soil.'

Half an hour passed of listless deliberation before Shaun finally stood up and made his excuses. Ireland had decidedly lost its appeal. Irish politics remained dark and dismal with faded words and lies hanging from old rafters and Shaun was drawn like an electric current to the glistening lights of progress downstairs.

Jessica was on a break. Shaun took in the full length of her body when he saw her at the bar and emboldened by an awakening for change, he moved to her side with confidence.

'Jessica, I'm Shaun, I've wanted to meet you.' Shaun detected a look of relief. Had she been awaiting his return?

'Good to meet you,' she smiled. She studied him for a moment. 'You're here on Friday nights. You always sit here in the same seat at the bar. I was wondering if I'd ever get the chance to speak to you.'

Shaun did not expect to hear the reply that Jessica gave.

'That was a beautiful rendition of a classic,' he said.

'Which song?' Jessica replied.

'Upside Down. You played it before I went upstairs. Your voice is spellbinding.'

Jessica's eyes were deep brown and they burnished in the wake of the compliment.

'Spellbinding huh?' she laughed, resting her elbow casually on the bar.

'Yes, spellbinding. And I'd love to hear it again, next time over dinner.'

Jessica removed her arm from the bar and stood up straight. Shaun could see that his confidence was contagious.

'You don't know anything about me.'

'That's why I've asked you to dinner.'

'I don't know anything about you.'

'I can fix that,' said Shaun. 'I live here in Bethesda. I work at CUA. I have a son who is crazy about baseball. I drink here on a Friday night and I go to church every other Sunday.' Shaun wasn't entirely sure why he mentioned his church and wondered if Jessica might think it was an odd admission.

'I need to do the same for you in case you change your mind,' she smiled.

'I am sure I won't, but please do.'

'I live in an apartment downtown, I'm in my final year of Economics at Georgetown University. I tried medicine first and relinquished that ambition when I recognised my aversion to blood was hindering my progress. I've been a student for eight years. No children. I would much prefer a baseball game to dinner and I change my place of worship according to where the wind blows.' Jessica held out her arms and added, 'And I sing here at the weekends.' She looked around and stooped slightly as she whispered, 'Don't tell the owner, but I today I auditioned for a swanky hotel downtown.'

'I'm thrilled that you prefer baseball to dinner,' Shaun said, and lowering his voice, he added, 'and I hope that you get the gig at the swanky hotel.'

'Me too,' Jessica smiled.

'So, tell me more about all those churches.'

'I have been offered direct debit forms for every church within a twenty mile radius of Georgetown University,' said Jessica, her eyebrows raised.

'That's a whole lot of spirituality.'

'I'd better get back to singing.'

Jessica reached for a pen and scribbled her number on a beer mat. 'Here you go, I sing most weekends, so I can only do baseball through the week. I play softball as well. How old is your son?'

Shaun was pleased that Jessica had asked. 'He's nine and a half. His name is Toby.'

'Maybe Toby could join us at the batting cage some day. I'd better go. See you later.'

Shaun took the beer mat and slipped it into his jacket pocket. 'I'll be in touch,' he said watching Jessica's frame move back to the stage.

He walked out of the bar, energised, and determined never to return to Flanagan's or the Irish Society again. Flanagan's was his father's bar, the Irish Society his grandfather's calling. Everything he had was borrowed from the past and Shaun needed to build something new. He removed the letter from his pocket, took one last glance at it and realised that Annie was merely describing the landscape of a life he would never know. Shaun's life was in America. He crumpled the letter and placed it in a trash can outside the bar. It was time to end the letters to Annie. This time for good.

PART TWO

THE RED SHOE
1993

Annie stopped, her head swirling, spinning in the dark. Where did all the vehicles go with their lights shining on her hand? A muted din and now, so peaceful. It was a sunny day, a crisp October day. It was Andrew's fifteenth birthday.

The Shankill Leisure Centre. Annie smiled. Jean was bouncing on the waves. The waves were red, blood waves, rising and falling, Jean drowning in blood.

Blood, was there blood in her ears? She checked. What were the patterns, the colours on the side of the wall? There were soldiers. How many? Too many. James and his Saxons and the SA 80s. Annie reached out her hand and Jean touched it and pulled her under the water. Was she drowning too? But there was no water. There was only sunshine, blistering sunshine and clear skies casting off a cool, dusty air.

Annie laughed. Dancing through Snugville Street in the morning, holding the little girl's hand. Hop over hop back hop back two three four, hop over hop back hop back two three four, and out hop back hop back two three four.

So young. Her little girl.

No, it was Shelley, Shelley in her ribbons and her red patent shoes.

'Ma'am, are you okay ma'am?'

Annie Steen always looked into the eyes of soldiers. Didn't

he know? Crystal blue eyes, framed in a wide, metal helmet.

And a kind lady with tea. 'Come and sit down love, come here. Take this.'

Hop over hop back hop back two three four.

'Little Shelley Adams will never dance again.'

'Sorry love, what did you say? Are you okay?'

Annie, seated, looking around at lines of armoured vehicles, weeping, 'Little Shelley Adams will never dance again.'

***

Harry walked fast and heard the crunch of autumn leaves echoing from a near past. He wanted to run, but his feet were pulled in opposing motions from his will, and as his legs accelerated, they tripped the current of his mind.

Harry had to walk, his feet slain for the weight of his crime.

He had danced for the third autumn. He had danced in the bandstand, holding Linda's hand before the distant, deadening thud that had carried him back to Linda's house.

Harry could locate the memory of the transient shift. The rusty, crackling fingers of horse chestnut leaves had tiptoed along the ground and then lifted into a soundless flurry, a whistle of a warning as he danced in the park.

Sitting on the velvet chair, clicking buttons on a remote control box, Harry knew where he was supposed to be.

'I'll get Annie to collect them,' Jean had said that morning in a weary whisper through the receiver of the phone box on Cregagh Road, and then in a worn voice, 'Come home, Harry. I need to talk to you. Please come home.'

Why had Jean wanted to talk?

People tiptoed along Royal Avenue like cracked leaves, pointless leaves drifting in a subdued wind of autumn's war. Harry willed his feet to move faster. He approached Smithfield market, and he remembered. He pictured a family portrait, gold and brown and three strong smiles, but his feet dragged against the weight of the headline that had appeared along the bottom of the screen. His eyes, so strong, had been dim and weak, but there was a transient vision of being in the wrong place at the right time. Or, the wrong place at the wrong time, and two wrongs didn't make it right.

Bomb. Shankill.

Two words, and Linda had stopped moving.

A whisper. 'Go home, Harry.'

A pulse of voice. 'Harry, go home.'

***

Please God, give her pain to me. Please God, give her pain to me.

Shelley, Shelley, listen to me. It's your mammy here and I can't speak. My voice is in my hand and it's holding you.

You'll be okay, Shelley, because I can feel it in your hand.

Please God, give her pain to me. Please God, give her pain to me.

Shelley, I'm not hurting you when I squeeze your hand. I'm taking your pain away. I want you to share it with me. Remember how we share.

Share your toys, girls. Learn to share. Why should you share your toys? It doesn't hurt anyone when you were playing with them at home by your sister's side. It's okay. When we get home, we won't worry about sharing. We'll buy you a new toy. And we'll buy you new shoes. We'll go to Clarkes and we'll find the same red shoes. We'll take a bus or a taxi.

'Mammy, I want the red shoes.'

'The patent ones?'

'The red, painted ones with the bows.'

'Patent, Shelley. Patent.'

'Daddy, do you like look my painting shoes with bows?'

One shoe.

Please God, give her pain to me.

***

'Shaun, have you heard?'

It was Stella from Project Children, her voice recognisable, yet strained.

'What is it?' Shaun asked.

Guilt surged through the circuit of his mind as he awaited the next sentence. Two years had passed since he had last spoken to Stella.

'Did you see the news this morning?' Stella asked.

'No, what is it?' Shaun's body moved slowly, responding to the realisation that something was wrong.

'I don't want to alarm you, but there was a bomb on the Shankill Road in Belfast. I went through some of the files to find out which children lived there. The first name I came to was Robert Adams. Have you spoken to him lately?'

Shaun's throat hardened, 'No, I haven't.'

'I thought maybe you could call his mom. See if everything is okay. I can do...'

'No, no, I'll do it. I'll call.'

'Thank you. And Shaun...'

'Yes?'

'We've missed you. It's great to hear your voice.'

'Thank you. I'll be in touch soon.' Shaun dropped the receiver. He walked slowly towards the TV and tuned into CNN. President Clinton's face reflected from the screen as a ticker-tape spelt out Stella's news, 'IRA bomb in Northern Ireland.'

Shaun moved to the kitchen and reached into a drawer, searching for his address book. Jean and Harry Adams were the first names he saw. He lifted the phone and dialled the number. A cut glass voice echoed through the receiver, 'Leave us a message and we'll get back to you later.'

'Jean, hi, it's Shaun. I've heard the news and I wanted to see if you are all okay. Call me.'

Shaun didn't know how to finish the message. He sat down and cleared his throat, 'Jean, I'm praying for you all.'

***

'Where the fuck have you been?' Sammy rolled down the window at the bottom of the Shankill Road 'Where have you been?' he repeated.

Harry jolted to reality.

'It's Shelley. Get in. We need to get you to the hospital.'

Harry's breathing was in his head and words slowly ruptured from his cracked, dry throat. 'What's happened to Shelley?'

'She was hurt. Harry, get in.'

Harry climbed into the car. 'Where is she?' he said, as voices and images pummelled through his mind.

'Daddy, can you collect us from dancing every week?'

It was Shelley and ice-cream was dripping off her chin.

'Daddy, are you coming home the night?' It was Hannah's stern voice, her hands on her hips at the door. 'Daddy, mummy says you're spending too much time with Uncle Sammy.'

'We'll have to try a few hospitals. Best bet's the Royal hospital for sick children. The roads are closed. We need to go round the Westlink.'

'What about Robert and Hannah?'

'They're safe, but they were all there.'

They were all there. Harry swallowed hard. Why?

Sammy responded to the silent question. 'Robert said he was going to meet his mate from the prison bus.'

The prison bus.

More than three years had passed since an American had visited his home. He looked out the window and stared at the stillness of the pale sky. He coughed, his throat dry from the long walk from Linda's house. Sammy reached into the side compartment and handed Shaun a tin of cola. Turning onto the Falls Road, Shaun found that same leafy stillness that he had witnessed in the city centre, the stillness of the flight of fear.

Sammy spoke again. 'There's going to be trouble.'

'Did you see her?' Harry asked, his mouth filling with syrupy bile as he sipped the coke.

'She was gone when I got there. Robert was with a friend of Jean's.'

'Annie.'

'I don't know mate, but I told her to take Robert and Hannah to Mrs McAdam. I've been sitting waiting at the bottom of the Shankill for an hour.'

Sammy parked the car in the hospital car park, as Harry's eyes roamed over grey concrete and up to the blue sky.

'Go,' said Sammy. 'Go.'

The car door swung open, and Harry's feet greedily commanded the black asphalt.

***

Roy gripped Annie's hand as they moved through the streets of Belfast in his new Vauxhaul Cavalier. The car picked up speed and lights streamed through the windows along the Shore Road. Annie wound the window down and gulped in the fresh air, images of the day merging into the light of the streetlamps, creating a film reel of incandescent colour.

A bright Saturday afternoon, Shelley and Hannah dancing by the front door. They had skipped from the car, a spectacle in their royal blue corduroy dresses and red, patent shoes. 'What did you learn today?' Jean had asked. 'A light double jig' two voices had chimed, a small choir of siblings, each child identical in height despite the two years between them. Annie had taken their hands and followed their lead around.

'Front and back, hop one two three.'

Shelley had tripped, scuffing the patent of her red shoe. Annie had squeezed her hands as she had moved on to the side step, at first stumbling and then gaining in rhythm as Annie had sounded out, 'Hop over hop back, hop back two three four.'

Annie pointed her right foot in the car. Her toes moved up and down, dancing out the movements of the jig.

'Come on in and we'll get you all some lunch,' Jean had said. 'And thanks for bringing them home, Annie. Harry didn't come home.'

Annie had studied the look of dismay on Jean's face. More than three years of disappearing and something had finally clicked.

And then the weightless time.

Was it a divine warning that had caused the strangled

acoustics of Jean's hollering voice? 'Shelley, Hannah, Robert,' over and over.

Snugville Street had been empty and Annie had followed Jean to the door and then towards the Shankill Road.

Annie's toes stopped moving, but Roy's hand shot volts into her leg. He pressed her knee and Annie twisted and turned around the dancefloor of her mind.

A deafening blast. A long, haunting silence and a thud.

She had moved her hands to her ears at the end of Snugville Street, instinctively checking them for blood, a sensation that liquid was pouring from them disorienting her in the din.

And then the serrated yell of Jean.

Annie cupped her ears as the engine droned.

There was Jean on the main road calling Shelley's name. Annie had moved toward the voice, but hundreds of voices all collided in a subdued stillness. People were running among ash clouds in fraught motion and the sound of indistinct voices fell flat on Annie's ears.

Annie had walked to the other side of the road and a mountain of debris had poured onto the road in a medley of bricks and dust. The buildings at each side of the Fish shop framed the mountain like a gigantic fireplace, its mantle remaining intact as it spewed grey coals and billowing ashes across the street. And people were slowly, painfully gathering.

Annie had moved aimlessly, consumed by the smell of burning ash and conscious that she was trying to take in each detail in a daze of disbelief and fear. Emergency vehicles had arrived to her left, carefully parking in uniform lines in the chaos.

Thank God. Robert and Hannah, Hannah in a puddle, sobbing, her brother holding her hand, both of them suddenly so small. Annie had lifted Hannah's slight body in her arms and cradled her soaking tights. Robert had called out 'mammy,' and Annie's hand had pulled him back as he had tried to run towards Jean.

And in the rubble, the red shoe.

Annie had swallowed hard, clutching Robert's shoulder, shielding his eyes from a sight he had already seen.

Jean had been close to the edge of a scattered mound of rubble in the middle of the road, bent over a pile of moving dust, a creature emerging from ashes. A stranger had lifted the bundle and he had walked towards the ambulance looking down tenderly as Jean gripped Shelley's hand. Annie had turned away from the black blood seeping through greyed tights and gulped back a flux of breath, her eyes averting the other red shoe dangling from a dusty leg.

Jean looked back. 'Please take care of my children.'

Robert had been mute and Hannah had begun to shake as the heat of her soggy tights had turned cold, and Annie, who had never been so far away from home, had walked, conscious of words sitting on the dusty plane of her dull ears as helpless people milled around; trampled voices on the Shankill.

THE LAST FLAMING SIGN OF PEACE

'There's something else,' said Stella, tentatively.

Shaun had been at Stella's for most of the afternoon. They had called dozens of families across the Shankill area and Shaun's emotions were spent. Everyone knew where they were at the moment the bomb had exploded and the world had stopped turning on an ordinary October day for so many people they had known.

'It's about the Irish Society,' she said.

'The Irish Society?' Shaun responded, surprised to hear the name after so long.

'Yes, I remember you were involved. Your name is still listed on the committee.'

'But I left two years ago. I didn't attend a meeting the whole time I was with Jessica,' said Shaun.

Stella spoke solemnly and Shaun's mind blackened.

'A man called Gary Ross has been arrested for gun running from Philadelphia. He's been in America for years. I don't know him, but I recognised the guy in the picture in the paper from an event I went to years ago. Here, take a look.' Stella passed the paper to Shaun.

His heart slowed as his eyes fell on the headline, 'Guns stitched into dolls. Irish terrorist arrested for gun running.' Shaun continued to read the short article.

'Gary Ross was born in County Down in Northern Ireland. He had been linked to an illegal Irish army at the age of seventeen and did not declare this to the US authorities. He was subsequently issued a US visa in 1979, at the age of twenty-two. He is reported to have been involved in fundraising activities in Irish heartlands in Boston, New York and Philadelphia and his arrest comes after documents, including his birth certificate, and a letter linking him to the address in County Down where the guns were received, were found under floorboards in an apartment he had rented in the Roxborough area of Philadelphia. He has been arrested for two incidences of gun-running in 1989 and 1990 and is accused of posting guns stitched into children's dolls. Since that time, he has removed himself from Irish republican strongholds, and retreated to Maryland, where he has been using the name Eamon Fitzgerald.'

Above the article was an image of a young man in his early twenties. Shaun stared at a black and white photograph of a fine serious face, embellished with a head of light curly hair and punctuated by piercing eyes that heralded memories of long meetings in a dark room above a bar. Here Eamon Fitzgerald was young, but equally intense.

An image of Harry Adams flashed before Shaun, his eyes saturated in disappointment. The Irish Society had not been Eamon Fitzgerald's, and yet he had seized it and turned it into something for which Shaun felt shame.

Stella's voice came again, gentle yet strong, 'Shaun. I need to ask you. Were you involved with Eamon Fitzgerald?'

'No!' The blood in Shaun's ears burned with the insinuation.

'Shaun, for your own sake, distance yourself from the Society.'

Shaun saw his grandfather's face pale into the distance as his mind raced with the same anger and apathy that had made him resent the Irish heritage he had once treasured. As he left Stella's house, he thought back to Annie and felt an intense regret at never having answered her last letter.

***

Annie clutched a mug of tea as James studied the TV screen.

'Bastard' lashed his breaking teenage voice, penetrating the uneasy calm that had surrounded them after all the names had passed. The last name was that of the bomber and the fire of hatred in Annie's son's eyes led her to say something that was not on her mind, 'James, don't speak ill of the dead.'

James turned to face his mother and his voice trembled. 'Why shouldn't I? He's dead now. What does he care?'

Another name, a familiar name, the other bomber, alive.

Annie's mind wandered and she was reminded of a sharp pain that had long gone. Why did he stop writing? The disappointment was there in her living room with her husband and her sons. She turned to Roy, attuned to a new thought. 'Would you forgive the man responsible for the bomb in the McNeill bar?'

'I did so years ago.'

Annie stared at her husband. Roy's voice had been flat like all the other voices clanging in her head.

She'd often thought that Roy had lost his spirit on the same day that he had lost his leg, but his eyes were now soulful with sincerity. No one had ever been convicted, but Roy had already forgiven the bomber.

'Have you?' Roy returned the question.

Annie hesitated. 'I don't know. I always imagined an older man, middle aged and aware of what he was doing. I've never pictured someone young.'

Roy's cheeks blazed. He coughed and cleared his throat. 'That's the best time to recruit them, before they have responsibilities and families, before their conscience has a chance to grow. You know that if any adult or child had been handed a gun on the Shankill on Saturday, they'd have committed murder.'

'I know.'

'I don't want to stay.'

Roy's voice was firm. Annie understood what was coming.

'I want to move to Holland. I want you and the boys to come with me.'

***

Through the front windscreen of Sammy's car, the Shankill Road swept up like a tide of tears. Harry wasn't ready to go home. He wasn't ready to face the tragedy of a people torn and battered, but he needed to see his family. He needed to touch the faces of Hannah and Robert.

'It's time for a rest,' the nurse had said after three days and nights on the ward, but Harry was blinded by flashbacks of Shelley, her angelic face blackened with bruises and cuts, wires running from her fine, pale body to a machine and blood pumping into the veins of her long arms through a plastic tube.

'Go home, the nurse had insisted. 'You need to sleep. Shelley is safe.'

Shelley is safe. Was anyone safe? And what use was Harry as a father if he couldn't keep his children safe?

He concentrated on the road ahead but the nine faces of the victims were ingrained in his memory and he knew that he held the pain of a city in his hands.

They turned right into Snugville Street and Harry began to feel more impatient to see his family. The repetitive reprieve of the window-wipers secreted his brother's voice, but Harry heard what he had to say. 'We need you back.'

Robert was the first to greet Harry at the door. Harry kissed his head, held him tight, and understood for the first time that the role of a father was to shield his children.

Hannah was on the sofa, asleep under a large, black duffle coat, and Jean was by the fire, seated, and dosing in the cold, dark room. Jean was still and Harry's home was lifeless. Harry removed his coat and placed it over Jean, and as the two arms surrounded her, a feeling of deep remorse compressed his chest. Only days ago, those same woollen arms had been wrapped around Linda.

Harry sat beside Hannah on the sofa, pulled up her coat and ran his fingers through her hair. Holding two fingers to his lips, he kissed them and set them on Hannah's freckled cheeks. He then looked up and prayed in silence. 'Thank you, God, for saving my children.'

'Daddy, can we light the fire?' asked Robert. 'There's no hot water.'

'Of course,' Harry stood up and switched on some lamps before going to the back yard for coal. He returned to find Robert crouched down, brushing the ash from the fire.

"Here, help me with these,' Harry said, opening an old *News Letter*. It was dated 25 September and the headline read. 'Hume-Adams joint statement on peace.'

The two Nationalist leaders had been talking behind closed doors about peace; Hume, the leader of a peaceful party in search of a United Ireland, and Adams, the leader of the political party behind the IRA. Harry shook his head. He hadn't dared to believe the words printed on the paper. Now, he wished he had believed in something because he had believed in nothing at all. The story had a beginning and no end.

He handed the newspaper to his son and lay the firelighters and wooden sticks on the grate. He sat back and watched his son carefully crease the wide expanse of paper into an accordion of pleats. Robert held a neat, oblong strip and folded it in the middle, one half running horizontally from his hand and the other vertically. His taut fingers tucked the folds in swift movements until a firelighter was created from news of peace. Harry lit a match to the firelighters and Robert mechanically raised a fresh sheet of paper across the fireplace, his deft fingers touching the brass that Jean had so carefully cleaned until a flame tore through the centre of the story, sucking the newspaper into the grate. Flames peeled back ash, circling around Zip firelighters, twisting towards the sticks that were singed black. Harry lifted the coal bucket and took another look at his son whose eyes were fixed on the fire that had parched the last flaming sign of peace. Harry shuffled the damp coal slowly from its bucket, hearkening the reassuring chime of coal on metal, the sound of warmth and of home, and a pile of black, glistening fuel quelled the dancing flames. Robert reached for the iron tongs and dug underneath the coal, turning over the red coated rocks and jabbing at the quiet fire that spread underneath.

'Daddy, what are they going to do?'

'Who, son?'

'Uncle Sammy. You. You, daddy,' Robert hesitated. 'Those men need to pay for what they did.'

Harry looked at his son through the eyes of a conscience quenched in sulphurous black, and he questioned if a man could shield his son without holding a sword.

***

'Who is she?' asked Jean as Harry coated the cooling embers in slack.

'Who?'

'Don't dare try to fool me.' Jean was still seated, the arms of the coat dangling and redundant by her side.

'It's not what you think,' said Harry, patting the slack with a shovel.

'Oh, I think we can both be sure that it's not what I thought.'

Jean had never felt so cold in her own home. She looked around at the untidy sofa and back to Harry. 'Who is she?'

Harry turned slowly towards Jean as his coat fell to the floor, a crumpled clap crushing the wintry silence.

'Linda,' he said, combusting the hope that had been burning in the back of Jean's mind for three long days.

'Linda,' she repeated, her mind churning, her mouth reacting. 'Where did you meet her?'

'The bank.'

Harry's voice was faint.

The bank. The mortgage application. The mortgage that had never happened. Jean looked down, the lines in the carpet pirouetting inches above the floor. She watched with double vision and wondered if she had known all along.

She looked up to the portrait of her children. It was real. 'At least it's real,' she murmured.

Harry raised his eyes in confusion.

'The portrait on the wall. At least it's real.'

'I'm sorry,' said Harry. 'I was wrong and I'm sorry. Linda

was…'

Jean jumped from her seat and spat sparks of voice towards her husband, 'I don't want to know anything about you and your fucking girlfriend, you stupid bastard!'

'Maybe we should talk about this another time,' Harry whispered. 'Robert and Hannah aren't long in bed.'

'No, we won't ever talk about it. I have a child in hospital and I don't care about you right now.'

'Shelley will be okay.'

'Shelley will never dance again.' Jean's voice broke and she held her head in her hands.

Harry reached out and placed a hand on Jean's knee.

'Don't,' she said, pulling his hand away, yet wishing that she could fall to the ground and be wrapped in his strong arms.

Jean could see him by Shelley's bed. He had held Jean and shared her pain, and she knew that God had answered her prayers. She had pushed from her mind what she had known when Harry had left two little girls, a six year-old with an eight year-old, both in red, patent shoes, sitting alone in a community centre ten miles from home.

'I hope that last kiss was worth it,' Jean shot, a cruelty igniting her sense of reason.

'What kiss?' asked Harry.

'The one that you lingered over, leaving your two little girls alone in Carrickfergus, the one that stopped you from taking them for a drive to the shore for their ice-cream. I hope to God that it was good, Harry, because I can tell you, it will be the last. It's over.'

Jean was standing and shaking and pointing as a mania took hold of her body. 'Tell her that it's over. Do you understand?'

'Yes,' Harry said, staring into the fire.

'Look at me.'

Two sincere blue eyes shimmered like abiding embers under the black slack of stubble on Harry's face. She looked into his eyes and remembered, and her voice broke in whispers. 'You were having an affair and you were still sleeping with me.'

Harry's lowered his head. 'I've always loved you.'

'Love? You don't know what it is. Love is putting yourself

before someone else. That's all.' Jean swiped her tears away with the back of her hand and looked down at her husband, 'You're not the only one dreaming of what it's like on the outside. I'd love to run off and have an affair, but I'm not Shirley fucking Valentine! And I have a conscience. Where was yours?'

Harry's eyes inched across the hearth.

'I'm going to bed and I never want to talk about this again.'

Jean walked to the door, paused and held onto the architrave. 'Open up a new bank account and apply for a mortgage,' she said calmly. 'We'll stay here and buy this house from the council. I want security. All I want from you is security.'

***

26th October 1993

Dear Shaun

You've probably heard the news by now. The world will surely know how ill we have all become. It has been a long time since I last heard from you, but I wanted to tell you about what happened because I need to share the muddled thoughts in my mind.

On Saturday, Jean and I were finishing lunch at her house when she suddenly got up and looked out of the window. I don't know what made her do it, but the children were gone from the front of the house. We ran to look for them and the world changed in the time it took us to get to the end of the street. The bomb exploded and I fell to the ground outside the Royal Bar on the corner of Snugville Street, less than one hundred metres from the fish shop. Robert and Hannah were standing on the footpath at the other side of the road, but Shelley was missing. I watched Jean running and I heard her screaming and realised that she had found Shelley. She was scrambling in the rubble with her bare hands and I wanted to help her, but I was with Robert and Hannah. A stranger stepped in and lifted Shelley. I won't describe to you what I saw, but I can't remove the images from my head. Hannah went into shock and has barely spoken since it happened. I think she feels responsible for losing her sister. Robert has been quiet too. A six-year old child ran across the road and got flooded in a surge of shrapnel and rubble on a beautiful October day and it doesn't seem fair that we continue to live like this.

When the ambulance doors closed, I tried hard to turn the children away from the site of the bomb, but they kept staring at the gigantic grate and at the people, the lines of heart-broken people, leaning in to help and surplus to the services already there. As I started moving the children towards Snugville Street, I took one last look back and an image that stays with me is the blue sky against a mass of grey below. My legs led me to Snugville Street through a tide of people, all moving like ghosts towards the scene.

I took Hannah to the bathroom and washed and changed her, but her body kept shaking in a house that appeared achingly still. Mrs McAdam from next door looked so pained when she saw little Hannah lying on the sofa. She spooned sweet tea into her mouth and then rocked her like a baby, whispering, 'my little Hannah' in her ear. I have never seen a love so clear.

Robert eventually put on the TV, but the external images were too raw and magnified. We heard how men with axes and crow-bars shattered the masonry, whilst others continued to claw at the rubble with their hands. Shapes wrapped in blankets were finally passed through the crowd. It took hours for the bodies to be recovered from the deepest part of the pile. I thanked God that Shelley had not been too close to the shop, yet a pain struck the back of my throat every time I thought of the blood on her tights.

Finally, Harry's brother, Sammy, called by at ten o'clock and told us that Shelley had lost her right foot. A piece of shrapnel had cut through her. All I could think was that Shelley will never dance again. It seems so unimportant when she survived, but images of her little pointed toes tripping on the pavement move around in my dreams. Even when Roy was hurt, I don't believe I cried so many tears. Maybe I understand Roy a little bit more today.

As I walked down the Shankill Road to meet Roy, the images that I had seen were on a loop in my head. There were army vehicles and blinding lights and I fainted on the Shankill Road by the Leisure centre. A lady from St. John's Ambulance Brigade helped me. I am not one of the fifty-seven people injured, but I am one in a population who will never forget the feeling of hurt that followed a hint of peace. Hope is a scarcity.

The funeral of a bomb victim coincided with that of the bomber who died and I thought about the strange meeting of those two bodies passing by, transported to another place by those who carry the past on their crooked shoulders and the future in their hands. The sleeping can't be enemies. Only those who carry their coffins can remain at war.

I looked out for a missing letter for some time after the last one I sent you because I was sure that you would say goodbye. Robert and James both still talk about you and Toby. We all miss you.

Yours sincerely,

Annie

HEALING PAIN AND SICKNESS

Shaun's hands felt their way across a ridge of wood and down a cold metal frame. A recording device rigged up with microphones and a series of coloured buttons emitted red rays in a semi-lit room, and a blacked out window shone behind the heads of two FBI agents. Shaun waited. Bill, his friend and attorney was seated to his right.

Agent Brady began, his voice measured.

'You're a history professor at CUA.'

'Yes.'

'You're Catholic.'

'Yes.'

'And your family is Irish.'

'Yes.'

'I understand that your Great uncle, Patrick Kelly, was a member of the Irish Republican Army.'

Shaun turned his head to Bill. 'Yes,' he confirmed.

Patrick had remained in Ireland when his brothers had emigrated to America. Shaun wanted to ask what relevance this information had. Half of Ireland was linked to the Old IRA around the time of Irish independence. He considered giving a fuller explanation, but Bill had warned him to stick to 'yes' and 'no.'

'I understand you're heavily involved in the Irish expat

community.'

'No.'

The agent lifted a sheet of paper and read, 'St. Patrick's Day committee, Project Children, The Irish Society.'

'I left them all more than two years ago.'

'Why?'

'I was in a new relationship and had no time.'

'When did you leave the Irish Society?'

'I don't know.' Shaun reflected. When was the last meeting? It was summer and he had received a letter from Annie about the Twelfth of July parade. 'July,' he confirmed. 'The last meeting I attended was in July 1991. Two and a half years ago.'

'Do you know this man?' Brady asked, laying a coloured photo on the table.

Shaun looked at the face of a middle aged man, eager to answer a question that seemed relevant.

'Yes. It's Eamon Fitzgerald.'

'And you're personal friends?'

'No. He was in the Irish Society.'

'And you know his name is Gary Ross.'

'I saw in the newspapers, yes.'

'And that his wife is Francis Ross.'

'No, I don't know his wife.'

In a moment of rumination when Shaun should have been worried about the repercussions of his involvement in the Irish Society, he found himself bemused by the idea that Eamon possessed the romantic proficiency to find himself a wife.

'Is this your signature?'

Shaun leaned in and silently winced. It was a photocopy of a cheque dated 3 June 1990. The value was $20,000.

'Yes,' replied Shaun.

Everything became clear.

The remainder of the interview was a blur as Shaun replied yes and no and tried his best to explain.

He had co-signed a cheque to Francis Ross. He had not questioned who she was and he had believed that the money was destined for a charity for prisoners' wives. Shaun felt all his years of education slip by as he spoke.

He returned home late in the afternoon and poured himself a glass of whisky. An Irishman had brought the politics of city bars in Philadelphia into quiet suburbia, and Shaun was now linked to a woman who had purchased guns that were destined for a country paying the price of a divorce scribed on a map.

Gary and Francis Ross had sent guns across the Atlantic ocean to fight for the restoration of a family with metal and fire.

The FBI had no further questions for Shaun, but the Irish Society's involvement in gun running was now global news. Shaun's mind was fixed on a bar down an alleyway in Belfast where he had once told Harry Adams that he was involved in the Irish Society.

Shaun drank his whisky and thought of Jessica, the young woman who had reminded him how uncomplicated life could be. She had been committed to Shaun, but she had wanted him to wait. She needed to explore Europe and do all the things that women in their twenties do. When she'd returned the engagement ring in the summer, Shaun had found himself alone once again.

He stared at moving images on the TV screen as he balanced the devil in a glass in one hand and a letter from Annie in the other.

***

Harry filled his lungs with cold air and followed the rhythm of his own footsteps. He stopped at the end of Snugville Street, looked back and scanned the long line of houses with people enclosed behind pulled blinds and unflinching curtains. He wanted to walk, to clear his gravelly mind, but he needed to get to Linda fast. He opened the car door and drove.

Harry drove through a city centre that was dead and still, with locked barricades and movement restricted to the flashing lights of army vehicles. He drove and his head didn't clear. Instead, his self-loathing and anger grew with the crunch of every change in gear.

The self-loathing was for the hurt he had caused Jean and it coursed around his body like blood.

The anger was a bedrock of hatred stripped from the pit of his stomach for the suffering of his children.

Jean's words about Shelley dancing had excavated deposits of rage towards an illegal army that had torn his country and his community apart. The Shankill bomb had finally dredged up twenty-four years of anger.

Harry had done nothing to serve his community. He had made a promise to Jean, a promise that didn't matter, and he had stood by and condemned the evil acts of men in his own community who had taken the law into their own hands. He had allowed his brother, Sammy, to carry the family burden of defence alone. The British government had failed to protect his family. The British army had turned into a wall of shields, a peace line of metal helmets hooked with guns they could not fire without condemnation.

Something needed to change.

Linda's house was in darkness, a stream of indigo through a crack in the curtains the only clue to life inside. Harry inserted his key in the door as he rapped gently on the glass. There was no response.

The radiator in the hallway was lukewarm. He had set the timer on the new oil heating system to go off at ten. Letters were piled up in the corner on the floor and his cup was on the windowsill above the kitchen sink, exactly where he had left it on Saturday morning.

'Linda,' he called, whilst pushing the living room door forward.

Linda was on the sofa in jogging bottoms and a loose, white, t-shirt. She looked up and paused the TV.

'What are you doing?' Harry asked, aware that Linda was watching footage of the bomb.

She clicked the off button, sending the room into blackness.

Harry turned the dimmer switch on the wall and Linda threw her arms up to shade her eyes despite the low light. Her eyes were shadowed with rings of black.

'How are you?' he asked, unsure how to begin when he had

come to mark the end.

Linda remained silent.

He looked around the room and sensed that time had stood still since Saturday. Linda's red coat from their walk was over the arm of the settee, and a crumpled leaf edged from the side of her boot on the floor beneath the coat. 'Have you not left the house?' he asked. 'Talk to me.'

'No, I haven't been to work.'

'What's wrong? Are you sick?'

'What do you mean, what's wrong? You know what's wrong.'

Harry knew that everything was wrong, but a presentiment of darkness that he had never felt in Linda's presence compelled him to feel less concerned about the end, and more concerned about the erosion of innocence in Linda's eyes.

'We paid the price,' Linda said, staring ahead at the TV.

Harry sat down on the arm of the chair as Linda raised her head towards him.

'What price?' he asked, afraid of the quickening movement in her eyes.

'I heard about Shelley. I called the bank and my manager told me that Harry's little girl was injured.'

'Harry's little girl,' Harry repeated, wondering how the manager had known his name.

'I told him. I called to resign because...' Linda pointed a wayward arm that fell back onto her lap. 'I called to resign because the bomb was my crime.'

'What?' Harry knelt down and spoke softly. 'You're not making any sense.'

'The bomb. It was me. I thought I could close my eyes from reality and have an affair with a married man, but God sent the bomb to warn me.'

She was speaking faster, her eyes flickering.

'I told him I couldn't work there anymore because I'd had an affair with a client. I asked him not to tell anyone, but I mentioned your name. He said he knew your family and that your brother had been there that morning. He said that Shelley had been injured in the bomb.'

Linda was sobbing.

'And so you see, Harry. The bomb was my crime. I did this to Shelley because I kept her away from her daddy on a Saturday. And now she's hurt and it's my fault because I thought I could ride out the bible in my own terms. Ha! In a minister's house.'

She looked around the room and Harry's mouth opened as he caught the rapid movement of her eyes.

'You didn't think I could pay for this by myself? No, this is daddy's house for when he retires. He'll sell it then. He'll buy something out in the country, but can't you see what we did? We danced with the devil in a beautiful home in East Belfast belonging to a man of the cloth and we didn't think that God would find us here, did we? But he did, and he sent a bomb.'

'Stop this now!'

Linda's eyes were stationary and startled.

'I can't stay here with you. I can't see you anymore, but you need to promise me that you will never ever think those thoughts.'

The room fell silent and Harry's mind stirred in an aggregate of blood and anger. He searched in his memory for the few vestiges of Christianity he owned, and all he could hear was Shelley's Sunday school song, 'Healing pain and sickness, blessing children small.' His voice emerged as he recollected the words, 'Jesus hands were kind hands doing good to all.' After a silent pause, he added, 'It's Shelley's favourite hymn.'

Linda collapsed from the sofa into Harry's arms and the anger that Harry had suppressed for so long cut through every last muscle that held her up.

'Listen to me,' he said, shaking Linda's limp body. 'You told me that God has always been your friend. You never had to look for Him. God is still here for you. We both did something wrong, but we did not cause a bomb. Do you hear me?'

'The devil's work is beautiful,' she said, her eyes wandering again.

Harry shook Linda's shoulders hard. 'Sit up and listen to me,' he said. 'I don't know religion the way that you do, but I can tell you that what we've lived through is not the work of the devil.'

He didn't know where he was going with his words, but his mouth kept talking.

'The devil's work is infinite. It goes on and on and doesn't know where to end. We both know that it's over. We did something that we shouldn't have done and now we can move on. We can make things better. I need to make things better.'

Harry released her body and sat back, still shaken by the mellowing hysteria in her eyes. 'You did not hurt my family. I hurt my wife and I let down my children, but you did not hurt them. You hurt yourself and you hurt God and I'm sorry for my role in that pain. Do you understand?'

Linda looked up, her eyes resting.

'You need to tell me you've understood.'

She nodded.

'I want you to go home to your parents for a while, until you go back to work. And you will go back to work. You'll find your way. Can you promise me you'll go home?'

Linda bowed her head.

'I mean it. I can never come and check on you, so you need to tell me the truth. You're going to go home?'

'Yes, I'll go home.'

Her eyes were clear for the first time. 'I'll go home,' she repeated.

Harry took Linda's hand and led her up the stairs. She lay on the bed and looked at Harry with eyes that were younger than the mistakes they had made. He kissed her on the cheek and took in the curtains and a memory of lace and a memory of Linda.

'Goodbye,' he heard faintly as he closed the door and walked away.

Harry parked his car on Snugville Street and stopped and surveyed the first house. There in the narrow confines of bricks and cement nestled a snug home that was happed up in peace and sleep.

Harry was sick in his stomach and sick in his soul and the

emptiness and the rock hard hunger were carving a schism in his body, precipitating salty tears that were cut from stone.

He walked briskly, paying no attention as flags turned from red, white and blue to green, white and gold, allowing the tears to dust freely from his eyes. He walked and he saw a familiar figure swaying by the side of a Republican bar. He approached casually, retaining his pace, walking with purpose. The figure was like a shadow of an old friend.

Harry checked again. The colours on the gable wall were not the colours of Harry's friend. He looked at Irish writing and back to the outline of the short, stocky figure, and as his fists solidified, he checked the angle of two security cameras, one pointing towards Harry and one pointing from the front door in the other direction. He bowed his head.

It's the saddest tale I ever heard, echoed an American voice.

Harry grasped the man's collar as a boulder of fist landed on the unguarded face. There was barely a cheep from the body as it grazed the ground, but a skull cracked off the tarmac and Harry knew that he was dead. He bent down and checked for a response. Not a breath. Not a pulse.

Harry walked back home along a different road, following the bright lights and sound of intermittent traffic. He raised his head and freed his hands from his pockets when he was at a distance from the bar.

'Your name, Sir.'

It was the voice of a young, Cockney squaddie. He was standing by an army patrol.

'Harry Adams,' Harry replied, exhaling a long expression of relief, his anger smelted through one act that he knew would dictate his time on earth. He needed to be free and he knew that he could not walk another inch carrying the weight of this burden. He provided the driving licence requested, and watched as a soldier unknowingly wrote down a witness statement for a crime.

***

October 30, 1993

Dear Annie

I hoped that I would hear from you one day, but I never dreamed I would receive a letter etched in so much pain. I feel like I walked through the streets with you.

When I visited Snugville Street, I missed my turn and walked as far as the fish store. I recognised the spire of the red-bricked building on the corner when I saw it on TV. I also passed the Shankill Leisure Centre, but there was no army patrol. It was a peaceful night, with an orange sky and the first hints of spring. I was confused that there could ever be war in such a beautiful place.

My memory of Shelley is of a little girl clinging to her mother's skirt. When I met the girls, Jean had them dressed up for my visit like princesses. I have a sister and two brothers and my mom used to dress my sister up like that. We have a similar portrait to the one in Jean's living room and it was always my mother's greatest pride. I often look at it and think of family, the family I thought I might have one day. I wish more than anything that Harry can absorb the hurt of his family.

You have asked about a missing letter and I don't know how to explain. I hope that this letter is safe when I say that a resentment within me was building and I snapped. The letters had become a distraction. Your words about love left me unable to live my life in a physical way. It had become a fantasy designed on a night that passed by like a whisper and I needed to find my feet. Events collided to bring me to a place of realisation.

I met Jessica a couple of years ago and we were happy for a while. We got engaged and we tried to build a future together. Things changed and the engagement was called off this summer.

I know you enjoy a little bit of history, so I will tell you a story that might make you smile. One of the students in my Scots-Irish course stumbled across a curious fact about King Billy. I already knew this, but laughed when he mentioned it because it seemed more human when he added, 'Man, that must have been a tense walk up the aisle.'

Did you know that King Jimmy was King Billy's father-in-law (and uncle)? Mary cried when she found out that she had to marry her cousin, William, but apparently they had a good life together despite William's relations with Elizabeth Villiers, and despite the fact that William knocked his father-in-law off a fine Roxboro horse at the Battle of the Boyne. Maybe it was Mary who was the hero, putting her family ties to the side and breaking a commandment of her faith in order to respect her husband over her father.

Annie, I have thought about what you mean to me, and I have finally comforted myself knowing that you are a friend.

Yours Sincerely,

Shaun

***

Roy could taste his youth in the oak, ash, beech and sycamore of Glenarm forest on the low lying slopes of the glen. He could see his past rippling among the mallards and the kingfishers and he could hear it in the water effusing and gushing over rocks of the high river, where he had once fished quietly for trout with his father. Glenarm represented the past and Roy resented its distance from the world where he belonged, as much as he felt grounded to its uneven, slippery terrain.

'Massacre at Greysteel,' was the headline that had come between Roy and his wife that morning as they walked through the old castle gates at Altmore Street.

Eight civilians had been gunned down by the UDA in revenge for the Shankill bomb and Annie had assumed that it was the reason Roy wanted to leave Ireland.

They had climbed the first mile of the forest walk in silence, each of them concentrating to avoid slipping on the damp leaves. At the crest of the path, they stopped to survey a collage of yellow-green, rusty-green and black-green square fields. The forest trail hooked back towards the town parallel to the first part of the walk, where they had been sheltered by trees and their own thoughts.

Annie spoke first. 'What message does that send out to terrorists if we run away to the Netherlands? Those killers will rule this country if decent people don't stay and fight for peace.'

'Your wording is interesting.'

'What?'

'You said, "fight for peace."'

'I meant "work for peace."'

'Peace has its own battle.'

'Maybe.'

'I care about peace as much as you do, Annie, but it's not for me to sort out this country. I've my work cut out with myself.'

Roy was unsteady on the rocky terrain of the sharp slope. 'Every man needs to start with himself, and this is not what I had in mind as a young fella.'

'The more that decent people flee, the more power those men have.'

Annie hadn't listened to a word that Roy had said. He knew that she had been planning the speech all the way around the forest. He stopped and placed his hands on Annie's shoulders to awaken her sense of hearing. 'What happened last night has nothing to do with why I think we should move. I want this for me, you, Andrew and James, and I need to be selfish when I say, I want this for me.'

'For you.'

'Yes. I've spent fourteen years being and I want to start living. I need a career.'

'You've got a career, a new career.'

'I can do something that I love in the Netherlands. Dirk is my only remaining relative and he is dying. I want to do this for Dirk, I want to do this for me and I want to do this for my father. If I move now, Dirk will be able to hand things over to me.'

'But you can't do that job anymore. You can't climb bridges, not every day anyway.'

'I don't need to climb bridges. I need to drive a car, man a phone and a computer and manage fifteen men. Dirk hasn't been up a bridge in more than two years. And more than anything, I need to look after Dirk.'

'That, I understand,' conceded Annie.

'Will you come to Holland? You know Dirk's will. There's the house, the business and the apartment in Leiden. The boys could go to university there and they'd have their own place. For once, we'd have no money worries.'

'We have no money worries now that we're both working.'

Roy looked out to the folding hills. 'We wouldn't have to live in an estate.'

'It's okay on the estate. I like it there.'

'You're lying,' smiled Roy. 'Your dream is to live back here.'

'I wouldn't say no to Glenarm, but it's too far away from work.'

'Annie, please do this for me.'

'I'm sorry, but I belong here. I can't move. I tried before and I can't do it.'

There it was, the pull to the land that Annie had rehearsed for so long. Roy led his wife by the arm to a summer seat where he had once proposed. They looked down on yellow bracken as a long parade of sheep passed by on the other side of the river and one thousand decibels of bleating drowned out the conversation they had had.

'I know what you're doing,' said Annie above the sound.

'What?' Roy smiled innocently.

'You think you can bring me to this spot and change my mind.'

'You could forgive a man for trying,' he said, his eyes begging Annie to buy his dream. He took his wife's hand, 'Annie, will you marry me?'

'Marry you again?'

'Yes, marry me again.'

'I dinnae think we're much o a match. We fight too much.'

'We aye fought before we walked up the aisle,' smiled Roy, enlivened by the language of his youth.

'Ay, we did,' said Annie. 'We didnae go into marriage blind, that's for sure.' She looked out to the fields in silent thought. 'Funny how you fall straight into it when you come home. Good old Ulster-Scots. It's like a warm bowl of stew.'

'It's an auld fella in a bar wi' a pint.'

'Or a farmer walking through the glen. It'll die out soon enough.'

'It will, ay. James and Andrew havenae a drap o it on their tongue.'

'No a bit,' smiled Annie.

'Did I ever tell you that your mum warned me before I married you that you'd start a row in an empty house?'

'She did not indeed. That's my sister, Katherine. I've always been mammy's favourite. Maybe I do fight with you too much, though.'

'I don't mind,' said Roy, his eyes focused on the continual stream of sheep.

'You don't mind?' Annie retorted with surprise.

'Folk trip over themselves to be nice to me because they know. You and James are the only two people who keep me on the five toes I have.'

'I'm not as bad as James,' Annie choked.

'You're cut from the same cloot, the pair of you. Try it for a couple of years. If it doesn't work, we'll come home.'

Annie looked out to fields and back to Roy. Roy knew that the river of sound below was blotting out the reality of the reaction Annie would have had to the same conversation in Whiteabbey.

'Two years, and we keep the place in Whiteabbey,' she agreed finally.

'It's a deal.' Roy smiled and kissed his wife on the lips. 'I'll make it work. I promise.'

'We need to tell mammy and daddy.'

'I taul them already.'

'You did not! You didn't know the answer. I've been manipulated. You've taken the han oot o me!'

'Ay, I know! Remember what we did after we got engaged last time?'

'Not a chance! Besides, we have an audience.'

Roy looked over at a lonely sheep standing by the edge of the river and smiled. 'A wee lost sheep.'

'A lost sheep. That's you!' elbowed Annie.

'In that case, you're the sheepdog leading that parade over

there. It's most likely a Protestant Parade being led through a Catholic area.'

'Are you suggesting I like to cause trouble? Those sheep have the right to retain their tradition of walking through the glen.'

'Come on,' laughed Roy. 'We can't solve peace in Northern Ireland, but we can report a lost sheep.'

***

'We could make it to Christmas,' Harry had said, and all of Jean's hope had been attached to that possibility until a blue light blared through the window ten days before Christmas.

Jean looked from Hannah to Robert. She had already explained to them that their daddy might have to go away, but she had yet to find the courage to speak to Shelley, the child whose fire-tinted cheeks were pale blue from the light outside.

'I punched a man,' were the words that had dredged a hole in what Jean had thought was rock bottom. She had awoken at six on the day that he had told her, and she recalled that the kitchen lights had been bright against a dark window as Downtown Radio nudged her into morning. Jean had watched the bacon bubbling under the grill, the first meal she had cooked in the five days since the bomb, and she had had a feeling that rock-bottom had passed, that life was somehow going to be easier. Harry had yet to tell Jean what he had done.

Later that afternoon, Mrs McAdam had joined Jean in the hospital where Shelley had been awake and responsive despite the heavy medication.

'You have a guardian angel taking care of you,' Mrs McAdam had said, and Jean had looked at her neighbour and allowed the numbness that she had felt for five days to spill over into pain.

She had cried thinking of a little girl that the world had never met, Mrs McAdam's own little stillborn angel in heaven.

Then followed the confession that had made the doctors and nurses laugh, 'Mammy, I don't like dancing anyway. I think I'll take up swimming instead.'

Jean had told Mrs McAdam about Harry's affair on the way back from the hospital. Mrs McAdam had said nothing at first. It wasn't until she had entered Jean's house and rolled up her sleeves that she spoke, 'The women of this town will never be beaten by bombs or betrayal.' She had then cleaned and dusted Jean's home, and as Jean had followed her neighbour around the house, she had recognised that reassembling her home was the first step in the restoration of her mind.

Jean returned to the reality surrounding her as the swirling light bellowed through the window, and she kicked herself for ever believing that rock bottom existed. Life had never worked that way for Jean. She had lost a mother, a grandmother, a father and a brother, and each time the same pattern emerged. There was the shock, and then the feeling of relief as anger and fear shattered the numbness like sustenance after a famine. The anger and fear would never entirely depart, a measure of residual emotion remaining until the next event.

Six weeks after lifting her little girl from the rubble, the sound of a bomb was still close enough that it rang continually in Jean's ears, and with it came the noise of bleeps from a hospital machine against the timbre of a voice telling a husband that he was a stupid man. There were so many noises, yet none of them had reverberated as far as the words, 'I punched a man,' and Jean had immediately understood that the tremor of those words would extend far beyond the pain in Shelley's leg.

The numbness had set in and the shock had lasted until the blue light transmitted emotions of anger and fear.

'It's only a matter of time,' Harry had said, but there was no way of predicting when the police would come.

Two weeks after the assault, Sammy had been arrested, and a further two weeks had passed by before an alibi had secured his release. Each night Harry and Jean had worked through their paperwork, assembling a future from the few pounds that Harry would leave behind. He'd spent time with Hannah and Robert, holding them while they watched TV, telling them stories of how things used to be, and he had visited the hospital every night after work. Money from the sale of the car and a small pot of savings from the mortgage deposit had been withdrawn from the bank and hidden to help Jean. Harry had checked rental prices on shops so that Jean could set up her own sewing business with the money. He had done everything he could do, living each day as though it were the last day of freedom, determined that his wife would not have to secure a livelihood from the Benefits Office across the road.

The door rattled and Jean was motionless with fear, an unfettered fear that was more amplified than the fear in the heart of a fifteen year-old girl who had lost a mother. Jean looked around at the three children and she knew she couldn't do it. She couldn't raise three children alone without Harry. She tried to hold back the tears but they tumbled from her eyes.

Harry kissed each of his children as the doorbell clanged. 'Be brave and take care of your mammy,' he said audibly to Robert. 'Look after your sister,' he whispered to Hannah. He then knelt down to Shelley, who was lying across the sofa, 'I have a special job for you, Shelley. You need to take care of Mrs McAdam. She'll need someone to help her put her curlers in her hair.'

Jean folded into Harry's arms like a child. 'I'll make amends,' he promised. He closed the door of the living room and spoke to the police alone.

Then the blue light was silenced and the room returned to the colour of fire. Robert lifted the poker and tipped a piece of burning coal, Hannah sat by the window, her eyes chasing each sound and Shelley's long limbs kicked under the blanket laid across them. Jean placed her hand on Shelley's legs. 'Stay there Shelley.'

But Shelley was distraught and a whimper rose and heightened into an elongated wail of voice and tears, 'Where are they taking my daddy?'

Jean placed her hand tenderly on Shelley's cheek, but Shelley tore the hand away and forced Jean to the floor. She leapt from the sofa and climbed onto the chair at the window and banged on the glass.

Harry was gone.

Jean tried to lift Shelley, but her fingers were clawing at the fabric of the chair and she was too heavy for Jean's arms. Jean stood back and cried again as Hannah placed her hand on Shelley's back.

Hannah led Shelley back to the sofa and Jean swallowed hard when she realised that her eight year-old daughter was soaking up everyone's pain. 'You stay here and I'll get Mrs McAdam,' she said to Shelley. 'Mammy, you sit down and we'll make some tea. God is taking care of daddy.'

WINTER SOLSTICE

Annie placed the newspaper on the kitchen table and revealed the page that had stopped her morning turning. Adjacent to an image of Northern Lights and an article about the winter solstice was a small photograph of Harry Adams, and an identical sized headshot of Shaun Sharpe, son of Deirdre and Arthur Sharpe, the victim of Harry's crime.

Annie pointed and looked at Jean, 'Why didn't you call me?

'You don't need to be near any of this,' said Jean, turning away and colouring in the last square of dry floor with her mop.

Annie's eyes slid across the gleaming black and white vinyl. 'What do you mean?' she asked, following the orbit of Jean's body around her.

'Harry is in prison for murder, Annie. You don't need this in your life.'

Annie looked back to the newspaper and tried to assemble her thoughts about Harry. She had been reminded of her own father when she had first seen Harry Adams with his daughters. Bobby O'Neill was a man who was rarely seen outside his workplace, his home or the pub, so when he had arrived to collect her from her dancing class at the age of seven, Annie had basked in the dazzling rays of his presence. It was a sad day because Annie's Granny O'Neill had died, but she would never forget the feeling of pride when holding his hand on the way home. Shelley and Hannah had borne that same look the first day that Harry had come to the dancing hall in Carrickfergus.

Annie, undaunted by Jean's glacial tone, pulled out a chair. 'Stop cleaning and come here and sit down.'

Jean did as she was told, but her eyes were set in the distance. She ripped a tattered tissue and spoke. 'It's nearly Christmas and I don't have a thing organised. It's a mess. Look at the state of the place.'

Annie surveyed the polished order of Jean's home and assessed her friend with a questioning tilt of the head.

'I forgot to put the bins out and the rubbish is piled up in the backyard, we've run out of coal, I forgot to make the sheep costume for Hannah's Christmas nativity play and Robert went out to school in yesterday's socks. If I let the house fall apart too, then it'll be the end. I need to keep it together.'

'What about the Christmas presents for the kids?'

'Harry laid everything out in the attic, so at least that's done.' Jean looked up, 'What am I going to do next year? I'm useless with things like that.'

'Don't worry about next year. Harry might be home by then.' Annie had spoken too quickly and she kicked herself for the being so insensitive.

'He's not coming home. He killed a man, and I don't think you belong here anymore.'

There was a short delay in Annie's mind before her body jolted with the pain of Jean's rejection. She looked at her friend and tried to interpret her cool, quiescent eyes.

'You've been kind to me but you're different and it's dangerous now.'

'What do you mean, I'm different?'

'You're a bit…' Jean repressed something resembling the onset of a smile and looked up. 'You shouldn't be here. It's not safe.'

'Look, I will admit that I was shocked when I read about

Harry, but that's got nothing to do with you or your children.' She handed Jean a packet of tissues. 'Get yourself a fresh hanky and I'll put the kettle on.'

Annie was distracted by the aurora of blue light at Jean's kitchen window as she poured water into the kettle. She shaded her eyes but, in an instant, the light had swept behind a dusky, blackened cloud on the afternoon sky. She turned away from the sink and looked at Jean and asked, 'When is the trial?'

'I don't know. It could be two years. There's a long queue of murderers in this god-forsaken country and Harry has admitted to the police that he murdered a man. Why couldn't he be like everyone else and say that he didn't mean to kill him? He could have pleaded manslaughter.'

'Can he change his plea?'

Jean's voice broke into tears. 'He said he knew what he was doing. He wanted to kill. He told me that only a man would understand why he wanted to kill.'

Silence pursued the four corners of the kitchen as Annie contemplated Jean's words. It wasn't only a man who could think like that. After Roy had been caught in a bomb, Annie had experienced a fierce anger that had eventually pivoted into a serene desire for peace.

The kettle clicked. Annie searched in the pristinely organised cupboards for cups and tea-bags, assuming Jean's role with a sense of purpose before settling in the chair opposite her with two cups of tea.

Jean was still staring ahead, her large, blue eyes watery from the brief storm of tears. 'Annie, what am I going to do?' Her voice was as tender as the voice of a child. 'I don't know if I'm coming or going. I lock up at night and I check the door four times because I'm so scared that I haven't locked it properly. And that chair.' Jean turned around and pointed through the living room wall. 'That chair by the window in the living room. That's where Hannah sits, but I don't like her sitting by the window.' A frenzied smile edged from Jean's lips. 'You know, Mrs McAdam and Hannah both look out the window and knock the wall when something's happening outside, but I can't let Hannah look out the window anymore.'

Jean was serious and Annie felt nervous as she witnessed the oscillating emotions on her friend's face, a face that was charged with particles of colour. Life was streaming from Jean's eyes and colliding with the black sheet of winter outside, and Jean was beautiful and alive with anguish.

'Drink some tea,' Annie said softly.

'No, I can't drink tea. I can't sleep and the tea is making it worse. I haven't slept since he left. What am I going to do? He'll be in for at least ten years. I can't survive ten years alone.'

'You can only take one day at a time.'

Silence fell between them as Annie chased a distant thought with her eyes. She was talking and trying to figure out if it was an appropriate question at the same time. 'Was he in the paramilitaries?'

'No, Annie, love. Harry wasn't running around with guns. He was running around with another woman. He had an affair for almost four years.'

Annie concentrated on her friend's eyes that were now crystal clear, as though the sadness had been washed clean. Annie didn't know Harry, but she could see clearly what it was about him that made the news a blow and not a surprise. Harry didn't have charm, but he had the kind of charisma that could lead a woman into a deep conversation and a long walk. Annie was in no position to judge him for his affair. She checked Jean's eyes and they were as still as the sun at the close of the winter solstice. Jean was dealing with the murder and the prison sentence, but her mind had eclipsed the affair.

'I can't think about that,' said Jean, confirming Annie's thoughts.

'You have enough to think about.' Annie looked around and realised why it seemed so dark. There were no fairy lights in Jean's home to compensate for the sun setting in a blue horizon.

'I took the Christmas tree down,' Jean said. 'It didn't seem right to have lights twinkling in the window when a mother had lost her son.'

Annie tried to silence her curiosity, but she wondered. 'Did you know this guy, Shauny?'

'No, but Harry knew his cousin, Johnny. He was older but grew up on the same street as Harry. Two Catholic sisters married two Protestant brothers and one sister turned Protestant, while the other remained Catholic. The families haven't spoken for more than twenty years.'

The atmosphere was solemn before Jean's face became alert with something new. 'I don't even have a turkey. I forgot to order the fucking turkey.' Jean held her tissue up to her face.

'You don't need one,' Annie stated resolutely. 'You, Mrs McAdam and the children are coming to our house on Christmas day. Roy told me to ask you. I'll come and pick you all up.'

'No, I couldn't. It would be too much for you. I'll sort something out.'

'You're coming to my house because I have ordered the biggest fucking turkey you've ever seen.'

Jean's jaw fell and the silence sluiced the sadness. 'Good lord in the heavens above!' Jean exclaimed. 'Did little Miss prissy Annie just say a naughty word?'

'Is that why you think I don't belong here? You think I'm prissy!'

'Yes, you are, but if you're making me Christmas dinner, then I'll put up with it.'

Annie tipped her head to one side as Jean tipped hers to the other. Jean dipped a bourbon cream into her tea and smiled, and Annie wondered why God had reversed the fortunes of the earthy woman on a bleak-mid winter's day.

In the bleak midwinter. Annie could hear the sound of a hymn from her childhood and she tried to recall the words as she looked back at Jean, a friend whose smile was summer and whose eyes were winter. The words of the song echoed and Annie promised herself that she would be there for Jean when snow was on snow and the water had turned to stone.

'The sun doesn't stand still on the winter solstice,' Annie said.

'What?' Jean's eyes were blizzards of confusion.

Annie pointed to the article beside the report of Harry's crime. 'I was reading about it this morning. The sun keeps moving slowly. Things will be okay. You'll have times of darkness and light and so will Harry, but everyone will keep moving.'

Jean's chin gathered into her neck and Annie smiled. She knew that Jean would never tell her she didn't belong there again.

***

Thermal vests, that's what Harry needed. The heating pipes of the Crumlin Road Gaol could not compensate for the draught that purged the cells of any form of comfort. The Victorian jail, located only a mile from his home was an austere distance from the warmth of his living room. The cold swaggered in windy strokes in tune with the clattering of gates, and it whistled from the wrought iron bars and clanged off the tiled floors. Harry warmed himself by stretching, and two dilemmas circulated in his mind as he moved around the cramped cell.

His prisoner status and his plea.

That morning at the carol service, he had been approached by both the chaplain and a Loyalist.

'Put your faith in God and you will never be alone,' was the first offer.

'You are entitled to be a political prisoner. You're not alone,' was the second.

Harry had always imagined that loneliness would be the one thing that might kill him in prison, but loneliness was not a choice. He was offered the hand of two families.

There was the family of God and God would be there for him at the end of his two year remand sentence in the Crumlin Road Goal, granting him peace of mind within a cell in the comparative comfort of a new prison at Maghaberry, where he would serve the remainder of his sentence.

There was also the family of terrorism and de facto political prisoner status that would reward him the freedom of the dismal compounds at the Maze prison, where he could live as a Loyalist soldier with a purpose and a routine.

Both prisons were located half an hour's drive from

Snugville Street.

The minister's talk of God was almost unnecessary because Harry had been talking to God all of his life. God was the label assigned by people of faith to the conscience with which Harry had conversed since he was a child. He had never needed preachings about Jesus to know that there was somewhere he could turn in times of darkness, and he knew that he needed to fix himself before seeking for the Lord. If he ever decided to find salvation, he would do so as a man praying for peace rather than a fool begging for pity.

He also knew enough men from the Shankill area to find a family at the Maze, but his conscience would never settle for the bloodbath of paramilitary belonging. Killing Shauny Sharpe was his own personal burden. If he joined an illegal army, he would carry the crimes of his comrades and he would suffer the tears of their victims.

The second dilemma was his plea. Everyone, from his solicitor to his brother, had advised him that he should plead manslaughter to reduce his sentence by a third, but Harry had lived a lie with Linda for four years, and the bars of deceit and denial had proved effortless compared to the freedom of the truth. Once Harry had decided to end the lies, he couldn't go back. He couldn't stand up in court and say that he didn't mean to murder Shauny Sharpe because he had meant it with all his being. Harry might never be free from the crime he had committed, but if he told the truth, he could at least absolve his crime from the consciences of his children.

Jean had begged him to plead manslaughter and Jean had begged him to take the hand of friendship offered. She had said that the IRA would catch up with him in a prison that was not segregated into Loyalist and Republican wings. She had said that the UDA would protect his life if he joined their ranks. She had said all the things that Sammy had told her to say.

Harry would plead guilty to murder and he would not accept the UDA offer. He needed to act alone and his greatest regret was that his wife would carry the burden of his conscience.

Jean's destiny was to travel on a prison bus, not knowing that she had made a man out of a fool.

***

Jean felt tired after dinner. The TV was blasting an uneven sound that amplified and abated in her ears as Shelley and Hannah watched The Wizard of Oz. Robert was upstairs playing on the computer with Andrew and James, and Harry was nowhere to be seen. Everything was the same except that Jean wasn't in her own home on Christmas day.

The noise continued to throb. An itch crept up her back and over her scalp. It travelled across her arms. She pulled up her woollen sleeve and patted her skin. The open fire was resplendent with orange flames, yet a cold current crawled across her body. Jean began to shiver. She replaced her sleeve and held the cuff tightly.

'When we move to Holland,' Roy began.

Jean saw the movement of the kick under the table between Annie and Roy, and the conversation ended exactly where it had begun.

'Have you not told anyone?' asked Roy.

'No.' Annie shot her husband a scornful glare and then addressed Jean. 'We only decided a few weeks ago. I had planned telling you in my own time.'

Jean's eyes closed and opened. She couldn't follow what they were saying because their voices were dull. She needed to go home.

'I'm sorry,' said Annie, her voice small.

Annie was Jean's brightest star and she was shimmering in lines and swirls from the fairy lights into a long sentence across the room, stretching and zigzagging, green and blue letters all joined together.

First son of eleven. First son.

Mrs McAdam was there in her red dress looking at Jean and the red was weaving in and out of the words as they fluttered across the wall. She needed her home and she needed sugar. She placed her spoon in the bowl and began to eat the last few drops of trifle. She swallowed hard and reached for some wine, but her hand was trembling.

'Jean, are you okay?'

It was Roy. Roy had been in a bomb. Like weightless time, he had said. Jean looked at Shelley, who was smiling at the TV and back to Roy. Weightless. There was no time anymore.

Annie's hand was on Jean's and it was warm. Why was the glass so light? It was crystal and it was cutting through the skin of Jean's palms. Blood was dribbling along her life-line. Was it blood, or was it the red from the long sentence formed in her eyes?

Roy reached for Jean's hand, Annie patted a napkin on the red sentence and as Mrs McAdam's lips moved, Jean exhaled one last thought. 'I can't do this anymore. I can't do this.'

Tears poured down her face blotting out the join of the lights. Everything was dark and Jean's body continued to tremor. Roy was peeling back red from the white napkin and there was a red cross on a white tin and the smell of the hospital ward and a long, shrill bell. Follow the yellow brick road. Follow follow follow.

Please Jean, can you hear me? Wrap it tight. Raise her hand. Get her some sugar. Is mammy okay? Go and sit down Shelley. Sit down. Your mammy's cut her hand. Come on. Upstairs. We'll see what the boys are doing.

What happens after the bomb?

Whispers drifting in. Whispers drifting back. What time was it? A fireplace with a wall of tiles like a chalet.

'What did you have to tell her for?'

The whispers rising, climbing up the legs of the spider plant.

'Why didn't you tell her yourself?'

'She's lost everything and you had to tell her on Christmas day!'

'This is one more excuse for you. One more reason. You never intended coming anyway.'

'I didn't know that Jean was in such a bad way.'

'And now you'll stay.'

'Oh for God's sake. I've had enough. Go by yourself. I

couldn't give a damn right now about Holland.'

Jean curled her legs up towards her stomach and placed her head on her hands. The noise was quieter, and Jean was cold.

'Here love. Put this wee blanket around you.'

Number four. Man at the door. Harry's jacket had slipped to the floor. Keep talking, Jean. Keep trying to make your voice travel and they'll hear what you have to say. Follow, follow, follow, follow. The stupid song.

'Has it happened before?' Harry's voice. Was it Harry's voice? Harry was in prison. It was Roy.

'Yes,' whispered Mrs McAdam, 'It has happened before.'

Mrs McAdam, a mother whose baby had died. Mrs McAdam, a mother. Yes, that was it. More than a mother.

'Should we call a doctor?'

Jean had never had a friend like Annie before.

'Could you take us home when she wakes up? I'll give her a wee cure when we get home.'

'Leave the children here.'

Annie, why did you make a friend like Jean?

'The children need to be with their mammy. We'll take her home.'

'I'm sorry, Mrs McAdam.'

'It wasn't your fault, Annie, love. It wasn't your fault.'

Annie's hand was on Jean's arm. 'I'm sorry, Jean.'

Annie was the brightest star.

***

Shaun unfolded the black and white newspaper and looked at an image of Harry that he barely recognised. The smiling, larger-than-life man was quietened by a still mouth and a darkness in his eyes, and beside him, another black and white photograph of man with a square face and a square jaw. Shaun's eyes fell on the name below the photograph and his fingers pressed the cutting.

Shauny Sharpe.

Shaun had never forgotten the tale of Johnny and Shauny, It was a Belfast Tale and it was no longer the saddest tale he had ever heard.

He pictured a pint of Guinness and a glass of whisky. The devil's work had only just begun.

1st January, 1994

Dear Shaun

Thank you for your letter. Unfortunately Harry Adams couldn't absorb the hurt of his family. He was arrested for one of the attacks after the Shankill bomb and he is on remand in Crumlin Road jail. He punched a known Republican terrorist and the man died instantly from the fall. I have enclosed a newspaper clip.

Jean finally collapsed with exhaustion on Christmas day. So many things have assailed her all at once, from the bomb to Shelley's injury to Harry's arrest. She also learned that Harry had been having an affair for four years. Robert and Hannah have been managing the house well alongside their neighbour, but Shelley is distraught about losing her daddy. I've seen people suffer all kinds of hardship, including death, but I don't think anything compares to this. Harry's wife and children are mourning someone who is still alive.

Jean is regaining strength every day. She has lost so much, but she loves with every muscle and tendon holding her together and she is standing by Harry. She is a better person than me.

As for William and Mary, your stories continue to intrigue me. Mary made a great sacrifice putting her husband before her father and her birth family, but I wonder sometimes if life is meant to be lived so piously. When we are all busy trying to do the right thing, trying not to hurt others, or in the case of religion, trying to avoid sin, where do we end up? Mary married William because she had to. Obligation was her lot in life and I suppose she had to mould her faith into her obligations. We all have to ignore a commandment from time to time. It's what makes us human.

I wish you peace and happiness for 1994.

Yours sincerely,

Annie

I HAD AN OCEAN
1994

The Irish February days were short with dusk settling in the late afternoon, but it was more than a fading light that had changed the outlook of Jean's home. There was something new, and Shaun recognised it despite the spritely greeting at the door. Jean looked well, a woman whose strength was reflected in her ability to ride out war, damp and rain without a single strand of hair falling out of place, but her eyes were beset with sadness, that same bleak look that Shaun had once seen through the rearview mirror of his car.

He walked into the living room and found everything as it had been before, yet a draught of mourning drifted from the short hallway to the living room, its cool current transforming Jean's home without changing a single thing.

'A true friend will visit even when the drapes are pulled,' Shaun's mother had often said. The drapes weren't pulled because no one had died, but a breeze floated through the space like a resounding farewell.

Shaun adjusted to the morbid climate around him until he heard an elongated 'hello' whistle through the narrow walls like an old kettle. A small lady with curled white hair stood before Shaun in a red dress.

'It's awfully nice to meet you,' she said in an accent that

Shaun didn't recognise as a Belfast one.

'Shaun, this is Mrs McAdam,' said Jean.

'Good to meet you,' smiled Shaun.

'I didn't have the pleasure of your company last time you were here,' her voice tinkled.

'I think I saw you by the window,' said Shaun. 'I never miss a pretty lady.'

Mrs McAdam blushed and reverted to a Belfast brogue. 'See what happens when they call your number!' she winked towards Jean. 'Number forty-eight. United States.'

'You need to update your flag, Mrs McAdam,' Jean stated. 'There are fifty stars.'

'Well, there were forty-eight the night that a GI tried to steal my heart.'

'You should have let him have it,' said Jean. 'The thief could have kept you warm instead of those thermal bloomers you hang on the line. You'll have to excuse us,' Jean added as she directed Shaun to the kitchen table with a drying cloth. 'I forgot we were in polite company.'

'You shouldn't be discussing my bloomers in public,' scolded Mrs McAdam.

'Discuss them! Satellite TV reported that the Loyalists of the Shankill had surrendered after seeing your bloomers from space.'

The two women conspired like naughty school children in laughter.

'Now I'm all red,' said Mrs McAdam, whose cheeks were pearly white. 'But I'll take a wee cuppa,' she added.

'I thought you might,' laughed Jean as she walked to the kettle.

Shaun relaxed and the draughty atmosphere lifted amidst the syrupy smiles and powdery perfume of Mrs McAdam. 'I'd love to hear more about the GI,' he ventured.

'Oh now, son. I don't like to talk about myself,' Mrs McAdam smiled coyly.

Jean turned from the sink and placed a hand on her hip as her jaw gaped open.

'Well, since you asked,' Mrs McAdam said leaning towards

Shaun. 'I lost my husband in the Blitz in forty-one and to tell you the God's honest truth, I'd no interest in finding another man. But the American GIs came in their droves with their shiny teeth, and they were everywhere.'

'What was it my father used to say?' interrupted Jean. 'They were overpaid, overfed, and worst of all, over here!'

'That's what all the men thought,' nodded Mrs McAdam. She then addressed Shaun, 'At that time, you could have counted the number of teeth on a man from the Shankill with one hand.'

'How many GIs were here?' Shaun asked, thrilled to find another aspect of Irish history that he had overlooked in his studies.

'There were three hundred thousand of them in this wee country,' said Mrs McAdam with eyes alight. 'Anyway, this one GI gave me his pocket guide to Northern Ireland.'

'I'd love to see that,' said Shaun, already forming a thesis for one of his PHD students in his head.

Mrs McAdam pulled a small booklet from her pocket. 'I thought you might. You can take it away and read it.'

Shaun flicked through the booklet with wide eyes. 'What an amazing piece of history,' he observed. It says here, "In other matters of morality and personal conduct, the Irish may seem puritanical to men used to America's free and easy ways," Well, I have to agree with Jean's father. They do sound like a threat to the men of Belfast.'

'Look here,' said Mrs McAdam. 'It says that Ulster is a saucer circled by rolling hills. My fella told me he'd be my cup if I'd be his saucer.'

Jean choked and set her cup back on the table.

'What?' scowled Mrs McAdam in Jean's direction.

'Nothing, Mrs McAdam. He sounds like a real poet, your GI! Are you sure you didn't imagine him?'

'Don't you be so cheeky little Miss Jean. I was a catch in my day!'

Shaun laughed inwardly and read, 'Argument for its own sake is a Scotch-Irish speciality, and arguing politics might almost be called a national sport.'

Jean and Mrs McAdam were silent.

Shaun's eyes scanned the pages until a word caught his eye. He delivered the passage with a smile. 'While there are temperance advocates and a few prohibitionists in Ireland, you won't see much of them.'

Mrs McAdam laughed, 'The only thing that's changed since the war is that the prohibitionists have all died.'

'You know,' said Shaun, 'when I last visited Ireland, Harry told me he was a non-practising man of temperance.'

Jean looked into the distance. 'Yes,' she said. 'Now he gets to be a non-practising husband and father.'

Shaun immediately regretted the observation and flicked through the book to find something else.

'Irish girls are friendly,' he began, and paused and looked up as he remembered. He continued, 'They will stop on the country road and pass the time of day. Don't think, on that account, that they are falling for you in a big way.'

'Well, they're not all the same,' said Mrs McAdam. 'I could fall for you in a big way if you stopped to talk to me.'

Mrs McAdam was blessed with words. The atmosphere was restored and laughter steamed up the eyes of the old lady in the red dress.

'You're a disgrace,' said Jean, as she flicked her tea towel at her neighbour.

'Whereabouts are you staying?' asked Mrs McAdam, ignoring the impact of linen.

'I booked the same hotel as last time. Carrickfergus.'

'GI George took me to Carrickfergus.'

'George!' exclaimed Jean.

'Well that's why I couldn't court him,' Mrs McAdam said to Jean before turning to Shaun. 'He'd the same name as my husband, you see. Anyway, we went on a trip that day.'

'Where to?' asked Jean.

'The Gobbins cliff walk in Islandmagee. It was closed at the time, but we snuck through the gate. It was a glorious day with the sun splitting the stanes. A walk along a cliff with the waves lapping against the shore and a kiss from an American soldier. Now, there's something I'll never forget.'

Mrs McAdam continued to entertain Shaun with stories of the war years, whilst Jean rolled her eyes like a daughter who'd heard it all before.

'I'll need to start moving,' said Shaun eventually. 'I've got a date on the Crumlin Road.'

'You've plenty of time,' said Jean.

'I wanted to buy a gift on the way,' Shaun said as he stood up. 'I'll be back for dinner Mrs McAdam, so I'll see you then.' He reached over to kiss her cheek and consumed the scent of synthetic flowers from the curls in her hair. He then paused to enjoy the silent acknowledgement that preceded a riotous laugh.

Mrs McAdam waved Shaun out of the kitchen. 'Oh you'd better get out the door son before my face explodes. I'm sure I'm beetroot.' She fanned her face with an envelope. 'Here, she said. Take the guide and this wee letter with you. You might enjoy it!'

Shaun reached for the letter from the snow white hands. 'I look forward to reading it. And I promise I'll bring it back.'

'You'd better not forget the prison pass,' said Jean, passing the document across the table. 'I hope you enjoy your visit.'

The doorbell rang as Shaun walked through the living room.

'Coming! called Jean, whizzing past Shaun.

'What are you doing here?' Shaun heard as he stalled by the portrait of Jean's family.

'Well, that's a fine welcome' the voice replied.

'But you're not meant to be here!'

'I'm here and it's freezing and it's wet, so are you going to let me in?'

Shaun stood still. He was sure it was Annie. He smiled and waited before a gale of hair and an abundance of purple wool gusted into the room.

Annie stopped in the middle of floor and looked.

'We have a visitor,' Jean explained to Annie.

Annie said nothing, but the centre of a pale face and small red nose emerged as Jean unwound the lengthy scarf from her friend.

'It's not that cold,' Jean censured, holding up a scarf that was longer than her own person. 'Where's your car?'

Annie kept looking at Shaun and Jean stood between the two of them, assessing the situation.

'Do you two not remember each other?' she asked with a look of confusion. She then pulled a strand of Annie's hair. 'You need that hair cut,' she said, patting down the tousled, dark locks that fell below Annie's shoulders. 'A woman of your age should have short hair.'

Shaun wasn't sure if he should laugh, but in his efforts to see a face in the midst of the disarray of a woman before him, his own instinct was to lift the hair away from her face, look at her and pull her into an embrace.

'Thanks Jean,' smiled Annie, stretching out a hand to Shaun, 'Nice to see you,' she said.

Shaun ignored the hand and hugged Annie, her hair cold against his chin, her shoulders hidden in layers of clothing. He stood back and watched as confusion deepened her brown eyes and colour filled her wintry cheeks

'Och, if it's not wee Annie,' swirled a voice from the kitchen. 'Are you not meant to be away, love?'

'I'm staying here for a week,' said Annie. She then looked at Jean as she addressed Shaun. 'I didn't know you were coming.'

'Well, I didn't think of telling you since you weren't supposed to be here!' said Jean.

Shaun realised that Annie mustn't have received his last letter.

'How's James?' he asked finally.

'Up to mischief as usual!' said Annie. 'And Toby? Is he here too?'

'No, he's at school. I travelled alone.'

Silence lingered as impossible questions assailed Shaun.

'Will you stay for a wee cup of tea?' Mrs McAdam asked Annie. 'I was just telling Shaun about the Gobbins and the GI sweetheart.'

'The Gobbins,' said Annie. 'I was there once when I was wee. It's a shame it's closed.'

'It was the main tourist attraction in the whole of Ireland once. My mother took me there on the train in 1933.'

'I need to see this place,' said Shaun, following the three women into the kitchen.

Jean and Mrs McAdam both looked at Shaun with questioning eyes as he sat down at the kitchen table. Jean cleared her throat and Shaun became unnerved by the two tipped heads.

'Excuse me,' said Jean. 'I don't mean to be rude, but do you not have a jailbird to attend to?'

'Oh, yes,' said Shaun, standing up.

'I bought Harry a wee packet of thermals,' said Mrs McAdam. 'Why don't you take them to him as a gift?'

Annie laughed.

'I'm sure he'll be delighted,' said Jean. 'Well, that's it settled. Another round of tea. I tell ya, I don't see a sinner from one end of the week to the next and then you all arrive like buses. Sit down, Shaun. Mrs McAdam, away in and get the thermals for Harry. I'm going to pop to the shop for a bit of ham for a few sandwiches. Are you two okay?'

'Yes,' said Shaun, his face burning.

Shaun and Annie spoke simultaneously when the front door closed. 'I tried to tell you,' said Shaun. 'Why didn't you tell me?' asked Annie. They laughed and Shaun began again. 'I wrote to tell you I'd be at the same hotel.'

'I didn't get it. I don't work at the factory anymore. I'm...' Annie looked nervously to the living room and back to Shaun. 'It's a long story. How long are you here?'

'Four days. I'm staying at the same hotel as last time, but I'm going to Dublin for a history conference after this. I thought the conference was a good excuse to visit Belfast.'

'Are you here tomorrow?'

'Yes.'

Annie lowered her voice. 'I'm free in the morning.'

The front door opened and closed. 'That'll be Mrs McAdam with the thermals,' she smiled. 'I'll pick you up at the hotel at ten.'

'Are you sure it's okay?' said Shaun.

'Yes, it's okay.'

Mrs McAdam took a seat in between Shaun and Annie.

Annie coughed and looked at Mrs McAdam's hands.

'What?' said Mrs McAdam.

'The thermals,' said Annie.

'Oh ay, that's right. I forgot the thermals. It's this big Honky Tonk man beside me. He's got me all confused!'

Shaun hugged Mrs McAdam before leaving the kitchen, 'I'll be back for dinner. As for you, Annie, it was a pleasure seeing you.'

'Goodbye,' said Annie.

The Crumlin Road Goal was a Victorian edifice built from terracotta stone. It was located between a handsome row of terraced cottages and a gothic-style red-bricked hospital. Opposite presided a magnificent courthouse painted in peach and cream and accessorised with a mass of barbed wire. It was typical of Belfast, a city made up of grand architecture enclosed in serrated metal.

Shaun had spent half an hour in the waiting area, enough time for anxiety to pillage him of the self-assurance he had enjoyed at Jean's house. He was frisked by a burly prison officer with the Troubles etched all over the lines in his face, and then led across an old stone courtyard to meet Harry in a room where the affected airs of the exterior disappeared into faded plaster walls and lacklustre tiles.

'How are you?' asked Shaun, his confidence crumbling in the wake of Harry's cold handshake and stony glare.

'Why did you come here? This isn't Project Children.'

Shaun passed a polystyrene cup of milky tea towards Harry, unable to find a response to his words. 'I needed to see some people,' he replied eventually, feeling the breadth of the Atlantic Ocean in his bones.

'Did you need to see Annie?' Harry asked.

Harry's eyes were stern and wrapped around Shaun's like fists.

Shaun's reply followed after a pause in a strangulated voice, 'What made you say that?'

'I saw you at the train station four years ago.'

Shaun settled into the hostile climate. 'The train station,' he repeated, assimilating an image of a pink dusk and wrought iron trellis.

'I was on the same train as Annie.'

Harry's blue eyes and long features were as hypnotic as they were harrowing and Shaun was unable to articulate clear thoughts. Why was he on the same train?

'The night after I went drinking with you, I took a woman called Linda to a B&B by the seaside and returned home on the first train the next day. I was disciplined back then, coming home in the early hours of the morning. I got complacent in the end. I forgot about home.'

'You saw nothing at the train station.'

'I saw nothing. You're right. I saw nothing and I saw everything. You were watching the train move off and a woman opposite me was crying. Two black lines of mascara travelled down her face and I couldn't take my eyes off her because I was trying to figure out if she was happy or if she was sad. She was fixated on her own reflection in the window.'

Shaun listened. He bowed his head.

'I met Annie when the kids got back from America. You know, the last thing I saw when I left Whitehead that morning were two long tears. I had told a woman that I loved her, and it was hard to tell if she was happy or if she was sad.'

The background noise of the other visitors amplified.

'I had an ocean,' said Shaun.

'And I had a river with a bridge.'

Shaun coughed and made his confession. 'I didn't kiss Annie and I didn't touch her skin, but I wrote the first letter.'

'This is the price I paid, Shaun.' Harry looked around. 'This is the price.'

'No, this is the price for killing a man.'

The words lingered in the silence.

Shaun spoke again. 'I came here to tell you something.'

Harry's demeanour was cool as Shaun narrated the story of Eamon Fitzgerald against a blockade of deadly silence.

Shaun finished and Harry leaned in and lowered his voice. 'Do you know how many men in Northern Ireland were serving sentences for murder the year before the Troubles began?'

Shaun was motionless, aware that an answer was not required.

'Less than twenty. Today, there are more than four hundred, and if you look around this room, you'll see what a murderer looks like.'

Shaun's neck reddened. His eyes circled the room as he felt closer to the trigger of the cheque he had signed.

'I sent my son to America in good faith, Harry said. 'I trusted you with my son.'

'And I fulfilled that duty of trust.'

'By sending arms to Belfast.'

'I've explained everything to you. I had no part in that.'

'How do I know that you're telling me the truth?'

'You need to take my word.'

'Can you see why you don't belong here?'

Shaun took a deep breath and unlocked Harry's grasp on his eyes. 'Neither of us belong here.'

'What about Annie?'

'I'll do the right thing.'

'You're a better man than me.'

Shaun settled in his seat again. 'I don't know if I am. I just saw a married woman in your house and there was no ocean between us.'

'You saw Annie?'

'Yes.'

'I thought she was in Holland. She moved to Holland.'

'I saw her.'

'They aren't together,' Harry said flatly.

'Who?'

'Roy and Annie. Jean said they aren't together.'

'You said they'd moved.'

'That's all I know.'

Shaun tried to register the implication of the split between Roy and Annie, but in the prison walls surrounding him, he felt only penance for a confession he hadn't intended making. It was hard to feel anything else in a place where mistrust and deception hung from the rafters like condemned men.

Harry sipped some tea and looked at Shaun, 'Welcome back to Belfast,' he said.

'If that's what you call a welcome, I'd hate to see you punch a man.'

Seconds passed before Shaun recalled why Harry was in prison. He looked Harry in the eye and a smile edged from Harry's lips. 'You don't want to get involved in a country like this,' Harry said. 'You belong in America.'

'Peace will come.'

'I always believed that a stranger would come to town,' Harry stated, his eyes set in the distance.

Shaun awaited an explanation, but it rested in the gallows of silence and remained unanswered. Shaun stood up and prepared to leave. Face to face, the two men shook hands.

'Thank you,' Harry said. 'If I had a Guinness in my hand, I would make a toast to Toby. May he be a great man.'

'If I had a whisky in my hand, I would make a toast to Robert. May he be a great man.'

Shaun began to walk away. He stopped and looked back. 'With a great father,' he added.

'With a great father,' echoed Harry, his voice trembling.

Shaun took one last look at Harry before moving towards the door and Harry's stony eyes had turned to water.

***

Annie led Shaun down an untamed grassy path towards the sea. To the left a lighthouse stood tall at the helm of a basalt cliff and across the water Scotland could be seen clearly against the white-blue sky. Annie stopped beside a solitary blackthorn tree, and ran her hands across a gnarly, fissured bark. 'It's a faerie tree,' she explained to Shaun. Do you have a dime?'

'I do,' said Shaun, looking at Annie inquisitively.

'If you can carve a little cranny in the trunk of the tree, you'll get a thousand years of luck.'

Shaun's eyes continued to question Annie.

She laughed. 'Actually, I'm not entirely sure what you'll get.

My knowledge of Irish mythology is about as strong as my knowledge of Irish history, so I've no idea what benefit this tree beholds.'

Shaun set a dime between two spindly branches and stood back. 'It's a hell of an ugly tree, if you don't mind me saying.'

'You've offended the faeries and jinxed the coin. Say something nice quickly.'

'Okay, so am I speaking to a tree or to you?'

'The tree, obviously.'

'Faerie Tree, you look like the kind of tree that is full of the wisdom of the past and the wisdom of present and I entrust you with this coin for good luck for the future. How's that?'

'Better. I admire your poetry.'

They continued along a northbound trail that sloped down towards a bay and slowed down when the path narrowed around the cliff's edge. They approached the gate to the Gobbins, where the sea slept on a pillow of rocks glimmering like coal, inhaling and exhaling pale turquoise and white surf against the ice-cold air. Shaun pulled an envelope from his pocket and revealed a faded postcard with a watercolour painting of the curious shape in the rocks.

'The Gobbins' was scribed onto the left side of a hole in the rock and 'Wise's eye' printed in white letters along the bottom. Annie read the back of the postcard.

Dear Edith.

I know you belong in Ireland, but I will always remember holding your hand here at the tubular bridge at the Gobbins. May you live a beautiful life and find peace with your angels in heaven.

Yours,
George.

'That's lovely,' said Annie. 'The tubular bridge fell into the sea a few years ago, mind you. And I had no idea that Mrs

McAdam was called Edith.'

'I think it's like a state secret. George wanted her to marry him and move to America, but she declined his offer and stayed in Belfast.'

'I didn't know that.'

'No. She said she didn't tell anyone. Her first husband was also called George. If the poor guy had had a different name, he might have been more fortunate.'

'I don't know,' said Annie. It's a big thing moving away from home. I should know.'

'Harry said you'd moved to Holland.'

'Yes. I moved last month and came back to sort the house out. We have some tenants now. '

Annie couldn't face a fuller explanation. She climbed the old stone steps through Wise's eye, where she was met with a crooked and rusted sign alerting trespassers that danger lay ahead. Annie read the sign and then read the sea. It was still calm but it was beginning to rouse from its slumber and beat gently against the cliff path. The railing of the narrow walkway cut from rock had been washed into the sea, but the old support pillars remained engineered deep into the basalt rocks. She held onto the rocks jutting from the cliff face and followed the walkway, aware of Shaun's presence close behind her.

She stopped at a rusted bridge of about ten feet in width between a ravine of rocks. The cry of a gull and the awakening water were the only sounds.

'It's safe,' she confirmed, as she walked to the other side. She stood back and watched Shaun cross, the sea below gushing vertically towards the old bridge that had been reclaimed by the birds. Behind Shaun, spleenwort burst from cracks in the rocks and scurvy grass clung to the sides of the cliff.

They passed by an opening to a cave as the sea stretched up to the level of their feet. Annie continued to pace her brown suede gloves across the cliff face and marvelled at how the rock had been chiselled to create the path on which she walked. She climbed a spiral of stone steps, holding onto the rock with her left hand and pillars with her right hand, consuming the wind that slapped her cold cheeks. At the peak, she looked down upon a long expanse of black cliff line fissured with glints of green and purple. White kittiwakes nested in the basalt with their yellow bills and as the wind rose, their angry cries ascended.

'That sure is something!' exclaimed the American voice.

'I don't think we can go any further,' Annie shouted into the tide of sound. 'The next bridge doesn't look safe.'

The bridge was at a distance from their vantage point and it was no more than a long concrete beam. It looked sturdy and Annie had no doubt that it was embedded deep into the rock, but the lack of support ropes made it a tightrope across a cove of tossing waves.

'We should turn back,' Annie said, conscious that the water was kicking hard against the side of the cliffs.

'It's a spectacular place,' Shaun said. 'Maybe some day, someone will rebuild those bridges.'

'It'll be a sure sign of peaceful times.'

They returned to the entrance of the cave.

'Come on, let's take a look,' said Annie.

Sheltered from the elements, the cave was illuminated by a long stretch of golden-emerald light that bounded off the back wall, exposing a bare wall of crystal, green rock. Annie stood in the vertical rays and looked up. The cave was at the centre of a ravine that narrowed into a long thin line of sky above.

'It's amazing,' said Shaun as he stretched his neck.

Annie was face to face with Shaun in an isolated cave with a shaft of light between them, and the impulse that had once sent her walking straight into Shaun's arms was stronger than before. His brown eyes were bright, the stubble on his dark face almost blond in the light. She reached out her hand. He received the offering without hesitation as his warm breath cast clouds between them.

'We're here again,' said Shaun, tucking a stray lock of hair into Annie's purple woollen hat.

'We're here again,' smiled Annie.

'I've been trying to find a way to ask you since we left the hotel.'

'Ask me what?'

'Harry said you and Roy weren't together.'

'Harry is right. Roy and I split up.'

'But you moved to Holland.'

'We split up on Boxing Day after a massive row, and after a lot of talking, I realised that I could keep everyone happy if I moved to Holland. If Roy had gone alone, the boys wouldn't see him and I couldn't do that to him. Anyway, I don't think I'd be good at controlling two teenagers on my own. It turns out that my fear of moving away was related more to the fear of being in the wrong marriage.'

'And you live together?'

'No, I'm staying in Dirk's flat in the centre of Leiden, and Roy is in Dirk's house outside the town. The boys are enrolled in an international school. They're with me through the week and with Roy at the weekends.'

'Are you guys happy?'

'Relieved maybe. It's all new. We left at the start of January, so it's been a case of sorting things out so far.'

Annie watched Shaun's eyes explore her face and knew she had to speak. 'All those years ago, I wanted to kiss you and you stopped me because I was a married woman. This time, I want to stop myself because I have just split up with Roy.'

'You're still a married woman,' Shaun said gently as he touched Annie's cheek.

The cave was secluded and safe, but Annie was still trying to heed the rusted sign. It would crush Roy to know that she had walked straight into another man's arms.

Shaun finally broke the silence. 'Do you believe in God?' he asked.

'Sometimes,' Annie replied. She waited, but there was no response. 'And you?'

'I have a troubled relationship with God. At Carrickfergus Castle, I didn't kiss you and afterwards, I couldn't help but think that God was guiding my fate. Today, I'm just a man and I am alone and I want to kiss you more than ever.'

'At the castle,' Annie began 'you were in the company of a

completely irrational woman. I was exhausted and emotional and I don't know where I got the adrenaline to walk all night. Today you have before you a better person, but I will give you this.' Annie reached up, closed her eyes and kissed Shaun on the lips. Shaun's arms encircled her body as the kiss made its own journey against time.

Annie stood back, placed her hands in her pocket and smiled. Shaun blinked and raised his eyebrows before smiling back.

'What changed?' Shaun asked.

'Nothing changed. Marriage was easier than the truth and the truth was that we didn't want to be together. If I hadn't met you four years ago, Roy and I would have split up.'

'I'm not sure that makes sense.'

'I felt so guilty that I had tried to kiss another man that we ended up staying together. We had both wanted to walk away.'

Annie raised her eyes to the slice of sky in the crevice as clarity surrounded her. 'If I'd known you were coming here this time, it would have confused me, so thank you for not telling me.'

'But it's very early days. How does Roy feel?'

'Roy is sad. His marriage is over and his uncle is dying, but he's got his job and he's excited about that.'

'What will you do?'

'I don't know. I'm busy looking after Dirk at the moment, but there are plenty of jobs for English speakers in Leiden.'

'We should get back,' Shaun said quietly. 'It's safer if I stay behind you. Lead the way, Madame.'

'Thank you sir,' Annie smiled.

Shaun was quiet as they followed the path back to Wise's eye. He stopped on the steps. 'Wait,' he said. 'Don't go outside yet.'

Annie held her hands up to the clear blue sky. 'We're outside.'

'We're still inside the Gobbins.'

'We are.'

'And we speak the truth inside this path and then when we exit, we return to reality.'

'What reality?'

'The reality of knowing that there is a chance you will get back with your husband.'

'There is no…'

'Stop.' Shaun placed one finger on Annie's lips. 'Don't say there is no chance, because you are still married.'

'What's the truth?'

'The truth is that when you wrote to me that you felt love, I disregarded your words.'

'Why?'

'To survive.'

'I see. And now?'

'And now, we both know.'

Annie smiled and reached her hand out to Shaun as she climbed through Wise's Eye.

'Back to reality,' Shaun said, looking up towards the lighthouse.

Annie held onto Shaun's hand as they passed the Faerie Tree. She removed the dime and placed it back into his pocket. 'You don't need luck,' she said. 'I think you have something greater on your side.'

'What do you mean?'

'You said you had a troubled relationship with God, but I don't think you do. I think you have a troubled relationship with your own conscience. Maybe God took care of you.'

'Maybe.'

'And this is reality right here,' Annie said, her hands spreading from the hill to the bay. 'The same reality as the cliff path below.'

Annie enjoyed Shaun's contented silence as they walked to the car.

'You're going to have some difficult months ahead,' Shaun said when they arrived at the hotel.

'I know. I'll write to you.'

'I look forward to that.'

Annie kissed Shaun on the cheek and sat back.

'Do you have to go?' he asked, his cheek reddening.

'I have to go.'

'I understand, but a kiss on the cheek is not enough compensation for the pain I'm going to be in until I go to Dublin tomorrow.'

Shaun kissed Annie on the lips.

Annie said goodbye and held onto the tears that were stirring in her eyes. She drove to Whiteabbey and the Shore Road became a blur of colour as she relived the guilt she had felt on the train four years before. That guilt had given Annie's children four more years with their parents, but still there was a loss for a love that had passed her by. Annie had betrayed her husband, but she felt ready to forgive herself and to begin her life again with a wider stretch of water between her and the man she loved.

PART THREE

THE FRONTIER
1994

A haunting melody of choir singers pierced the air and lingered on as a graceful dancer with red curls and long toned legs moved around the stage like a feather. Roy was pretending not to look at the TV, but he was as captivated by the movements and pulsating sounds of the dancer as he once was by a lively girl in a quiet bar in Glenarm. Roy's uncle had died, and he and Annie were alone in Dirk's home after the funeral, doing something that ordinary couples do, sitting quietly, watching TV. Except, they were no longer an ordinary couple.

The beat intensified as the brusque march of heavy shoes thumped through the room. A man was dancing, moving swiftly, raising his arms, tapping furiously in a battle of drums and feet. The girl joined the stage, she too joining in the raucous chorus of tapping. The fiddles and drums heightened into their final throes of fervour, the audience erupted and Roy turned to Annie. 'Sex and Irish dancing! Did ye ever see anything like it in your life? We've only been away for four months.'

'My old dance teacher would turn in her grave,' smiled Annie, clearly in awe of what she had seen on the Eurovision Song Contest.

'I fell for you when I saw you dance in the Schooner.'

'You never told me that before.'

'You were beautiful. One minute you had these skinny, short legs and next thing they were long and toned and making the most amazing impression on my young mind.'

'Roy, I—'

'Can you remember the first time we kissed?' Roy interrupted, knowing that Annie would have something to say.

'Why now? Is this not hard enough?'

'I have memories. At least, I've started to remember things.'

Roy hadn't realised it until he'd said it. He had started to remember things, beautiful things and sinister things that had been buried alongside them as the sweat poured off his skin through the night. In dreams, it was Nina who would follow Roy. She would follow him to a quiet corner of the bar and she would unbutton the denim jacket with its belted waist. She would be there before him, her bulging breasts soft and threatening. He would look down and the fine waistline would be replaced with a curved stomach and Roy would be on his knees, his ear against the skin of the stomach like a fetoscope listening to the tick tock of a timing device on a terrorist bomb.

Roy's eyes fell as he recognised a feeling he had been trying to recapture for years. He loved Annie, and he had spent so long loving a figment of his imagination and pretending that he loved his wife, that the difference between pretense and reality was as bewildering as it was heartbreaking.

The pretense hadn't only been about marriage. The pretense had been entwined in every detail of his personal circumstances. He had found a job in Belfast that facilitated his disability, but that had done nothing to restore the ego that the disability had embalmed. Only his children and his love for his family had been alive, and that had been enough for a long period of time. It was no longer enough.

Annie was looking down. Roy reached out a hand and clasped Annie's in his. 'We're allowed to look back and remember. You're the mother of my children.'

'But you're not one for talking about the past. I thought it didn't matter to you until we were in Glenarm before

Christmas. You were full of memories that day too.'

'The past didn't matter to me for a long time because I didn't see the point in trying to recapture what life was like before the bomb. I resented that life.'

'Because of your leg?'

No, was the answer that he clenched between his lips.

Roy had lost his innocence, and an innate love for the people around him. Nina had hurt him, cutting a wound through a soul that had been innocent and believing.

He carefully composed the response for Annie, giving her enough to understand him, but retaining the secret he had cherished and despised. 'No, he said. 'It was harder to get over losing my innocence.' Annie's eyes were searching for an explanation and Roy stalled. He wanted to tell Annie the truth, but he didn't know if the words would ever find their way from his lips. He smiled. 'I had dreams before then.'

'I know that. I remember them. I tried to get you to remember them too.'

'It wasn't just dreams. I wanted to succeed at something other than family, which is ironic since I failed at family and I'm sorry for failing.'

'You didn't fail. Neither of us failed. We're only human and I wonder sometimes where all this pressure to have perfect marriages comes from.'

'Religion is to blame for that.'

'I think religion is separate to what goes on in someone's mind. Sometimes I try to talk to God, but I always find myself back at me.'

'Back at you?' Roy questioned with a smile.

'Yes, I have to forgive myself first before I ask God to forgive me.'

'But you didn't do anything wrong.'

'I did. I stopped believing in you.'

'I'm sorry that I didn't give you something to believe in.'

'I stopped believing in you because I…'

Annie looked down.

'What is it?' Roy asked.

'It's nothing.' Annie touched the corner of her eye with the back of her hand.

'Can you remember the day that you pushed me?'

Roy could see Annie's body harden at the memory.

'I stood back and let you.'

Annie's eyes were black and distant.

'I decided then that I'd had enough of everything, of the house, the role of looking after the boys, of you.'

'Of me.'

'Of life. I wanted out. I wanted to leave you.'

'I know.'

'How did you know?'

'Roy, that day, you used words that were so ugly that I kept thinking that I couldn't live with someone like you anymore. I couldn't do it. I wanted to walk away too.'

'Why didn't you?'

'Because I...Why didn't you?'

'Because I knew that I had to keep us together. And now I know why. I love you, Annie. I just couldn't remember some things.'

Annie looked away. 'It's too late.'

'I know it's too late. It's all I've thought about for weeks. We got a round of applause, remember?'

'When?'

'The first time we kissed.'

Annie smiled. 'That's because no one could believe you had a chance with a tough girl like me. You were gye an soft, ye know!'

'Ye may hae run wild through the hills, but you were a fine girl, Annie O'Neill. You still are a fine girl,' he said, his words fading.

Roy could feel his eyes sting with tears and he didn't know if he was crying for the past he had buried or for the one that was still alive. He spoke carefully. 'Thank you for coming here.'

'It's the best thing for the boys. I can see that. I never thought about how nice it would be to have money, but it is. Life is easier here, although I don't know how long James will last at that British school.'

'He's no dozer.'

'He's no dozer,' smiled Annie.

'He wants to work with me when he's sixteen. We'll get him an apprenticeship.'

'The slip jig's a mournful dance, you know?'

'What's a slip jig?'

'It's the dance you fell for.'

'I didn't fall for a dance. I fell in love with you.'

'Seventeen years haven't been wasted.'

'I know that and I also know that I can't keep you here forever.'

'I like it for now.'

'You like it because you know it doesn't have to be forever.'

'Maybe.' Annie stood up, lifted her coat and reached out her hand to Roy. He held it and understood that it was over. All he had were the exhumed memories of a love that had passed and a weighty sense of loss for the present.

***

Annie was perched on a confiscated box of cider in a tent pitched by a lakeland of hushed waters and sleepy rain. County Fermanagh was as far away as Annie could persuade Jean to travel for their four day adventure, and as close to Belfast as necessary if she needed to go home.

Jean, meanwhile, was on her feet, orchestrating happiness among ten boys. Minutes previously, the sixteen year-olds from each side of Belfast's peace-line had been blissfully united in the consumption of illicit cider, a bootlegging exploit that had ended when Jean had pulled back the flap of the tent and guldered, 'Busted!'

Operation Adamsteen was what Jean had code-named the plan to bring some of the Project Children alumni together in Northern Ireland, and Annie wondered how she would find the energy to board a plane to America immediately after the sporting pursuits that had cracked her shoulders, pulled at her ligaments and brought her closer to a physical acknowledgment that a thirty-eighth birthday beckoned.

While Jean had stayed true to form, arranging lunches and

dinners and clearing up endless dishes in the Share Centre kitchen, Annie had been soaked to the oxters and slarried in mud every day. She had been ejected from a banana boat at speed, capsized from a canoe every day and tipped from a windsurf board more times than she had held onto the sail.

She was exhausted. Six months of change had taken its toll and she could neither eat nor sleep thinking about her next journey.

After Fermanagh, her destination was Washington, D.C. She was to be a Project Children volunteer for three weeks, helping Stella with the administration of the D.C. chapter, and it was a trip that filled her with as much anxiety as excitement.

There was the prospect of falling into Shaun's arms and making love, a dream sparked night after night, heightened in the fire of Annie's imagination and quenched by the fear that desire had been mistaken for love. There was also the worry that she and Shaun might agree to complicate life further by making a commitment to stay together.

Change was painting a landscape in Annie's mind that was so foreign that she felt lost, unsure of her future and unsteady in her mind.

'Thank you.'

An unexpected voice cut across Annie's hazy future. It was Aaron, a boy with cheeks as pale as water, a boy who hadn't been subject to the July sun percolating through clouds that had turned Annie's skin to chestnut.

Annie responded with a questioning eye, unsure if she was being thanked for the holiday or for not completely losing her cool when she realised that the underaged boys in her care were all inebriated.

'Thank you for bringing us here. It's been good.'

'Glad you enjoyed it.' Annie said with a sense of accomplishment.

'The water skiing was brilliant. We're all coming back in August.'

'Who all?' asked Annie.

'Us.'

'Are we not invited too? Me and Jean?' Annie teased.

'No chance!'

'Are you going to meet up in Belfast?'

'I dunno. Maybe in the city centre.' he shrugged.

A lengthy pause followed. Annie was familiar with the disjointed pattern of teenage conversation. She waited.

'It's good to see these boys again,' Aaron began. 'I went to America for four summers. I haven't seen them in a while.'

'You must have liked it if you went back three times.'

'I didn't like leaving my ma with my da being away, but it was good. The family were in Virginia. They had a swimming pool and all that.'

'Where was he? Your dad?'

'My da's in prison.'

'How long?'

'Most of my life. He went in in 1981 after the hunger strike. I don't remember him ever being at home.'

The realisation that Aaron's father was in the IRA settled around Annie like misty lakeland rain. She was as close as she had ever come to a Republican terrorist.

She remembered the Hunger Strike. The Troubles at that time had become a sickening backdrop to the reality of caring for two babies and Roy after the bomb. She also remembered the scale of IRA support when thousands of people had poured onto the streets for Bobby Sands' funeral, an event that had passed her by in the midst of sleepless nights and reckless dawns.

'He was in prison for handling a gun.' Aaron said.

'Your dad?'

'No, Bobby Sands.'

'Oh.'

'My da hated Thatcher. She could have intervened. He would never have joined if it hadn't been for Thatcher.'

Annie was taken aback. Aaron was too young to have remembered any of it. A teenage boy was explaining to her why a martyr was made of a man who had starved himself to death for political status, and Annie was listening closely to what he had to say.

'You're a Protestant, aren't you? You and Jean both?'

Annie felt her cheeks burn. It was strange to hear that label from the son of an IRA man and it stuck like an insinuation despite the boy's gentle voice.

'Yes, Jean is from the Shankill. I live in the Netherlands now. Do you miss him?'

'Sometimes. Sometimes, I hate him. He's my brothers' hero. Both of them worship him. I'm proud of him, I suppose.'

There was another pause and Aaron's cheeks reddened.

'Did your husband take your kids to football?' he asked.

'Yes he did,' Annie replied, embarrassed by her response in the face of Aaron's keen stare. Roy had taken his children to football and, in their eyes, he was brave and steadfast and loyal. Roy had always been a hero to his children.

'He said that he did it for my future, that I wouldn't have had the same rights today if they hadn't fought for equality.'

'Aaron, love,' she said. 'Your dad may have fought for something he believed in, but this country let down its children.'

'You're okay you know,' he responded.

Annie laughed, 'Thank you! You still can't drink the cider.'

'It was worth a try,' he smiled.

***

Shaun applauded the sound of the gentle virtuoso flautist who had followed the dancers in their war of feet and drums. The lights dimmed for the last two speeches and Shaun awaited Annie's arrival on stage.

It had taken time to acclimatise to Annie without her armour of wool. In the four years he had known her, Shaun's fantasies had been fixed on a continual loop of treacle eyes peering over scarves and a face that was as fearless as it was apprehensive. The woman he had met at Stella's house that morning had been stripped back to a short summer dress with tanned skin stretched across fine ridges of muscle, her untamed hair tied back from her face, and Shaun soon realised that all the images created in his mind for years had been naked of the real voice and the real laughter that had made a bright day in one hundred degrees celsius come alive.

It had been a last minute decision to add Annie to the programme for the Project Children fundraiser in the Kennedy Centre, and Shaun was consumed by nerves for her. Stella had invited President Clinton to make the closing address and Annie had seemed unfazed, her distance from Washington D.C. and US politics serving as an interface to the magnitude of the task. Like the Irish children who had stood in the middle of the stage and recited their stories from the Project Children experience, Annie was oblivious to the number of dignitaries the evening had attracted.

Shaun held his breath when she appeared. She stood alone after Stella's introduction, shimmering in a black satin dress like a fleck of dust trapped in the light.

'In 1990,' she began, 'my friend Shaun from Maryland visited his host son in Belfast.'

This was not the speech she had practiced and Shaun had not expected to hear his own name.

'He told me how bemused he was that Robert, a boy from the Shankill area of Belfast, had a dream of travelling on the prison bus.'

Shaun looked up. His eyes converged with Annie's. He had recited the prison bus story earlier that day by the Lincoln monument, and Annie had listened quietly.

'The reason that Robert wanted to be on the prison bus was that his friends travelled on it every Saturday morning to visit their dads. There was free lemonade and chips for the kids. When you're eight, that's a great incentive to be somewhere.'

A gentle hint of laughter stalled on its journey through the ominous, black silence of the auditorium.

'Last October, Robert walked to the prison bus to meet his friends. It was a normal Saturday afternoon.'

Her voice started to break. She looked into the audience and Shaun's eyes gripped Annie's with all their might.

'Robert didn't meet his friends that day. Instead…'

Annie coughed and an auditorium held its collective breath throughout a long pause.

'Robert survived the bomb, but his little sister, six year-old

Shelley, who had just been to her dance class, was injured.'

Shaun's eyes began to shatter, the pain of one family magnified in the thick silence of the room.

'In response to that tragic day, Robert's father killed a man,' Annie said, looking up towards the beam of light that was suspended above the audience. 'He is in prison now and Robert no longer wants to travel on the prison bus.'

Annie had wrapped her story around the audience and her words had clasped the heartbeats of a thousand people.

'This is 1994 and a war has been raging since 1969. Robert Adams won't get to play football with his father for another decade, until he is an adult, Jean Adams will raise three children alone, Hannah Adams will always be sorry that she let go of her sister's hand and little Shelley Adams…'

Annie's voice ruptured. Her eyes circled the audience, 'Little Shelley Adams will never Irish dance again.'

Annie paused as an auditorium collected the pain of one family in Ireland.

'I hope,' she said, as Shaun's eyes braced Annie's. 'I hope that the bombs will stop falling, that the prison buses will stop rolling and that it will soon be safe to send your children to stay in our homes. Thank you.'

The speech was over and the applause rippled in considerate beats as the hope of Annie reverberated around the room.

Shaun's mind was still on Annie when Stella took the stage and began to speak. He couldn't focus on anything else but Annie when President Clinton thanked Stella and the Project Children volunteers for their work. And Annie was still there with her potent eyes when President Clinton pledged his support for the peace talks that had already begun.

Shaun loved Annie, and he didn't want to spend another day of his life without the woman in whom his love was vested.

***

Jean surveyed the girls scattered along the stone walls in their burgundy, velvet dresses at Carrickfergus Castle and felt an intense satisfaction in her craft. She had tailored costumes for the entire dance school in the seven months since Harry had gone to prison, earning her a steady salary of £100 per dress.

Two dresses each week were required to pay the bills, and her work occupied her fingers and her mind almost every day. She attended to the cutting and the stitching in the mornings when the children were at school, and at night, after a routine of prison visits, housework, homeworks and dinners, she would crochet and embroider with one eye on the TV soaps. On Saturdays, Jean was in perpetual transit.

There was an early rise to walk Shelley to her swimming lesson, a return train journey to Carrickfergus for Hannah's dance lesson, a bus from the station to see Harry in prison, a walk into town for an hour's shopping and a visit to McDonald's on Royal Avenue for dinner. Robert played football on Saturdays and walked into town to meet Jean and the girls every week, conceding his obsessive preoccupation with his friends to guarantee a Big Mac and fries before the taxi ride home. Jean had spent her Saturdays doing housework when Harry had been at home.

The dancing festival was outside in an open area surrounded by strong walls and heavy, black canon. Seats had been placed at the front of the stage, but the castle was open for the usual trickle of tourists. Unsuspecting visitors stood around the side of the chairs with delighted bemusement on their faces whilst four year-old girls skipped their one-two-threes like chicks splashing around the make-shift stage.

The festival gathered momentum as the more experienced dancers skilfully moved through their reels. They hopped and birled, the finesse of their interlaced feet as they rocked from side to side, reminding Jean of what could have been.

Pretty girls with natural hair adorned in ribbons moved to the slow, pensive beat of the slip jig. Like ballet swans with clipped wings, their hands were locked by their sides, their black leather pumps kicking up a light dust from the stage.

Hannah was at the corner of the stage. Jean folded her programme and stood up to wave.

'Is that your daughter?' the woman beside her asked.

'Yes,' smiled Jean. That's Hannah.'

Burgundy velvet fanned across the stage and Jean waved enthusiastically. She looked at the woman beside her. She wanted to boast that the black, velvet waistcoats that were tied with criss-crossed laces were made by her own hands, that the golden embroidery looped along the knee-length hems and rising up through the centre pleat had kept her up for three nights, that the white, rounded collars were filled with the fine detail of crocheted flowers that couldn't be seen in any of the other dresses. She wanted to tell her that the burgundy, velvet capes were attached with silver brooches embellished in green and gold stones that were gifts from her grandmother.

Jean turned back to the stage and took a deep breath.

Her daughters were positioned with their toes pointing and their hands raised. The background noise closed to the gentle sound of gulls singing, and a sharp silence cascaded the audience before the fiddle began.

Jean was seated under a canopy of blue sky, yet her mind was fixed on a covered prison and a husband with lamenting eyes. She had taken Shelley and Hannah to see their father that morning and the memory of black pumps sliding across the polished tiles of an echoey prison floor invaded the light atmosphere of a cloudless July day. She could see Harry breathe deeply as he watched his daughters skip around the floor, his chest moving up and down, his hand covering his lips.

Hannah and Shelley switched arms on the stage, and moved onto their side step, Shelley's blond hair rippling as they twirled. Her body stuttered from side to side when moving to the right, but Hannah provided her strength and her footing as they returned to the left, the energy in Shelley's body and bright eyes compensating for the turn and drag of her right leg. Hannah's hair was tied back in a plait with ribbons entwined through the threads of hair, and her blue eyes were large and fierce and filled with pride.

Tears had escaped from Harry's eyes as he had watched his daughters. Jean had seen them fall and she had taken Harry's hand as the girls had danced in the space between two tables. The visitors in the prison had been grateful for the girls who had been dancing. Jean had seen it in their smiling eyes. Shelley and Hannah had brought life to the tiles of a prison floor like daffodils sprouting from a tired, stone grave.

They stopped after the second step and bowed. They waited. The pianist played on for a moment, then realising the dance was over and that there was no third step, silenced her keys.

There was a fissle of bags and coats.

Jean's face was motionless. She had seen the dance that morning in the prison and had already shed tears in its wake.

People began to stand. Jean followed their lead and looked around. Women, many of them friends who had come to Jean for dresses and who had heard Shelley's story, were applauding and the woman seated next to Jean turned around with glassy eyes and a tear-stained face and smiled. The tourists were smiling and clapping, the dancers were standing on their chairs and clapping, and Jean cried tears of happiness under an awning of love from strangers and friends. She looked back to the stage. Hannah was holding Shelley's arm in the air and smiling at her sister.

'I'm sorry I can't be there today.' Harry had said as he held Shelley and Hannah in his arms.

'It's my last dance,' Shelley had responded with confidence. 'Mammy will have to bring you photos because I can't swim for you in here.'

Harry had laughed, and only Jean had seen his sorrowful eyes when they were leaving. 'I'm sorry I didn't pick them up that day,' he whispered to Jean. 'If I could change anything in my life, that's what I would change.'

***

Shaun was seated in the same French restaurant in Georgetown where he had once read a letter from Annie. This time he was not alone. He stretched his hands across the table after dinner. 'I still can't believe you're here,' he said.

There was a glow about Annie, a fresh energy that was radiant among the flickering fairy lights and melting candles of the restaurant.

'Nether can I,' Annie replied. 'A walk through the Mall with a handsome American, a speech on the same stage as the President, a tour of the Whitehouse and dinner in a fancy restaurant. I might be the luckiest woman alive.'

Shaun smiled, the Irish music of Annie's voice was ever more compelling. 'I want to hear your voice every day.'

'But it wouldn't be like this every day. I'm in America for the first time in my life and I feel alive.'

'I want you to live here.'

Annie's luminance subsided. 'That's not going to happen,' she said quietly. 'You must know that. James is at school for another three years. We can see each other. Once a month might be possible.'

'Once a month is financially impossible.'

'You could apply for a sabbatical.'

'Where to? Ireland? The Netherlands? And what about Toby?'

'This was never going to be easy, Shaun.'

'The offer still stands for you to stay with me on this trip.'

'It's a generous offer, but I don't want to confuse Toby. It's easier to be near the Project Children Office if I stay with Stella.'

'Toby stays with my mom at the weekends. We've got three weekends.'

'Three weekends? Okay. It's a deal.'

'Starting tonight.'

'It's only my third night at Stella's.'

'She'll understand.'

Shaun was already walking hand-in-hand with Annie towards the door.

'Where are we going?'

'Home,' said Shaun, leading Annie to his car.

'I have a feeling you might take advantage of this situation.'

'What situation?' Shaun asked, opening the car door.

'The situation of a single woman, alone and so far away from home.'

'It's a perilous thing to cross the Atlantic.'

'What plans do you have for me?' Annie said, climbing into the car.

'I plan to demonstrate the American dream for you.'

'The American dream?' Annie laughed. 'On the third day of my trip?'

'Your ancestors didn't wait around.' Shaun was driving and enjoying the note of intrigue from Annie.

'What do you mean?'

'Your ancestors were men and women of the wild frontier. You should follow their journey.'

'How do you know?'

'One of John Roxboro's grandsons came to America in 1755.'

Annie straightened up. Shaun could feel her eyes on the side of his face.

'You found my ancestors?'

'I sure did.' He glanced to the right. 'You forgot to tell me that John Roxboro was a plantation settler from Scotland and that he was Presbyterian. Presbyterians got a pretty raw deal after King Billy left town and so, Henry Roxboro arrived in Philadelphia with dozens of other Scots-Irish and made his way to the wild frontier.

'How do you know all this?'

'I made a trip to the Public Records office in Belfast in February and did the rest of the work here. Actually, I got a Master's student to take it on and he is still following the trail of a ship load of Ulster-Scots from 1755.'

'You're full of surprises.'

'Your uncle settled in Tennessee. So, how much do you like me right now?'

'I like you, but I feel you have solicited my affections with the tools of your trade.'

'I feel you made the first move in that regard.'

'And how do you figure that?'

'Some talk of King Billy, is all.'

Shaun held Annie's hand as he drove to Bethesda, narrating details of his student's findings.

He turned off the engine in his driveway and watched

Annie's curious face.

'So, this is the mansion with the laundry room and three toilets.

'The what? It's a normal four-bedroom house, I'm afraid.'

'Jean once told me about this Honky Tonk man.'

'I see.'

Shaun guided Annie through the front door and straight up the stairs to the right of the hall.

'Can I interrupt the story to say how amazing your house is?' Annie said, her eyes scanning the hall.

'You can end the story and follow me.'

'Before I've seen the three toilets.'

'Before you've seen the three bathrooms.'

'And the laundry room.'

'The laundry room can also wait, although…' Shaun opened the door to his room.

'Although?'

'Although, I do need this dress.'

'My dress doesn't need to go to the laundry room.'

The dress was on the floor and Shaun was unfastening the clips from Annie's hair. He pulled the long strands around her neck before removing his clothes. Annie's face was fierce with beauty in the shadow of a thicket of long, disordered, dark hair.

The room was in semi-darkness and Shaun watched Annie remove her lingerie in the threshold of the door, her silhouette lighted by the hallway lamp below. A body of fine copper was revealed, tenacious and wild, and burgeoning with the soft surrender of white breasts.

Shaun stood naked of years of wondering and reached down to kiss Annie. He pulled her to the bed and learned every peak and trough of her skin, responding to her breath as her body twisted and turned to Shaun's attention.

He made love with abandon, his mind untamed and free from the restrictions of religion, marriage and mourning.

Annie belonged to Shaun, and he was controlling the rising pitch of her voice as her body writhed in torment and pleasure. He responded to Annie's cries, giving and taking in measured strokes, preventing the fall of her conflicted body. He could feel her shrinking back, yet rising inexorably to his will until they both fell.

Annie had thrived and withered, and she curled into a cluster of limbs beside him. He placed his arm around her and huddled in silence.

Shaun had conquered Annie's body, but she did not belong to him when the battle of flesh was done.

He lay awake as Annie slept and contemplated how his love was vested in a woman who was still married to another man. His devotion to the Catholic values he had always cherished had been dismissed in the pursuit of his desires through letters he had written, the call he had made and the long drawn-out dreams of the reality of the present. He may have broken the code of his religion and the code of his conscience in respect of another man, but Shaun knew he could not ignore his instincts. Annie belonged to him. Annie belonged in America.

A STRANGER COMES TO TOWN
1995

'Oh come on to the city centre. You'll enjoy it!' Annie enthused.

'I'm up to my eyes,' said Jean, pointing to a row of dresses that were suspended from the ceiling on a wooden PulleyMaid. 'I've three to do this week.'

'Are these dancing dresses?' Annie asked with confusion, running her hands along the glittery lycra.

'Yes and if I see another sparkle, I'll take a turn in my eye. A wee woman on the Falls Road has started sending me work. Her girls have adopted glitter, and you can blame Michael Flatley for that! I had twenty to do for Mr President's arrival.'

'What for?'

'The girls are dancing today at the city hall before he turns on the Christmas lights.'

'And so you're going to sit here and sew when you have the chance to see your own handiwork on stage? Come on Jean! Mrs McAdam is with the kids anyway. This is exciting. There's an American President in town!'

'But it's Harry's trial tomorrow. It wouldn't be right to go out celebrating.'

'Harry wouldn't want you to miss it.'

'Oh alright then.' Jean placed the lid on a sewing machine

on the kitchen table. 'Wait till I get my bag,' she said, brushing up some threads on the kitchen floor with her hands.

'I heard on the radio that you should leave bags at home.'

'Oh for God's sake,' said Jean. 'My life's in my handbag.'

'Have a day off life, then. Come on! Stick a wheen o pound in your pocket for emergencies and bring your keys. That's all you need.'

'Alright. Alright. You always come back here and put me out of sorts!'

'Good! I'm glad I can be of service! Now, quit your yammering and come on!'

Jean was quiet as they walked briskly down the Shankill Road.

'A penny for them?' Annie smiled.

'I was thinking,' said Jean. 'Bill Clinton or Tony Blair?'

'I don't follow.'

'Which one? You know…' Jean winked at Annie.

Annie stopped and looked at her friend with exasperation. 'I thought something deep and meaningful was troubling you. Does the Prime Minister not get a mention?'

'John Major? Well, if he's your type, love, work away!'

'No, he's not my type. I don't think any of them are my type. I'm not into politicians.'

'Who are you into? You can't stay single forever?'

Annie had been trying to find a way to tell Jean about Shaun. She had attempted writing a letter and had torn it up, knowing that she needed to see Jean's face, and she had almost mentioned it on the phone before arriving at the same conclusion. Jean was a woman whose emotions were contained in the twitch of her head, the flight of her hands and the movement of her body, and Annie needed to be present to see Jean's reaction. Now was the time to tell her friend about the relationship she had been having in secret for more than a year.

'I might not be completely single,' Annie ventured.

'Oh, might you not?' said Jean, her chin puckered into her neck.

'There is someone.'

Jean whacked Annie's arm with the back of her hand,

'Who?'

'An American.'

'An American?'

'An American.'

'Well, which bloody American?' Jean said, her arms gyrating in the air.

'A sort of Honky Tonk type of American.'

Jean stopped walking and grabbed Annie's elbows. 'The Honky Tonk man?' she squealed.

'Yes,' Annie laughed.

'How? Where? When? Why?' darted Jean's voice.

'Well...I've been to see him twice, three times if you count the first time, which was just after we got back from the Share Centre. The last time I saw him was two months ago for my fortieth birthday. And I don't know why. Does there have to be a why?'

'So, you're telling me that you've been seeing him for more than one year and you didn't think to tell your best friend?'

'It was early days and I didn't want anyone to know. I'd only been apart from Roy for about seven months before we got together, and I'd only been apart from Roy for about four weeks before we kissed.'

Jean gasped. 'Hang on a minute. When was that?'

'The time he came over to see you.'

'The time he came over to see me! He could have been mine. You stole my man!'

'You didn't want him,' Annie laughed, and after an unsettling silence, she added, 'Did you?'

'Don't be daft. I'm more happy for you than anyone in the world. I just wish you'd told me sooner. Wait 'til I tell Mrs McAdam the good news.'

'Actually, we went to the Gobbins, where Mrs McAdam courted her GI the day after she told Shaun about him.'

'It didn't take you long, did it?'

'It looks bad. I didn't want Roy to think I'd run straight into someone else's arms.'

'But you did run straight into someone else's arms. Poor Roy,' said Jean, looking down.

'Oh stop it, you! I feel bad enough!'

'What about Roy? Has he not seen anyone yet?'

'I don't know. Roy's a mystery, and that's okay. He can live his own life.'

'I always liked Roy,' said Jean wistfully. She was strolling with her head in the air and her eyes set in the distance.

'You barely knew him,' Annie replied.

'He was always good to Robert. And he was so...I don't know...foreign. I got Harry from the Shankill who's in prison for murder and you got Roy, the sexy Dutchman who set you free.'

'Set me free? I'm not sure I'd say—'

'Annie, what were you doing here all these years when you could have been living in a nice house in Holland? Why could you not have made things work with Roy?'

'I don't know. I think I hated him so much at one stage that there was no going back.'

Annie didn't mention the encounter with Shaun that had played its part in the failure to rebuild her relationship with Roy, or the fact that Jean had acted as an intermediary between two people who had been sent off together on the same train. Self-preservation had condemned the beginnings of the relationship to their own solitary confinement and Annie couldn't dredge up the guilt again to divulge the truth about when she had fallen in love with Shaun.

'Well, Little Miss Secretive, what are you going to do with this big Honky Tonk Man?'

'I don't know. He's trying to convince me to move there and I think he might be getting impatient.'

'No wonder.'

'I know but the boys have another year and a half at school. James is going to do an apprenticeship with his dad, so he'll stay in Holland, and before I came here, Andrew asked me about doing a degree in America.'

'That's convenient.'

'I know. I was surprised! I think he regrets that he didn't get to do the whole Project Children thing.'

'You'll have to go then.'

Jean's voice and body had quietened.

Annie hooked Jean's arm in hers. 'James is only fifteen. He's still a child. I can't leave him.'

'Child! I don't think so love. That Robert one's more grown up than me. I think he's trying to fill his father's shoes and keep us all in line.'

'He's a good boy, Jean. You should be proud of him.'

Annie caught a shy smile and a blush from Jean and walked on in silence thinking about the possibility of leaving her boys in Holland. She couldn't imagine the profound guilt entailed in that decision despite the small amount of face-to-face time involved in raising her children. A parental taxi service wasn't necessary in a country that jangled with bicycle chains, and both boys earned their own money during holidays at their dad's business. Annie's role as a mother had been reduced to washing clothes, providing a healthy range of microwave meals and fighting the feeling that her work was done.

The remainder of her life revolved around a swivel chair in the Heineken offices from which she communicated with the world. Shaun would send her updates of the day-to-day events of his life, which principally involved an evening and weekend taxi service for his son. Katherine, her eldest sister and only email user in her family in Glenarm, would narrate emails about who was dead or dying, and her customers would acknowledge their orders and send greetings from all across Ireland.

Annie would return home to an empty apartment and the realisation that her life was conducted across cyberspace and that she could literally live anywhere without making a difference to anyone but herself.

Annie observed the circulation of people in the city centre after crossing the West link. Roads that were reserved for buses and cars were filled with people converging from every artery.

Jean led Annie right on Royal Avenue towards Donegal Place, a defiant line of architecture that had retained its grace of character despite the scars of bombs. Thousands of feet were softly teeming along the tarmac, light with a sense of disorientation in a space usually defined by barricades, buses and the steady gait of shoppers. Annie assumed the pace of the people as they walked towards the green dome of the city hall.

This was not a ceremony to illuminate Christmas lights, Annie realised. Nor was it a vast welcome committee for a famous American visitor. This was the biggest cry for peace that Belfast had ever made, and Annie wondered if Mr Clinton knew that he was travelling towards the scene of a resuscitation that had already taken place.

She looked back when she reached a towering security line and realised that the same number of people were behind her, all flowing like blood towards the heart of the city.

'Mam, please come this way,' a monumental, black security guard said to Annie.

Jean's bewildered blue eyes were lit up in veneration and Annie struggled to contain a smile.

'Do you have a purse, Ma'am?' the man said to Jean.

Annie stood back and enjoyed the wonder on her friend's face. The security guard was part of an American blockade of men who looked as foreign in Belfast as the giant jeeps lined up behind them.

'No, sir,' said Jean in an American accent. 'You're very welcome in Belfast,' she added.

'Thank you, Ma'am, and ya'll have a good day.'

Jean walked away in slow motion, the American voice trailing across the dusky sky. 'God Bless America!' she said, much to the amusement of the students who were walking beside her.

Expectant eyes were revealed as people assimilated close to strangers, and it was hard to unravel how everyone came to be so tightly approximated in what was silent and unsaid.

It had been more than a year since the paramilitaries in Northern Ireland had laid down their arms, but Annie had been so removed from it all, that she couldn't quite feel the pulse of the people. Since the IRA ceasefire, there had been a sense of foreboding that rotated like the sound of the helicopters whirling overhead, but a micro-nation was gathering around the city hall of Belfast, a nation that was intimately engaged with an American President and distant from the two countries that had made their claim on the city.

Annie hadn't been prepared to believe that weapons could ever be silenced until they were removed from their masters, but as her eyes circled the thousands of faces on a cool November afternoon, she started to believe in something. That it might be over, that the promise of the end was near, was as palpable as it was imaginary.

Young people were laughing as they swaddled together in the diminishing light. Among them were secondary school pupils who had finished school for the day, and a vast number of university students clad in denim jackets and jeans. Two of them were attached to Jean, chatting animatedly as they all settled on a spot about fifty yards from the stage.

Annie heard the tail end of a Jean's discourse with the girls, 'My friend here answered John Major.'

She nudged Annie. 'Annie, love, these are my friends from Queen's University and they both voted for Clinton.'

'Did they indeed?' laughed Annie.

The girls were giggling and Jean, who was in a black leather biker jacket zipped up to the neck, could easily have passed for the same age as their new companions. The students' voices were confident as they chatted and laughed. They belonged here among all the young people of a new Belfast.

Annie danced to keep warm, swaying with Jean and the students as Van Morrison's vaporous voice fell on a microphone like dewy rain.

The physical touch of the people around her, the connection of their voices and the anticipation of something more than a President's visit, held everyone together until cheers and whistles ascended and Clinton's floodlit face smiled sincerely from a giant screen. Annie's throat filled with emotion when the crowd that had been so peaceful erupted jubilantly. She hooked arms with the man beside her just as Jean had hooked arms with the students, and she became part of a long line of strangers watching a river of magic cascade through tens of thousands of tear-stained eyes.

Annie was enraptured by a Belfast she had never known. She watched the President's lips smile through the words he had prepared. The words didn't matter, although Annie listened to his hopes for the future as he had perhaps listened to her own over a year ago in the Kennedy Centre.

The crowd was chanting numbers, the countdown to turn on lights on a tree that had been brought from Nashville in Tennessee, the state in which Annie's ancestors had found a home, and all the connections across the Atlantic, all the Irelands and all the religions moved together in a white flood of electric light that blared across the startled faces of tens of thousands of people. Annie adjusted her eyes. The lights of the Christmas tree twinkled in yellow stimes and the crowd heralded American flags and cheered.

'I pledge you America's support,' the President said, the President who was a stranger and a friend.

The speeches ended and the crowd was in introspective motion, Annie and Jean swinging arms with the students to the sha la la of Van Morrison soul-instilled voice.

'Who would you chose?' laughed Jean as they turned back to take one last look as a micro-nation unfurled.

'Clinton,' Annie replied with a smile. 'I'd pledge my undying love to Clinton.'

***

Harry was at the washstand stooping down to the mirror. A pale, drawn face reflected back. It was a last look at his own reflection before his trial, a farewell to the man that had been made in the Crumlin Road Goal.

He had always had colour in his face before he came to prison, and he recalled being conscious of the weight gained around his neck as he had approached middle age. Vanity had frequently compelled him to think about his own appearance when he was trying to impress Linda.

After two years in prison, the weight had gone. Harry hadn't been so toned and thin since the day he had got married in the fitted, tan suit that Jean had chosen. He had mastered youth in his body, but the listlessness of prison life had begun to drag at his eye-lids and draw the blood from his face. He was certain to spend at least another eight years behind bars, and he wondered what face would be looking back at him at the age of fifty.

He saw Brian in the reflection of the mirror. He was lying on his side on the top bunk, his legs curled up towards his chin. He was having a bad day. Harry could tell the good days from the bad by the position of his body. Brian would lie flat with his hands underneath his head when his spirit was awake. Today, his spirit was dead because Harry would be leaving.

The news the night before had been all about the commotion of the presidential visit. An hour of solid reporting on his journey across the province had been watched by weary eyes. The President had turned on the Christmas lights in a spectacle that couldn't have been more removed from the reality of the stone, cold despair that rattled through the bars of the Crumlin Road Gaol.

Clinton had given the prisoners gold, and they had seen it glimmer from the television screen before drifting back to their cells like vagabonds searching for the first crop after a famine.

Brian was a vagabond who had given up searching for food. Harry had been assigned to a cell with a man who believed in nothing, his own self-worth long ago condemned to the gallows. When news had arrived about the ceasefires a year before, the cheers and the clanging of tin and metal hadn't stirred the emotions of Brian Hamilton. He had been silent, and the blankness on his face had engineered a shift in Harry as he realised that he was travelling on the same desolate road. Harry had already started to question how he would survive the seemingly interminable pain of coming face to face with his own person day after day, but it was Brian's eyes that had made him change his own destination.

Brian had been a drinker, and when he was curled up in a ball sweating and crying, Harry knew what medication was required to soothe his mind. He was a sick man, and no different to those men without political persuasion who had joined paramilitaries to find a sense of belonging from the isolation of their minds.

One day Brian would talk in full sentences, narrating stories of his childhood on the streets of the Shankill. The next, his eyes would stop. Harry would watch him slip away, and he would track his breathing and his movements in the bed above him and pray that God would take care of Brian.

Harry had started to pray. He had started to pray the first time he had seen the light leave Brian's eyes, and he had started to pray because he knew that he could not help his fellow man.

He didn't think about whether it was a Christian God or the God of any other religion. He prayed because prayer was cutting a tunnel from his prison to the world outside.

He couldn't keep his children safe every night from the narrow bunk bed where he had learned to find rest, but he could pray for them from a place of peaceful solitude. He had found the spiritual part of himself that had lain dormant on the outside, and coming face to face with his own person became easier the more he talked to God.

Harry prayed for Linda because he was reminded of the oscillation of Linda's eyes each time he looked at Brian.

Brian had killed the man who had raped his girlfriend, and so, he could not claim the crime he had committed. He had been drunk and motivated by blazing instincts. Manslaughter would be his plea, and, as Harry watched life leave Brian's eyes, he wondered if Brian would live long enough to serve the sentence.

Harry buttoned up his shirt and took one last look back at the man who was about to walk underneath a tunnel leading from a prison to a courthouse and plead his guilt for the conscious act of murder, the act that unlocked the cataclysmic meeting of the physical and spiritual that had occurred when he had followed his instincts with Linda.

He knew that if his days were numbered, he would have no regrets about Linda. He would be sorry for the pain he had caused Jean and his children, but he was glad that he had experienced the fall that had brought him face to face with his own person. Harry was certain that God would give him a long life and a long sentence for the crime of the lucidity of his actions with Shauny.

***

Only two weeks had passed since the President's visit, but the memory of it was beginning to splinter into sights and sounds. Jean could still hear the songs and she could see the lights and feel the buoyancy of eighty thousand people dancing, but she could not touch the magic among the tenacious shoppers and impatient buses in Donegall Place on a cool Monday morning. Clinton's visit had become a lost diamond in a ring that had been betrothed to a people starved of peace, and Jean was the first to notice the missing stone on the day that Harry had been sentenced for murder.

Harry had been moved to Maghaberry prison, twenty miles from home. There was nothing unexpected about the sentence, but as Jean stood in a line for a bus, she counted eight more years of bus journeys and promised herself that she would learn to drive.

Her husband would be released in December 2003, a faraway date that Jean could not reconcile in her imagination.

Hannah's lips had quivered when she'd said, 'Daddy will be home when I'm eighteen.'

The conversation with Shelley had been surprisingly painless. Shelley had held up her hands and conducted a vision of how life would be from now on, with plans to make her daddy a pillowcase with their names sewn onto it, plans to make diaries of all the things they were doing in Belfast, endless plans to give their father some comfort in his distance from home.

Shelley's empathetic fear centred on the notion that her daddy was about to fall off the edge of the world, a world that was defined in her eight year-old eyes by long rows of terraced houses bordered by distant hills, and not by the flat, wet fields and the cows and the hedgerows that had been slick with dark rain on the first journey they had taken with their uncle Sammy to Maghaberry prison.

It was Robert who had been more distressed by the verdict than anyone. He had said nothing, but his hands had made their own protest on the doors he banged and on the stairs upon which his feet were heavy. He would be a man in his own right by 2003, by the time his father had served a ten year sentence, and Robert had realised that his chances of a childhood with his father were over.

Jean looked at a line of people awaiting the bus to Maghaberry prison. A well-dressed elderly man with a leathery face stood to her right, purposefully holding onto a wheelchair where a woman was seated, her face drooped on the left side.

Jean smiled at the man as she pondered why he might be travelling on a prison bus. Was there a son in Maghaberry prison, a son whose crime had stopped the blood flowing to his mother's brain, a mother whose head was tipped forward and whose eyes were climbing up towards Jean?

Jean leaned over and addressed the woman. 'Are you going to Maghaberry?'

'Yes,' the man replied, after a pause. 'Nell's going to see her son, our son.'

The woman's eyes were animated and Jean knew that she was trying to communicate back.

Jean knelt down. 'It's my first time,' she said. 'Does the bus have heating?'

'Oh ay,' replied the man, giving his wife the chance to respond with her eyes. 'The heat would kill you.'

'I'm off to see my husband. He's just moved from the Crum.'

Nell's eyelid declined over the pupil of the right side of her face, the side that had not been touched by the stroke that must have dragged the left side down.

'Och, don't you worry about me,' said Jean. 'The Crum made my blood run cold. I like Maghaberry. It's nicer. Do you not think?'

Nell's eyes didn't change expression. Jean held out her hand, squeezed Nell's and stood up to find that that a lady with long, mauve, woollen coat and a beady head wrapped in a paisley-patterned scarf had joined the queue. She had been listening closely to the conversation and had flinched when Jean had looked into her eyes. Her stare was fixed on the shop on a spot on the opposite side of the street, her lightly wrinkled face, frail and dignified.

'Excuse me,' said Jean. 'I think I know you from somewhere.'

The woman's eyelids widened to Jean and then narrowed back to the spot she had rehearsed.

'I'm Jean,' she continued. 'Are you from the Shankill?'

The woman's body flinched again and a cold wind gusted up Jean's back.

She shivered as she realised that the women beside her was the mother of Johnny Sharpe.

Jean gulped back air and looked back at the wheelchair where Nell's husband's smiling eyes greeted her like a hug. She breathed in deeply and spoke in measured words.

'You're Johnny Sharpe's mother. Kathleen, isn't it?' Jean asked, the warmth of the couple to her left sustaining her against the cold wind to her right. The woman didn't answer, but her nod alerted Jean to the movement of people towards the bus that had arrived.

She busied herself helping Nell, but the blood pumped around her body, mercilessly filling her with dread.

She took a seat near the front of the bus on the opposite side of the aisle from Nell.

'Is it okay if I sit here?'

Jean was startled to hear Kathleen Sharpe's voice. She nodded and looked around. There were rows of empty seats behind her. Jean clasped her hands as the bus sped through the city, the droning heat stifling her neck. She unzipped her leather jacket.

'I'm not Kathleen,' the woman said once the background noise of the engine on the motorway drowned out the sound. 'I'm Deirdre.'

Deirdre Sharpe.

Jean could see the name printed in black and white beside a coloured image of Northern Lights.

First son of eleven.

Jean clutched her bag. She looked out the window and the green fields of County Antrim blurred as an image of Robert filtered by.

First son of Jean Adams. She closed her eyes.

'I'm sorry,' Jean said, her voice weak.

'Your husband already wrote to me.'

Jean turned to Deirdre and blinked away the half-formed tears.

'Harry?'

'Yes. He said he was sorry. He said he knew what he was doing and that he was sorry.'

Jean swallowed.

'It's better in Maghaberry,' Deirdre said.

Jean nodded and sniffed back the overwhelming shame that was culling her breath. She looked at Nell. Her husband was cradling his arms around her as her head lolled with the sway of the bus.

'Who are you going to see?' Asked Jean.

Deirdre removed the prison pass from her bag. The name at the top of the pass was James Sharpe. Jean leaned in closer. The name of the visitor was Kathleen Sharpe. She looked up.

'I'm going to see my nephew,' Deirdre whispered.

There was silence. Jean didn't know what to say.

'Have you seen him before?' she asked finally.

'Once a month. I go to see his brother in the Maze once a month too.'

Jean's eyes questioned Deirdre and her soft voice explained. 'Kathleen is my twin, and our families haven't been able to see each other for nearly twenty-five years. We had threats in the early days. And we saw what happened to the girls who were accused of being informants. It was easier to split the two families apart to protect the girls.'

Deirdre's words felt like a confession, and Jean was overwhelmed by the trust the woman was vesting in the wife of the man who had murdered her son.

The sweat poured down Jean's back. She removed her coat and the words were there again. First son eleven. Son of Deirdre and Arthur Sharpe. And a dramatic skyline of green and blue light.

'Kathleen is my twin. We've worn the same clothes every day since we were born.'

Jean concentrated. Deirdre was trying to tell her something.

'Even when we don't see each other. It just happens.'

She wondered if the old lady had lost her train of thought, but her sincerity was rich and warm and Jean began to understand. The prison pass.

'She has a coat like this, and a scarf like this one too. We bought them in the sales years ago. We always buy two of everything.'

Jean sucked back tears as perspiration gushed from her glands. She had cried for herself and for her children many times, and she had often thought about Deirdre with compassion. Now she was crying salty tears for the mother of Shaun Sharpe and they were warm and overflowing.

Shaun's family hadn't attended Harry's trial. It was an undramatic trial with an admission of guilt and a confirmation of regret and it was over as quickly as it had begun. Now Jean was in a courtroom and Shauny Sharpe's mother was touching her hand.

Deirdre rummaged in her bag.

'Here, love, I don't have any water with me. Take a wee sweet.'

Jean unwrapped the plastic covering of a brandy ball with trembling hands. She put her head back on the seat and breathed deeply.

'Do you see your sister?' Jean asked, once she had sucked the sweet to a thin line of glucose. She was curious about the two families who lived on opposite sides of a peaceline.

'Every day.'

'Every day?' repeated Jean, surprised.

'We find our own place of peace,' replied Deirdre. 'We drink tea and exchange prison passes. There are four boys in prison. The girls all stayed out of trouble.'

That's lovely, Jean wanted to say, but she couldn't dissect her mind from the shame.

'We're getting too old for it.'

'For what?' Jean asked, lost in her own thoughts.

'For hiding. It feels colder when you get to my age.'

Jean observed that Deirdre was still clad in her coat and scarf with no obvious indication that the suffocating heat of the bus had affected her.

'Our children were raised as brothers and sisters before the Troubles. We were pregnant at the same time every year for eight years. I kept going until eleven.'

Jean nodded. She wanted to hear what Deirdre had to say. She wanted to hear how this woman had overcome the suffering of a severed family, but her mind was focused on the heartache of a mother who had lost her first son. Was Deirdre sitting beside Jean because she had forgiven the assailant, or did she merely pity his wife?

Jean looked at the leather handbag the woman was holding. She used to see bags like that all over the Shankill when she was first married. It was fabricated in thick brown leather with a black stem stitch and strong brass buckle. It belonged in the 1970s, but it looked as good as new.

'I have a few of these,' Deirdre explained as her eyes followed Jean's to the buckle of her bag.

'It's nice,' said Jean, relieved to be in a safe conversation, able to form words without shame.

'My son made it for me. He was in the Maze in the seventies. The women on the prison bus used to joke about the bags. They used to say that if there was ever peace, they'd buy themselves a designer handbag. Every Christmas and birthday, we all got the same hand-made bags and purses from our sons and husbands.'

Jean laughed. Deirdre had led her back to a safe haven.

'When there's peace, I'm going to wear a flower in my hair and have a picnic in a park,' said Jean. 'I promised a man I'd do that once.'

Deirdre smiled. 'I've had a picnic in a park every day for twenty four years. I might have a day off.'

'Is that where you meet her? In a park?'

'Kind of,' Deirdre replied, her eyes and lips smiling.

A SAIL POINTED TO HOPE

The whisky was still on Shaun's breath as he poured his coffee and settled at the kitchen table with his newspaper, his mind anaesthetised from another Friday night of needless drinking. He looked down. Words were dancing on the front page of the newspaper, swirling and taunting at his lapsed concentration until his eyes adjusted and focused on a headline that was as black and cold as the dawn.

IRA return to terror

Shaun stared at the words and tried to make sense of them. The bomb had happened the day before. He checked the date of the paper, 10 February 1996, exactly one month after Annie's visit was cancelled. He recollected the lines of Annie's email about the Clinton visit before Christmas, words that had skipped from the screen in naive excitement.

He scanned the first paragraph and read on.

The bomb struck at the heart of the peace process when the 17 month IRA ceasefire came to a bloody end. Prime Minister John Major attacked the bombing as an 'appalling outrage', while Ulster unionists demonstrated their disgust at this stain on the IRA truce. More than 100 people have been injured in the attack in East London where a six storey building at the recently regenerated Docklands area collapsed. One man has been confirmed dead, another missing. Washington has pledged its continuation of negotiations and Mr Clinton has not broken off contact with Gerry Adams.

Gazing at the picture of London, Shaun marvelled at how a bomb could reduce a finished building to threads, a building that was draped in filaments dangling loosely in several shades of grey, only a murky hint of sepia hinting that it was a coloured photo, and he marvelled at the wrath of terrorists who had plunged a country into darkness once again.

He pictured Annie standing with two children underneath a pile of scattered grey rubble, Robert in a bright green football shirt, Annie in her purple scarf, and Hannah in the red velvet dress in the family portrait, and he pressed his head to quell the alcohol cutting through his temples. His vision was distorted. His vision was of Toby holding his mother's hand in the rubble.

Shaun put down the paper as whisky tears dripped from his eyes. He had been drinking until the early hours of the morning. He had been drinking since the January day when Annie's flight had been grounded in Amsterdam because of a blizzard in D.C. Four weeks of temperamental weather had followed, and Annie hadn't been able to fit another flight around her work commitments. It would be Easter before they would see each other.

Shaun thought about Sarah. She had been there every day despite the career in law that often kept her at the office when she wanted to be with her husband and her son. She had been his wife and his friend and Annie's friendship was becoming too distant, dragging at his patience throughout another long winter of emails and phone calls. She wasn't truly present in his life. She was in the Netherlands, taking care of her children, taking care of Roy, and Shaun had done everything he could to bring Annie to America.

He had asked her to bring James and Andrew to

Washington D.C., but the ocean had torn her in two. Five long months had passed since he had held her, and the ceaseless blizzards and floods felt like a warning, a plague upon his claim on another man's wife.

How close was Annie to Roy? The question tormented Shaun night after night. Annie would casually mention in passing that she had had Sunday dinner with him, or that he had visited her flat to see them mid-week, and the jealousy was blazing a fire through Shaun's sense of reason.

Love is patient. Love is kind.

Love. Shaun could feel it each time he spoke to Annie, but he couldn't feel it now. He couldn't feel it because he was irritated and angry.

He closed the paper and stood up. He walked to the dresser where the wedding photo stood. He ran his hand across the veil. He closed his eyes and tried to connect with the man who once shared his problems with God, but he felt nothing. He didn't believe in anything, his faith tattered into threads dangling from a bombed edifice of his religion.

How much longer did he have to wait? James and Andrew both had exams that would end in June 1997, another spring, another summer, another autumn, another winter, another spring.

Shaun couldn't do it. He couldn't wait that long. And he couldn't ask a woman to choose between a man and her sons.

He placed the photograph back on the dresser, walked back to the living room and poured another glass of whisky.

***

To: Shaun Kelly
From: Annie Steen
Subject: Where are you?
Date: 16 February 1996

Dear Shaun

I tried calling you last night. I haven't heard from you for almost a week. Is everything okay? Please reply to this email.

Love
Annie

***

A loose strand of hair swathed its way from her swan-like neck into a river of brown silk on the white pillow. Shaun lay on his side, his eyes roaming over a fine, pale shoulder to a glittering white gown. It was strewn across the chair beside the bed, and it was evidence of a hurried night, as two people, whose bodies had already lived out their fleshly desires, met in a melee of whisky and the veneration of skin. Shaun closed his eyes and wished for more time before the morning rays would bring him to reality.

He slowly pieced together the night. Another email from Annie that he couldn't answer, a long walk in freezing temperatures from his office to the Hay-Adams hotel, the heady scent of cigars in the hotel bar, a crystal glass glistening in brown particles of light, the warmth of Glenfiddich single malt on his lips, a vision of white rising through phlegmatic plumes of smoke and the throaty rapture of a voice swirling through the vapor of La Gloria cigars.

The distance between two springs would be too long, and Jessica was there in her white dress, lit up like a celestial invitation, her song calling him in the middle of a long winter. She had been singing for Shaun and the sultry voice was bidding him to keep his eyes on her lips. Her brown eyes had skipped over the microphone and temptation had ascended as Jessica's hands caressed the stand. The bar had emptied and Jessica had walked past Shaun, leaving her room card on the table.

Shaun had been there by the threshold of the hotel room when Jessica had arrived. They had kissed and made love by the door, Jessica's dress hitched up over her hips, Shaun's body still wrapped in the suit he had worn to work. It was a fleeting dance of lust after two hours of supplication.

Morning sliced through the gap in the curtains. Shaun placed his finger on Jessica's spine and moved it gently towards her neck. He kissed her shoulder and awakened her from an even sleep. Closing his mind, pushing back regret, he allowed himself to fall weightlessly again.

He was making love, kissing the back of Jessica's neck and clasping at her firm breast as her body stirred.

'I love you,' he said, as his mind and body merged, but Jessica's body faltered. She removed herself from Shaun's arms and turned to face him.

'Why did you say that?'

Shaun, his head still cast in semi-darkness with need still pumping through his body, remained still, his eyes resting uneasily on Jessica's blushing face.

'Why did you say that?' Jessica repeated and Shaun's mind eclipsed his body as he looked into Jessica's eyes.

'You said you loved me, but you didn't mean it. You can't even look me in the eye.'

Shaun's eyes remained blank, as he tried to disentangle from the night and the whisky.

'I'm sorry,' he said.

'I should never have done this with you.'

Shaun wanted to sit up, but his head was weighty. He remained on his side facing Jessica.

'You know, one of the things I liked about you was that you were a decent man. You didn't drink, you were raising this amazing kid alone and you were a—'

'A widower.'

'I didn't say that. There was something deeper about you, I guess.'

'And now?'

'Now you seem a little emp...You seem a little lost.'

'You mean empty?'

'No, I mean lost. And I know that you don't love me. You don't love me in that way. And I shouldn't be here. I've been dating someone. I made a mistake. You were there in the bar and your eyes were burning my skin. I've been so foolish.'

Jessica sat up and pulled the white cotton sheet across her body. She reached for an overnight bag beside the bed. Shaun was aware of clothes being stretched across limbs, but his eyes were fixed on the white ceiling.

'I'm sorry,' he said gently, not fully grasping his own words, but knowing that their meaning would become clear to him later when the alcohol evaporated from his breath. 'I didn't mean to hurt you.'

'You didn't hurt me. We're two adults who loved each other once and we got a little mixed up.' Jessica was still dressing as she spoke. She turned back to Shaun. 'Is it Annie?'

Shaun sat up.

'I know. I knew.'

'You knew what?' Shaun had had no contact with Jessica and couldn't imagine how she knew about Annie.

'I found a box of letters from Annie.' Jessica held her hands up. 'I promise I wasn't looking for anything. I came across it and I looked inside.'

'You read my personal mail?' Shaun retorted, his voice elevated, his tone unbridled.

Jessica shot up from the bed. 'Don't raise your voice to me!' She flung the bag down with frustration. 'I forgot my shoes,' she muttered as she tied on the high, strappy sandals.

'Wait!' Shaun said, attempting to stand, but swaying as the weight in his head dragged him back down.

Jessica began to fold her dress and then grabbed it, crumpling it into a ball in her bag. She turned to face Shaun. 'I was with you for almost two years and there was always this missing piece. I thought it was Sarah. I thought you still loved your wife, but one day, I saw the box with the letters, and I couldn't help it. I needed to know if there was someone else, and then I began reading this one letter. She said that she was trying to make things work with her husband. She said she'd loved you. And when I asked you about that trip to Ireland, you walked away.'

'Is that why everything went cold?'

'No. It hasn't got anything to do with it. You wanted a

family and I wanted to travel. When I got back from Europe, I went to your church one Sunday, thinking I could surprise you, but your lawyer friend said you were in Ireland. I guessed why you were in Ireland.'

'Jessica, don't go away from here thinking that this meant nothing. I can't explain why it did, but I promise you, it did.'

'It was skin on skin Shaun. You know that. That's all it was. We were impatient and greedy and didn't even take the time to remove our clothes.'

Shaun lay back, defeated. Jessica was right. The songs were a lust-filled dance of lips and hands moving, and the remainder of the night was greed.

'What's with the drinking? You told me you didn't drink because of your father. What happened?'

Shaun bowed his head.

Jessica lifted her bag. She stood at the door and looked back at the bed. 'Straighten yourself out. You're better than this.'

Shaun held up his eyes to a chink of artificial light from the hall. 'Goodbye,' he said to a door that had already closed.

***

People were delivered to the city centre, tens of thousands of them, stunned, fallen, reborn. The peace rally was illuminated by a February sky that was fresh blue with flitting white clouds, and people were swaddled together without a plan. There was no dancing, no singing, no orchestration. Jean was standing behind the gates of the city hall with a view of Donegall Place, where tens of thousands of hand-crafted white, paper doves floated thoughtfully from the hands of knowing children. Hannah and Shelley held one in each hand.

Jean tipped her head up to the sun and bathed in the breezy quiet. The quiet of the peace rally wasn't as still as a one minute silence after a bugle's call, or as mournful as the descent of a coffin. It was a moving quiet, rocking back and forth, cradled in the nurturing hands of peace.

And Jean needed peace for her son.

Robert had lost his compassion and empathy. Jean knew

that it was normal for a teenage boy, but there was something else, something darker than anger. She had stripped Robert's bed right back to the valance the day after she had put her Christmas decorations away, part of the deep clean she executed throughout her home at the start of every January.

She had lifted the mattress off Robert's bed, hesitating, suddenly aware that she might find something hidden, an adult magazine, perhaps.

She didn't find a magazine. She found a black balaclava.

Jean shuddered despite the warmth of the peaceful flight of white paper doves around her.

She had walked to the fire, where the coal had turned grey. She had poked at it, stirring red coal from the bottom. A flame had arisen and Jean had moved the balaclava around with the poker, shedding tears as the flames clung to the wool. She had buried it in coal and waited. The flames roused and the uniform of paramilitary anonymity slowly burned in Jean's grate.

She didn't mention it to Robert and she couldn't find the courage to talk to Harry.

As she looked across the blanket of people, she closed her eyes and prayed for peace for Robert and peace for his country's future.

***

To: Shaun Kelly
From: Annie Steen
Subject: Call me
Date: 25 February 1996

Dear Shaun

You're not answering my calls and it's breaking my heart. I know that it has been a long time since September, and I'm sorry that life has been on hold. Easter is only weeks away, so please don't lose faith. I'll be with you soon.

I know you want me to bring Andrew and James to America, but I can't do that. I can't do that to Roy.

Let me know if I have done something to hurt you.

I love you,

Annie

***

The head-splitting sound of the dial-up connection pierced Shaun's resolve. He rarely used his home computer, but he needed to check his email. He needed to reply to Annie. He lifted the whisky glass and stared at the fingerprints around the side of the glass, cloudy clues as to how far he had fallen.

I had a river, Harry had said, and Harry was serving time while Shaun still had an ocean.

He swiped the whisky glass from the desk and tossed it at the wall. He sat back down and watched a brown stain grow across the carpet. The glass remained unbroken, his smudged fingerprints visible from the chair.

'Dad, what are you doing?'

Shaun looked up, startled. It was Toby. It was a Sunday morning. It was too early for Toby.

'What are you doing here?'

'You didn't come,' Toby said.

Shaun's mother was standing behind Toby, pain sweeping across her anguished face. She was wearing a smart navy suit and heels, her bobbed hair gleaming silver around her pale face.

'Mom, what are you doing here?'

'We came to see if you were okay. Did you forget?'

Shaun's mom was looking around, her eyes taking in the discarded plates of food and the unwashed dishes in the kitchen. Shaun stood up and blocked her view of the whisky glass by the wall, but a shadow was in his peripheral vision, a shadow of a man who rarely travelled into the city.

His father was walking around, opening curtains. Shaun caught a reflection of dishevelled hair and untamed beard in the patio window. He ran his fingers through his hair.

'Dad, did you forget?' It was Toby. His voice was broken glass, his face sullen.

Shaun concentrated on his own father, who betrayed no emotion. He was in the kitchen and Shaun followed him in pyjamas and bare feet, his body shrinking to that of a teenage boy before the might of a well-groomed father. His father lifted the whisky bottle from the bench. He opened it, turned on the tap and slowly poured its contents into the sink. He walked to the wine rack in the kitchen and checked, returning with a bottle of vodka that had been there for more than ten years. He emptied it, its potent smell filling the kitchen and clinging to Shaun's lungs. He walked to the door and stopped by an upturned frame. He lifted it, looked at it and placed the picture of Sarah on the shelf. The back door was open and a cold draft transported Shaun back thirty years in time.

The dread and the shame were there in his weakening limbs, the shame of a teenage boy who had been caught smoking his father's cigarettes. There were three of them on the jury in their small kitchen back then; his mother with a tender look of sympathy for the retribution that Shaun was about to pay, his sister, Arlene, with her questioning face that lowered Shaun from the pedestal he had occupied in her eyes, and his father, removing his belt, coming towards him. 'I hate you!' Shaun had screamed repeatedly with every muscle and tendon in his body. His mother had turned towards the sink and the belt was buckled as his sister sobbed. Shaun was lifted a foot off the floor by the scruff of the neck. 'Don't ever disrespect your parents,' his father had said with large brown eyes that were dark with disappointment. He had then dropped Shaun and walked out the backdoor, returning later with the usual stench of alcohol on his breath. Shaun had despised his father, the hypocrite who had made him feel like dirt when his own venomous vice had often left his mother crying by the sink.

There was a shattering of glass. His father returned from the garbage and raised his head to indicate to his wife and grandson that they should leave. His father was walking towards him. He placed his hand on Shaun's shoulder and led him to the table. He coughed. 'You're a man, but you're my son. And…' His father's eyes were filled with water. He wiped away a tear. 'I'm here for you, son,' he said.

They each remained unmoving, Shaun's eyes resting on his own shaking hands.

'When you were a boy, I was your hero.'

Shaun pressed his hands tightly. The shaking stopped.

'And then when you were a teenager, you hated me.'

Shaun looked his father in the eye.

'It wasn't me you hated. I know that now. It was the man with the drink. I thought I was something when I was drinking. I took pride in the smiles on the faces as I told stories at the bar. And then I'd come home, and my only son would look at me with hatred in his eyes.'

Shaun rubbed his leg with his hands. The hatred never lasted. That's what he wanted to say, but his voice was suppressed in his throat. He had loved his father every day, the father who had provided for his family and who had worked hard to get his son an education. He had loved that father. It was only at night, when a half drunk would come through the door that hatred would emerge. Shaun's father had never been a whole drunk, splayed out on the sofa singing rebel songs like his brother at family gatherings. He had just enough to throw the weight of his voice around. On Saturdays and Sundays he had been a real father, working Shaun to the bone fixing car engines, mowing the lawn, painting fences. He had loved that father in their backyard in Silver Spring, the one who taught him everything he knew about being a man.

'I'm sorry, son,' his father said. 'I'm sorry for the drinking. I stopped in the end. You need to stop.'

'I know,' Shaun replied, offering his tired eyes to his father.

'Have you been going to work?'

'Yes.'

'Do you drink every night?'

'Yes, a little. And then a lot.'
'And through the day?'
'No. Never.'
'Is it the Irish girl?'
'The Irish girl?'
Shaun had never hidden Annie's existence from his parents, but he had yet to introduce her. She hadn't seemed like a real part of his world until Jessica and his father had mentioned her by name.
'The Protestant,' his father said flatly.
Shaun's back straightened defensively, and then catching the glimmer in his father's eyes, he stopped and smiled.
'My father had the same problem one time with a Protestant girl.'
Shaun's eyes widened. 'Before Mary?'
'Before he met your grandmother, he fell in love with a Protestant girl. Those girls know their own mind, he warned me.'
'They sure do,' smiled Shaun.
'Is she divorced?'
'Not yet, but almost.'
'And did she leave her husband for you?'
'No, I don't think she did.'
'Then stop drinking. Stop punishing yourself for this.'
Shaun saw something in his father's eyes.
'What were you punishing yourself for?' Shaun ventured. He had never discussed his father's drinking with him before.
'I don't know. My father handed me a beer and a cigarette at the age of fourteen, and that was that. I left school and worked and smoked and drank.'
'Did you want to leave high school?'
'No, I didn't. I didn't want to leave school and I didn't want that for my son. I wanted you to be your own man, and you've made me mighty proud. I never imagined my son would be a professor of history.'
Shaun smiled and ignored the ringing telephone.
'We want to meet the Irish girl.'
'The Protestant?' smiled Shaun.

'We can work on that.'

'You do realise your own ancestors were Protestant?'

'Your great grandmother was saved,' his father said, mimicking a Donegal accent.

Shaun laughed. His great grandfather had married a Protestant girl from Donegal, a family secret that was retold each time the New York family assembled for weddings and funerals.

'Arlene is pretty cut up that you missed the Christening.'

The Christening. Shaun had forgotten his nephew's christening. His mother was coming towards the kitchen door.

'Shaun Kelly and Shaun Kelly, if you've finished, could we get this show on the road? There are thirty people sitting around waiting for us before they eat.'

'I don't feel much like eating,' said Shaun. 'You guys go ahead and I'll meet you for coffee after lunch. There's somewhere I need to go.'

Shaun squeezed his mother's hand. 'Sorry, Mom,' he said.

He laid his hand on Toby's shoulder as he passed through the hallway to take a shower. Sorry, Toby,' he said. 'I'm gonna fix everything, I promise.'

Toby's face remained sullen, his shoulders stooped, and Shaun understood his own father for the first time.

***

Annie stood on the bridge by the Beestenmarkt, a wide market square bustling with the anonymity of people and bicycles. There was the windmill, the flea market and the pleasure boats on the canal draped in patriotic, red, white and blue flags. People were assembled on a frosty Sunday afternoon in their padded jackets, sipping their coffee and talking to friends on the terraces of cafes. The same scene in Northern Ireland was unimaginable, a country where life was lived indoors and at a distance from the damp.

She looked back at the windmill and recalled her first visit to Leiden with Roy. He had stood on the same bridge and pointed to the position of the static sails on De Valk windmill.

They had been upright, the latticed white wood of the four blades spread out like a compass, pointing north, south, east and west. Custom had it that the sail moved anti-clockwise according to life's cycle of birth, marriage and death. Today it was titled close to the upright position. The windmill was pointing to joy for a birth, a marriage, or a celebration. Roy was outside the Pannenkoekenhuis. Annie waved and walked across the square to him.

'Why's the sail on De Valk windmill tilted to joy?'

'I don't know. Maybe you have some good news for me.'

Annie looked away. 'Let's go inside.'

She was staring at the menu when Roy spoke. 'Why do you always look at the menu for so long when you're going to have appel en spek.'

'Why do you mind so much?'

'Because it's what you do every time! You spend half an hour reading the menu, no matter where you go, and then you order the same thing as always. Back at home it was always chicken and champ.'

'Well I might have something different today.'

'You always say that!' exclaimed Roy.

'And does it bother you?

'Ay! It would drive a man insane!'

'Well, it's a good thing we couldn't afford to eat out much at home or we'd never have lasted as long as we did.'

Roy's face was solemn. 'Sorry,' he said. 'It's hard to break old habits.'

The waiter was beside them. Annie looked at Roy and then back to the menu. Roy rolled his eyes and placed his order in Dutch. Annie cleared her throat and spoke in clear English. 'I'd like the apple and bacon one please.' She chewed on a smile and waited for Roy's reaction.

'Annie, you're a pain in the ass.'

'Oh am I now?'

'Yes you are.'

'You're a misunderstood plant in that case,' she laughed.

'What?' Roy's brow was folded in confusion.

'Isn't that what you said about the weeds in our garden?'

Roy pushed back his chair and laughed.

Annie occupied him with small talk about the boys until two gigantic Delft platters arrived. She thought of something and looked up.

'It hasn't escaped me that since we moved to Holland, your garden is perfection!'

'You're right. And I'm busier than ever. Sorry for not taking better care of the garden.'

'Don't be silly. I'm not here to go over old ground, but I need to talk to you.'

'If there's someone else, it's okay.'

'What made you say that?'

'Well, why else would you be buying me pancakes?'

Annie blushed. She wished she'd sent Roy a long text instead.

'Who's the lucky fella so I can warn him not to chide you about your restaurant habits?'

'Shaun.'

Roy sought clarification with his eyebrows.

'Shaun from America.'

'Shaun?' Roy set down his knife. Annie watched and was surprised to see a flicker of disappointment on Roy's face.

'Did you know?'

'I had no idea.' Roy's head remained bowed as he slowly picked over his food with a fork.

'He wants me to move to America.'

Roy wasn't listening. Annie watched as he calculated something with his eyes hitched to the left.

'Is that why you went there on holiday? You should have said.'

'I didn't know if it was going to work out,' she replied. 'Anyway, I don't know what to do. The boys are here.'

Roy continued to prod at a piece of bacon, his demeanour crestfallen.

'Are you alright?' Annie asked.

'Yes. I'm fine. Did you meet him in America?'

'Sure you know that I went there twice last year.'

'No, I mean, did you meet him there the first time?'

Annie hesitated. 'Roy, is there something wrong?'

'You wrote a letter to Shaun after the Shankill bomb. I remember that.'

'Yes,' Annie said, her neck reddening. 'I did.'

Roy cleared his voice and looked up. 'I met someone.'

Annie breathed deeply, her face flooding with the heat of relief, her eyes smarting with guilt. She nodded, unable to speak.

'Just recently,' he said, sitting upright. 'Her name is Saskia.'

'Saskia,' smiled Annie, blinking to soothe her eyes.

Roy's body was more confident as he took another bite of his food.

Annie began to cut through the buttery pancake, her mind as static as a sail of a windmill pointing North. She ate in silence thinking about a letter she had written before her husband's eyes. She had been trying to prove that she and Shaun were merely friends and that she could openly communicate with him. The result was a look of heart-ache on Roy's face that reassured Annie that she should never offload her guilt about Shaun. It was a burden she would carry alone.

'Annie, be careful. You don't know this fella.'

'Shaun?'

'Yes.'

'Did we ever know each other?'

'Yes, we did. We grew up together and it was safe.'

Annie's head was still bowed. Roy's advice was incongruous with the fact that she had felt perpetually lost in her marriage. Although Shaun was far away, and she risked everything by going to America, she felt sure of her path with him. At least, she had convinced herself that she felt sure of her path with him until the recent unexplained absence of calls and emails.

'The boys will be okay here.' Roy said with sincere and sober eyes.

'What about Saskia?'

Roy smiled and shrugged. 'She's nice, but we're a quare bit away from tilting any windmills for joy. It's early days.'

'Maybe the windmill is just shy of joy,' Annie smiled. Maybe it's a sail titled to hope.'

LIFE IN SACRAMENTS

The familiar sight of evergreen trees around Chevy Chase circle tempered the heart-breaking call that Shaun had made to Annie.

'I slept with another woman,' were the words that had widened the ocean between them, and Annie's silent response brought Shaun ever closer to the realisation that she was on the wrong side of the Atlantic. He had carefully explained the drinking, the shame as his father had poured the vodka down the sink, and the deep regret when he realised that he might lose Annie, and when Annie had finally spoken, she simply said, 'It turns out that I don't know you, after all.'

Shaun had offered to fly to Holland the following weekend, but she had swiftly said no. Then, after a moment, she had agreed to book a flight to Washington, D.C., and that was the hope that Shaun clung to as he drove through the gates of the church.

The Shrine of the most Blessed Sacrament church hugged a corner of Western Avenue like an inglenook of dusty pink stone kindling the north-west of Washington D.C. It had been Sarah's church, and walking through its gates, Shaun could plot the cycle of Sarah's life in sacraments.

There was a baptism in a white gown depicted in the black and white photograph on her mother's piano only yards away from the church. There was a first confession, and Shaun found it hard to imagine Sarah accumulating any sin to confess at such a young age. She had led a charmed childhood, the cherished daughter of a couple who had begun a family late in life. A first communion followed, a blessed sacrament, when a young girl of seven had sipped the blood of Christ and consumed the body of Christ, narrated in another photograph with another white dress lit up against green trees in the church yard.

A confirmation was next, a deepening of the faith that Sarah had inherited and practised with the axiom that it was safer to believe in something than nothing at all. 'Just in case,' she had once observed with a smile when they were dating.

Just in case she was dead and gone before her family was complete, before she'd given birth to the little girl she had openly desired.

It was Shaun who had pulled back a veil on a face that was fine, pale and determined during the sacrament of Holy matrimony. He had held Sarah's hand with pride in his fingertips as her white dress swept along the stone flags of the church underneath a starry green sky of golden fleur de lis.

The anointing of the sick was the last sacrament before Sarah had returned to the church in a coffin lined with white satin.

She had worn each sacrament well.

And Shaun was there under a vaulted ceiling of pale green with fleur de lis speckled like stars on a dusky sky. He was en route to a confession, but he had chosen not to hide behind the confines of the confessional booth. He was facing the world as much as he was reconciling himself to God, and his cheeks flushed with shame when the nostalgia of his past and the reality of his present collided.

There was a ritual he'd once followed before a confession. He would gather his thoughts, the examination of conscience, but Shaun had been trapped in his own mind examining his conscience for months. He had lost a winter in whisky and thinking and his conscience remained awash with the birling, golden liquid that had cleansed him from loneliness. He had numbed a craving for physical touch with a drink that had stirred up feelings of lust and sent him into Jessica's arms.

A clack of footsteps struck the ground in even paces as Father Marshall walked towards Shaun. He was dressed in a white habit from the mid-afternoon mass and his arms flared as he shook Shaun's right hand. He spoke slowly and sincerely. 'Welcome back. I'm glad to see you.'

'Thank you for your time at such short notice,' said Shaun, following the priest to his office.

'What's troubling you?'

Shaun began, 'It's been a long time since my last confession, and I don't know where to begin.'

'Take your time.'

'I've been drinking.' Shaun looked up, knowing that he'd confessed nothing at all.

He waited, pressing his heels into the carpet. He cleared his throat and allowed the words to form of their own accord. 'I've been having a relationship with a woman who is separated but still legally married, and I'm supposed to be the kind of guy who sets an example to the students in the college. I feel like a fraud every single day because I don't have any faith in anything at all.'

Shaun told the story about Annie and Father Marshall held his hands together and closed his eyes, assuming the stance of a priest listening in a confessional.

'Annie has two children. They're fifteen and seventeen, so she can't move here.'

'And you want her to move here?'

'Yes, it's the only thing I want.'

'The only thing?'

'The only thing with Annie.'

'Does Annie want to move to America?'

'She's in the Netherlands with her sons and her ex-husband and she said she can move here in a year and a half. I've been waiting for a long time already.'

'How long have you been waiting?'

'A year and a half, I guess, but it feels like a life-time. The problem is that there's no certainty in the future, and I don't have the patience to wait.'

'When did you start drinking?'

'I don't remember.' Shaun looked up to the pale winter sky through the window. 'It was a nightcap to begin with. Lately, it's gotten out of control and I slept with someone else.'

Father Marshall's eyes betrayed his curiosity.

'It was Friday night. She's my ex-girlfriend.'

'How do you feel about your ex-girlfriend?'

Shaun's body tensed. 'It was a mistake for both of us. I'd been drinking for hours and I got mixed up. I know I hurt Jessica and I know that Annie will be devastated, and I keep thinking about Sarah and what she would think of the whole mess, and I doubt Sarah would ever have married the man that I've become.'

Shaun was speaking to someone who knew Sarah and her family well. Father Marshall had been a young priest when he had married Shaun and Sarah. His black hair was now grey around the sides, reflections of all the sacraments that had passed him by. He blinked in thought before responding, 'How did you feel about Annie when she was married?'

Shaun's body pulsed with a conflicting mix of anger and passion. 'I fell in love with her.'

'I see. Did she love you?'

'Yes. Annie was honest and admitted it early on in a letter. I denied it to myself.'

'Did you act on it?'

'No, we didn't kiss. We didn't sleep together. We had this incredible night and then we were in different countries. If there hadn't been an ocean…' Shaun pictured Harry's watery blue eyes and a river with a bridge. 'I wrote the first letter.' Shaun said, recalling a confession he had already made.

'And you fell in love through the letters?'

'Yes, I think so. It's the only explanation, but then I don't know. That first night when we met in Ireland, Annie reached up to kiss me and I stopped and I don't know why. Something held me back.'

'Perhaps God set the ocean between you.'

Words from Father Marshall flowed as Shaun's body

restored itself. He was telling Shaun to talk to God and Shaun's eyes fell on the branches of wintry trees outside, trees that were twisted in the white sky like the gnarled knots of the faerie tree he had once seen in Ireland.

'Annie removed my dime from a good luck tree.' he said, his eyes still set on the tree. 'She said I had something greater on my side.'

'I think Annie understands you well. You have been on a journey and you still have some faith because you have found your way back home to this church, to your family. Your students will learn from no better man than one whose salvation flows as his faith strengthens in the face of doubt. With the grace of God, your journey will continue.'

Father Marshall closed his hands in prayer. Shaun followed, recalling the young boy who had talked to God when his father was throwing the weight of his drunken voice around his home. 'My God, I am sorry for my sins with all my heart,' he had often said to the night sky through his bedroom window, an act of contrition from a boy who had committed the mortal sin of hatred for his father, a sin that was merely a passion for a man who didn't show him the love that he craved.

***

Annie didn't want to talk about what had happened. Before she had put the phone down, she already knew that she had forgiven Shaun, and on the long flight to Dulles Airport, a calm had settled around her in the blissful skies as she shut out everything that was wrong. She knew she should feel angry, cheated and upset, but she didn't. Six years had passed since the night she had held Shaun's hand at the castle, and she wasn't prepared to give another year of her life to waiting and wondering. She no longer had time.

'We can start afresh,' Annie said after she had taken a shower.

She was seated at the kitchen table with Shaun, overlooking a leafy patio and long garden with a covered swimming pool. She lifted Shaun's hand to her face and tried to lead him away from the kitchen, but he resisted and Annie experienced that same feeling of disappointment that had troubled her so much many years before at a castle. She recognised it as the pain of not getting her own way, and her reflex after the long journey was to return Shaun's rejection with petulance. She shot Shaun a glare of irreverent eyes.

'I've seen that look before,' smiled Shaun, 'and as much as I'd like to follow you, we need to talk.'

Annie waited. Shaun clasped both her hands in his. 'This is not a question,' he said. 'This is a statement of intent. I want to marry you.'

Annie's neck burned with the initial slight on her desires and it grew hotter with the feeling of elation that Shaun was giving her what she wanted. Annie wanted to marry Shaun, but her voice spoiled the moment with a reality that couldn't be ignored. 'I've just come out of one marriage. My decree absolute hasn't even come through yet. I don't know if it would be the right thing to step into another marriage so soon.'

'I want to marry you, Annie. I love you and I want you to be part of my family. That's the first reason I want to marry you, but we need to face the practical implication of you living in the United States. You need to be married to get a visa.'

Annie had considered that necessity already, and as she had stood on a bridge in Leiden looking towards a windmill titled to joy, she had created a whole vision of her future in her mind. Something in the conversation with Roy only days before had given her the freedom to use her imagination once again, and she couldn't remove the notion of a child from her dreams. She was forty years old and she was free to build a new future without dependent children, but the realisation hit her that if she ever wanted another child, then she needed to think about it now.

'You're very quiet. I assume you knew the subject of marriage would come up sooner or later.'

'Yes, I did, and I would love to marry you.' She released a smile that was met by a composed look on Shaun's face.

'Annie, would you consider changing your faith?'

'Do you mean, would I consider marrying you in a Catholic church?'

'Yes.' Shaun's brown eyes were hopeful.

Annie knew enough about Catholicism to understand that she couldn't marry in a Catholic church if she was divorced, let alone Protestant. She had managed to avoid thinking about religion for at least twenty years, and Shaun was testing her spirituality in a way that it had never been tested.

'I believe in God, but I don't feel compelled to be part of one church. Anyway, how on earth would I go about becoming a Catholic?'

'Being a Catholic is simple. You need to repent, have faith and be baptised.'

'What about the fact that I've been divorced? Would the Catholic church even take me?'

'Your marriage could be deemed invalid.'

Annie's face reddened. 'I will never say my marriage was invalid.'

'Your divorce papers will surely attest the same thing.'

'That's not what divorce is,' said Annie, swallowing an unexpected rage that Shaun's words had provoked. Roy's face was there before her, safe and certain.

'What is it then?'

'It's the end of a marriage, not a statement about its worth.'

Annie had never been good at articulating her thoughts aloud, but she felt satisfied with her improvised response.

'Surely it's the ultimate statement about its worth.'

Shaun's voice was calm but unsteady.

'You never went through the pain of it. I know how much suffering the death of Sarah caused, but death brings certainty. Why can't we have a civil marriage? You could still go to church.'

'In the eyes of the church, it would be adultery.'

'My adultery you mean.'

Shaun's eyes gave a gentle response. His hand reached for Annie's and her heart felt scorched by the insinuation that she was less than Sarah for being alive. 'Why do you need the conventions of a church to have your faith?'

'The Catholic church has always taken care of me. I never felt alone until I walked away from my faith.'

'I will never ask you to walk away from it and I will never tell any priest that my first marriage was invalid, but if we have a child, I'd be happy for you to baptise it into the Catholic faith.'

Annie had yet to see the depths of scarlet to which Shaun's face could fall. She could feel his sweat in her hands.

'What did you say?'

She was unsure of his tone.

'Sorry, I shouldn't have said that. It's a silly idea and I don't even know why I thought of it. I was standing looking at this stupid windmill and—'

'Hey, slow down with the windmills and the silly ideas. This is not a silly idea, but I assumed that with your—'

'With me being old?'

'No! You've spent your adult life raising children. I assumed you'd want some freedom and that you'd be...What the hell? I'm going to stop talking. Tell me this, Annie, would you like to have a baby?'

'Yes.'

Annie finalised the notion in her own mind as she affirmed it, and she was completely baffled by her own confidence in wishing for something she hadn't thought about since the bomb in the McNeill bar. Here she was after an eight hour flight with no sleep and a man who had slept with another woman, and all she could think about was that it would be a beautiful thing to have another child. She wondered if she had lost her mind, but she felt certain within her body. Even as her imagination unfolded a landscape of sleepless nights, bottles and nappies, she couldn't see a single blot on that landscape that wasn't worth the pain. Nervous laughter released itself from the core of Annie's body. She looked at Shaun with as much hope in her eyes as she had ever had. 'Can we try? I mean, if it's possible. If it's not too late.'

'Yes,' Shaun said with a sweeping assurance that almost tipped the table and the coffee onto Annie's lap. 'Yes.'

Annie touched her neck and felt a potent mix of

satisfaction and fear at the control she gained from an impossible religious quandary. She hadn't tried to trick Shaun, but she had unwittingly cast a spell and Shaun had fallen under it and honesty and an unexpected bout of Catholic guilt played on her Protestant mind.

'Wait. You need to give this some thought. I'm happy to attend church with you and to allow any child of ours to be a Catholic, but I don't want you to feel you need to pray for forgiveness for the rest of your life for an unholy marriage. Can a house stand if it's divided?' Annie was puzzled by her own words.

Shaun laughed, 'I see you Protestants know your scriptures. A verse for a sweet is an effective mechanism after all.'

'Did I just quote from the bible?'

'You sure did.'

'There you go. It's my latent Catholic guilt. It must be genetic. Apparently the O'Neills were once Catholic. Where does that leave us?'

'I guess we're just two old fashioned Ulster sinners trying to find our way,' said Shaun.

Annie had never met a man whose emotions were so openly tied to his tongue. Roy had been a closed book, shifting around the house in his own silent brooding. The problem was that Shaun's conscience echoed the voice of his church, while Annie's echoed her own judgement.

'You've a lot to think about, and I have only four days on this trip, so between now and Easter, can you work it out? And can we try to enjoy the rest of the holiday?'

'Yes, we can, starting with my family. I got myself into some trouble over a baptism, so I've invited them all here tomorrow night to meet you.'

'I look forward to that!'

'Good. The priest is coming too.'

'Oh God.'

'Well, that's blasphemy off the list. Your first opportunity for a confession.'

'Very funny! By the way, I told my parents about you, and we'll be visiting them in April when you come over. Guess what the first thing they asked was?'

'What?'

'They asked if you had a swimming pool in your garden. When I starting seeing Roy, the first thing they said was, "Is he a Protestant?"'

GEZELLIGHEID

The Shankill rose in tattered flags and murals draped like connective tissue along the neck of Belfast towards its misty, darkened head. People bustled with their buggies and their shopping trolleys, unaware that the scraps of history patched onto their walls were a mystery to the people of Holland, whose ancestors had unwittingly clothed the city of Belfast in its brightest colours.

Robert was there outside the house on Snugville Street, skinny as before, his brown gelled hair crowning a cautious face. Jean was beside him by the time the car had turned, and Roy was surprised to find her pale face narrowed by the frame of a short bob.

He had been uncertain as he'd called Jean to inform her of the arrival of James and Andrew. She was Annie's friend, and although he'd spent many hours by her side watching James and Robert play football, he wasn't sure if it was appropriate to spend time with his ex-wife's friend.

He instantly felt at ease when she reached out to hug him. He stood back and watched her ruffle the hair of Andrew and James and he was reminded of the vitality of the woman as he took in her shiny boots, tight, black jeans, and suede, cropped jacket.

‘I thought maybe we could go for pizza,’ said Roy in the car en route to the city. The hire car was alive with the flowery scent of Jean.

‘Pizza, ye say?’ said Jean after the young men departed from the car.

Roy met Jean’s mocking voice with laughter. ‘Ay, he replied. ‘And I’m sure we could order a side of spuds for ye.’

‘Where are ye taking me?’ said Jean.

‘I dinnae know yet, Jean. D’ye fancy a pint?’

‘You’re driving! A cup of tea will do the job. What made you come over, anyway?

‘It was the 22nd March yesterday.’

Jean looked at Roy, and the indicator on the car ticked for as long as it took Jean to acknowledge the date with a nod. Roy drove through the winding, slippery multi-story car park in silence, as the automatic gears coughed on the crest of each ramp. He parked on the top storey of Castle Court carpark, overlooking the west of the city. Belfast’s mountains had borrowed the sun that had been shining in the belly of the city earlier that day and Roy and Jean stood side by side in a light mountain mist enjoying the elevated view.

‘They’re pulling the bar down,’ Roy explained as they drifted through the crowded Castle Court shopping centre. ‘I wanted to take a last look.’

‘Where is it?’

‘Not far from the Cathedral. We could go a wee danner if you like?’

‘Alright.’

‘And ye dinnae mind the drizzle?’

‘Och, you’ll no get burnt in the rain, Roy.’

Roy smiled as Jean raised a black umbrella.

He did get burnt in the rain. It was a damp and mizzly day when an explosion had cast off the cool air, charring Roy’s perceptions of everything he had known.

He led Jean on a detour of Bridge Street, passing an alleyway lined with forgotten red-brick warehouses. The alleyway narrowed into an entry and the graze of the cobbles against his shoes and the stench of stale smoke reminded him of that day. Roy pointed to a boarded up bar on the corner of Talbot Street. St. Anne's Cathedral stood opposite like a mother surrounded by the empty nests of children who'd fled to a more peaceful town.

'There she is,' said Roy, pointing to a dilapidated building at the corner of Hill Street. 'It's to be a carpark. I'd say they'll pull all the old buildings on these entries soon enough.'

'Where were you going that day?'

No one had ever asked Roy that question, and here was Annie's friend discussing the event that rain had long ago washed away from the cobbles below his feet. He led Jean to a wall by the bar and began telling her a story that he had never shared, and as an umbrella collected dusty drizzle, Roy's words faltered. He shared the edifice of his atonement with Jean, but he filled and pointed the bricks of his story in his own memory.

'I followed a girl to this bar,' he began, attentive to the flush of Jean's face. 'It was a Thursday and I'd had been to the travel agent to book flights to Holland.'

Roy looked along Talbot Street. Nina's blond hair had darkened, but bright highlights were sprayed like silk across her back, her athletic body shapely in denim flares, her chest rising over the tight belt on the matching jacket.

'Were you seeing her?' Jean asked with a nervous voice.

'No, but I knew her. I'd met her many times as a child. I followed her because I was curious.'

Roy had followed Nina to the bar with no expectations, but he had known well that it was a walk into a compelling darkness. Perhaps there had been a promise of touch on his mind as he had pulled up a chair at the bar beside her and felt the heat radiate from the bare neck. Perhaps lust had hindered his judgement as his eyes had followed the swell of breasts that had blossomed and rounded since he had seen them through the bewildered eyes of his youth, breasts that had been tightly wrapped in the outfit she had selected for her destination.

'I sat beside her at the bar.' Roy continued.

Nina had looked at Roy with fear and wonder in blue eyelids set under blue eye-shadow. Her face was peach with high cheekbones painted with a light, pink blusher, and her nose was small and sloped upwards, an appendage to the form of her perfection.

'She was pretty. When we were children, we'd creep under tables and look at each other and make faces. I'd move away and play with the boys eventually. The fathers would reminisce about the country of their birth and mothers would gossip about the ways of the men they had married, and Nina would follow me around. I thought she was mute for a long time. Maybe she was mute as a child. It happens to children, doesn't it?'

'It happened to Hannah after the bomb. She was fine at home, but her teachers said she didn't speak in school.'

'I fell in love with her,' Roy stated, and he could see the curiosity draw circles on Jean's cheeks.

'You hadn't spoken to her,' said Jean.

'No, I hadn't, but there's a love between children who grow up together.'

Roy had been to one last party when he was eighteen, the year before his father had died, and Nina had been there, more confident and aware of her own reflection. There had been furtive glances and smiles as the drink flowed through the bar, and yet, they had never spoken.

'Why didn't you ask her out? When you were older, I mean.'

'I don't know. I regretted it for a long time, and then I didn't see her after my father died. I found another girl I'd seen grow up and this time I had more sense than to stand about in silence!'

Jean smiled.

'I lost touch with the Nederlanders once my father died.'

'What happened in the bar? Did the girl get hurt too?'

Roy looked at the bar, with its emerald green crackled paint and shabby posters. Nina had stared at him for a moment and then she had stood up. 'I forgot something,' were the first words he'd ever heard her say, and her voice had been faint and fearful.

'She had this brown, leather satchel made from thick leather with black stitching and she kept footering with the long handle hooked around her knee. I spoke to her. I said I was Jan's son and I asked if she didn't know me.' Roy shook his head. Nina had remembered him and her eyes had lingered on Roy's face, but her mouth had been impatient.

'She told me that she had forgotten something and she left her bag sitting on the floor. I walked to the door with it. I can't remember how heavy the bag was. I can't remember anything about it except the leather. She was walking away and I shouted after her and held out the bag and she went here and there.' Roy pointed to the left and the right and he could hear it then. He could hear the clack clack of her heeled boots as they clamoured over the cobbles.

'She snatched the bag and threw it in that alleyway.' Roy's eyes fell on the alleyway as he recalled the ugly terror in her eyes.

He didn't know what to tell Jean about what happened after that. He couldn't remember why he hadn't run away. Maybe he had failed to understand what she was telling him. Maybe he had understood and he had been grounded to the cobbles thinking about why a girl with a Dutch father would be involved in anything like that. The Dutch parties had been filled with Protestant and Catholic men and women who cared little for the politics of the day.

'She told me that I needed to move, that it was a bomb, and then she said she was sorry.'

Jean's eyes widened as the umbrella loosened in her hand. A drip of rain cooled Roy's neck.

'God,' said Jean. 'I thought you were going to tell me that something happened to her too and I was ready for a sad tale. Well I got a sad tale, that's for sure.'

'Nina was the bomber and the only image I see over and over is the terrorist with her silk hair in flight.'

'A girl,' Jean said, staring at the spot where Nina had hovered.

Would Roy forgive the man responsible for the bomb in McNeill's, Annie had asked him, and Roy had replied that he had forgiven her many years ago.

The barman had given the police a description and the

barman had explained to the police how Roy had lifted the bag and followed the girl out the door.

It had taken weeks after the bomb for Roy to piece together the memories of Nina walking away. Now he realised that the shock of the loss of something pure had already cut through his soul before the shrapnel had severed his leg. He couldn't remember the bomb, but he could recall how his body had convulsed in shock when he learned that Nina was a bomber.

The knowledge was there in his dreams for years, pure and silent. He had loved her, and he couldn't connect with the reality of Annie because he had loved a figment of the past in order to deny the reality of his assailant. Roy had tampered with his own memory so successfully that he couldn't remember his love for his own wife.

'I didn't tell the police that I recognised the girl. The barman gave a detailed description and they never found her. She was probably the most beautiful woman in the country, but they never found her.'

'I don't want to judge you, but you should have told the police.'

'If anyone else had been hurt or injured, I would have spoken up, but it was just me and so I left it alone and said nothing. Some days I believed it had happened and other days I believed I was insane. Then there was this place in daydreams where I was giving her a second chance.'

'It wasn't your chance to give. Her sentence will be longer than Harry's, and I don't mean the prison sentence. You didn't do the girl any favours.'

Roy became aware of the strain of the umbrella in Jean's hand. He took it from her and shook off the weight of the rain.

'I know,' he said. 'I'm thinking of going to the police tomorrow.'

'What will you say?'

'I'll tell the truth, that I've been having flashbacks and I recognise the girl's face.'

'You'll leave out the part about falling in love with her.'

'Yes. I don't think the police would make any sense of that.'

'Withholding evidence is a crime.'

'I know, but I believed that there would be an explanation. I believed in her. At least, sometimes I did. Other times, I felt haunted by her. I thought I loved the girl.

'But you never touched.'

'No, we never touched.'

Roy pressed Jean's hand and watched her face turn red as the cool air between them turned to heat. 'Touch can stir many false emotions.' He wanted to kiss Jean, but a cold wind passed through his body like mourning and he shivered. Jean released her hand.

'There's a Dutch word that can't be translated into English,' said Roy. 'It's gezellig and it's warm and comforting and you can feel it in your bones when people are gathered for a celebration. Sitting there on the other side of the room from Nina as a young boy, I could feel that gezelligheid. And I can never understand what force of nature brought Nina to meet me in such a place. What cause had she to join?'

A long silence followed and the damp atmosphere penetrated Roy's skin as the gezelligheid he'd had with Jean subsided.

Jean's eyes widened and Roy watched her glossy eyelashes flash with pain. 'Roy, I found a balaclava. I was cleaning Robert's room and found it underneath his mattress. I don't know what to do. They get them young and they get them selling drugs and then they get stuck. What future does he have here in Belfast?'

Roy responded without a moment's thought. 'Would he work at the bridges?'

'He's too young. He's only fifteen.'

'When he's finished school then.'

'I don't know. Maybe. He doesn't think much of school. I hope to God it all sorts itself out and I never have to take up your offer. Roy, did any of the paramilitary groups claim responsibility for the bomb?'

'Yes.'

'Oh.'

'Why?'

'Nothing. I thought of something else. It's nothing. Listen, you near gave me a heart attack when you touched my hand. I turned forty-one last week and a clasped hand from a handsome man could be detrimental to the health of a prisoner's wife. Can we go inside?'

Roy laughed and looked towards the cathedral. A woman in a long mauve coat passed through the gates.

'I think I'm seeing double,' said Roy. 'That same woman has gone into the Cathedral twice in the last five minutes, but she hasn't come back out.'

Jean's eyes followed Roy's and she smiled up at him. 'Twin sisters. Must have been too cold today for their picnic. Come on. I have a better idea than pizza. There's a grubby wee pub with an open fire up the entries. The Duke of York, I think they call it. They do a great plate of roast beef and champ. What do you say we abandon the car and have a celebration?'

'A celebration?'

'For the peace.'

'What peace? The IRA said yesterday there'd be no ceasefire.'

'Oh there'll be peace alright. I feel it and it's like weightless time. Come on. Mine's a vodka.'

'A vodka! You're a geg!"

'Och well you know, I promised you one time that I'd have a picnic with a flower in my hair. Sitting on a wall will do instead. My arse is soaked. Sorry I didn't have a flower in my hair.'

Roy picked a dandelion from the side of the wall and placed it in Jean's hair.

'There you go! It suits you.'

'A weed. And a pee-the-bed! I suppose I should be grateful. It's been a long time since anyone gave me flowers.'

Roy smiled, 'You women are all the same. A weed is a misunderstood plant.'

'Ay,' said Jean. 'And you men frae Glenarm are gye an romantic!'

***

'My great granny taul me that the O'Neills were yinst Catholic,' said May.

Annie had warned Shaun that her mother would mention his religion within the first twenty minutes of his visit, and that she would, as was her custom, try to make him feel more at home by pointing out that there was Catholic blood in the family. It took fifteen minutes, and Shaun was already struggling to maintain the pace of May's Ulster-Scots patter. Whilst Annie would slip words into conversation that required interpretation, May's dialect felt more like a language that Shaun lacked the skills to decode. May looked at Shaun and whispered, 'She sid they turned.'

Annie intervened by way of translation. 'They turned Catholic.'

'I could take a look into that,' offered Shaun.

'Och, I dinnae know about that. You'd be goin' back a fair auld bit.'

Annie whirled around the room, lifting cups and laying out plates of ham and butter sandwiches on a thick, grainy bread that held the scent of the oven. Her sisters, Irene and Katherine, came and went in veiled whispers, whilst the feet of teenage girls and boys passed back and forth by the fire. Shaun could only dare to imagine what Annie and her sisters were discussing in the room they called the skullery. Who was this American friend of Annie's? Why was he here? What really happened with Roy?

May spoke again. 'What do ye think o Glenarm then, Shaun?'

'It's beautiful.'

Shaun smiled as he said the words and cast his mind back to the drive that morning over the hills. The Feystown Road was narrow and steep with a hairpin bend opening onto acres of warm fields, the hills rising and falling like waves with verdant shadows in the troughs. It was April, yet the fields were dipped in autumnal accents with brownish tinges on virginal green landscape. Sheep appeared as small white pebbles from a distance, dotting the uneven hills that disappeared into a grey-blue sea. Annie had driven the car over a grate into a carpark and when she had cut the engine, she had turned and said, 'Welcome to Sallagh, God's ain country.'

Annie's father, Bobby, had been seated in the corner of the living room in contented peace. His voice emerged in quiet fortitude when May had finished speaking. 'Shaun, did ye no see the graveyard, son?'

'Daddy, don't be going on about dead people,' smiled Annie. She turned to Shaun and added, 'Daddy has a thing about graveyards. The one we passed today is famous around these parts.'

'Oh ay', Annie's father continued. 'There's a mass grave thonner wi' hundreds o bodies. It was the cholera, son. Not yin o the folk in Castle Street survived it. The Great famine took o'er a million in Ireland, but it was the cholera that took the folk o Glenarm.' Bobby spoke as though he had lived through it himself. Shaun was in the land of tellers of tales and felt a little closer to the dust under his feet. There was a moment of quiet as the facts settled on the listeners before Bobby's voice was heard again, this time with a movement of his arm. 'And did ye know, son, that Glenarm is the aul'est town in Ulster? Belfast was jist a swamp when Glenarm was at its prime.'

Bobby talked and Shaun had a sense of having been there before. He was a child in the parlours of his uncles in New York, listening to the same iridescent history choreographed through the mouths of generations of people who had travelled. This was the same Ireland he had visited in Dunfanaghy in Donegal on the first Project Children trip. A distant cousin had recounted the tragedies buried in the quiet stone of a Famine Graveyard and spoken of the loss of Scottish fishermen and a starving village in much the same way that Annie's father re-lived the Glenarm of his past. Both coastal villages shared the same earth, yet they were separated by a political border that bewildered Shaun more in the Glens of Antrim, than it had in Belfast. This was an island people hemmed into the land by the same salt, and Shaun felt closer to the Nationalism of his grandfather than ever before. He was aware of the irony that this should happen to him in a Protestant home in a formidably Unionist county.

‘Annie tells me you served in the war,’ said Shaun.

Bobby stood up from his seat and reached into a drawer in an old oak cabinet. His arthritic hands pried open a black box with blue silk interior to reveal a cap badge and a row of four medals on coloured ribbons. Shaun looked closely at the badge and saw a silver harp and crown and the words *Quis Separabit* at the bottom.

‘Who will separate us,’ Bobby explained.

Shaun nodded. He was familiar with the motto.

‘We thought it was the last,’ came Bobby’s plaintive voice.

Shaun looked into Bobby’s eyes and saw the weariness of a man who had lived through battle. He sat back down again, as Shaun clutched the box in his hand.

‘When I was a youngster we stood outside the Catholic church with our caps by our sides and waited on our freens. Folk think religion caused the war, but tribalism was to blame.’

As he handed the box back to Bobby, Shaun felt the warmth of a cool hand on his skin.

‘Son, I’ll walk into any church that makes my daughter happy. I won’t stand outside.’

Shaun breathed deeply and looked around to check if anyone was listening. The background noise in the skullery allowed Bobby’s voice to be heard only by Shaun.

‘You’ll need a quare faith to take on our Annie, for she never pays heed to anything anyone tells her.’

Shaun continued to look into Bobby’s eyes. There was that hope he’d sought, laid bare in the smiles of a father, a gentleman and a hero, who had read between the knowing glances and spoken more words than Shaun had ever expected to hear. Shaun reached out and grasped the cool hand firmly in his own.

EPILOGUE
1998

Carrickfergus Castle was poised in stoicism like a wife accustomed to dusting the soot from the hearth. Tulips in red and yellow hues blazed through the spring bedding by a statue of a dead king, their heads swaying in the composed wind, their bodies erect in elegiac dance, and the skies that had cast their clout of thunder, precipitation and sleet over the hidden sunshine throughout Shaun's vacation, were resting to the tune of gulls squawking. Shaun could feel the swell of the sun on his cheeks, and as he stared into its core, he recalled two sun-starved Irish boys standing in his backyard in the midday sun, their skinny necks hitched to the rays. His eyes scanned the new apartments to the south but they were drawn back to a castle that emerged with vanity and grace, wrapping its long, impermeable walls around a body built by stronger men.

Shaun held a slim tourist brochure in his hand and looked out to the grey-blue lough after reading the first lines. 'Close your eyes,' he said to Annie, 'and imagine the scene over eight hundred years ago as twenty-two knights from Normandy and their small army drive the Gaelic rulers out of Carrickfergus.'

Annie, who was seated on a bench bordered by flowers, closed her eyes. 'Is this a history lesson?'

Shaun remained standing, his eyes set on the lough. 'Yes, sit at peace. Can you see Edward the Bruce arriving on a boat from Scotland to take over the castle?'

'No, but I can picture his brother Robert and he looks a bit like Mel Gibson,' smiled Annie.

'You're a disruptive student, Mrs Annie Kelly. Skip forward through centuries of plague and famine and the burning of the town by the Gaelics and Highland Scots.'

'That's a lot of flames,' Annie replied, her left eye opening and closing. 'I'm getting hungry.' Annie addressed the toddler with brown curls on her lap. 'What about you, Edith?'

'Enter James II, a Catholic King. He doesn't receive a great welcome, but his son-in-law, King William III is lauded in cheers and whistles in 1690.'

'I know that bit.'

'I know you know that bit,' smiled Shaun. 'Now back to the lecture. You may wish to cover your daughter's ears. In 1711, the last witchcraft trials take place. Eight women are charged with bewitching a young girl and are sentenced to a year in prison and four sessions at the pillory. There follows in 1990 a Protestant woman who bewitches a good Catholic man. Her punishment is a life sentence in the colonies that begins in 1996.'

'You're taking artistic freedom with the history of this castle. What about the greatest non-event in history?'

'What's that?

'A kiss,' said Annie.

'Ah. A kiss. You need to be patient because it's 1912 and every citizen of Carrickfergus is watching the RMS Titanic leave this very lough on its maiden voyage.' Shaun narrowed his eyes and imagined the length of the vessel and the sound of hands clapping and voices cheering along the shore. He turned to his wife and daughter. 'If you ladies would like to walk with me, I will make another momentous addition to the history of Carrickfergus.'

Shaun led Annie and Edith to a railing where he had once turned his head away from crushed, brown eyes. He kissed Annie and he lifted Edith from her arms.

'Billy,' Edith said, pointing to the statue of King William III.

'Billy!' laughed Shaun. 'I fear you have the Protestant ways, little Edith. If it weren't for that guy upholding the Protestant faith so that the O'Neills of Glenarm eventually turned in 1723, there'd be three Catholics enjoying this trip in the unity of their faith.'

'Edith, if it weren't for your mother, your father might be sitting in bars like some Honky Tonk man.'

Annie flashed a look of disdainful humour at Shaun. He had yet to become accustomed to the shift of her eyes, eyes that could be cool and judicious and captivating and charming, but he was compensated by the warmth and comfort of her hand as she led him to a restaurant at the marina.

Shaun pointed to boats through the restaurant windows and played with his daughter while Annie remained near the bar, her eyes fixed to a television set on the wall. He could make out the silhouette of Senator George Mitchell before Annie returned to the table with a curious look on her face. She sat down slowly and lifted the tourist brochure from the table. Shaun watched as she searched for a pen in her bag. She added a note after the last date in the timeline about the history of Carrickfergus and drew an arrow pointing to the castle.

'This is for your scrapbook,' she said to Edith.

The note read, 'Good Friday 1998, Peace agreement. No more bombs. No more fires. Edith was here.'

ACKNOWLEDGMENTS

Friends and Family
I am indebted to all of you for reading a raw manuscript. More than twenty of you gave me detailed feedback in the early days. The help continued throughout the three re-writes.
Thank you

Project Children Families
You did an incredible thing during The Troubles. Around 25,000 children had a holiday of a life-time in your care. During my summer internship in Washington D.C., I experienced that kindness first hand from my host parents, Patty and John Myler. Carol, I reckon I was lucky to work with you in the Project Children attic instead of Capitol Hill.
Thank you

Donna
You have been there as a friend, mentor and editor every step of the way.
Thank you

Readers
You are the reason I'm self-publishing this novel. The feedback you send to me by email and on social media compels to give more. I write for you.
Thank you

ABOUT THE AUTHOR

Angeline King was born in 1975 in Larne in Northern Ireland. She graduated from Queen's University of Belfast, where she studied Modern History and French. She went on to complete a Master's Degree in Applied Languages and Business and had a successful career in international business for fifteen years. Angeline now lives in her beloved home town of Larne with her husband and children.

Snugville Street, the prequel to *A Belfast Tale*, was published in September 2015.

Angeline's blog can be found at:
www.angelineking.com